Daphne du Maurier

maurier   Daphne du maur

Daphne du maurier

maurier   Daphne du maur

Daphne du maurier

KU-628-060

GREENWICH LIBRARIES
3 8028 02135310 4

maui   du maur

Daphne du maurier

VIRAGO

MODERN CLASSICS

498

Daphne du Maurier

DAPHNE DU MAURIER (1907–89) was born in London, the daughter of the famous actor-manager Sir Gerald du Maurier and granddaughter of George du Maurier, the author and artist. A voracious reader, she was from an early age fascinated by imaginary worlds and even created a male alter ego for herself. Educated at home with her sisters and later in Paris, she began writing short stories and articles in 1928, and in 1931 her first novel, *The Loving Spirit*, was published. A biography of her father and three other novels followed, but it was the novel *Rebecca* that launched her into the literary stratosphere and made her one of the most popular authors of her day. In 1932, du Maurier married Major Frederick Browning, with whom she had three children.

Besides novels, du Maurier published short stories, plays and biographies. Many of her bestselling novels became award-winning films, and in 1969 du Maurier was herself awarded a DBE. She lived most of her life in Cornwall, the setting for many of her books, and when she died in 1989, Margaret Forster wrote in tribute: 'No other popular writer has so triumphantly defied classification . . . She satisfied all the questionable criteria of popular fiction, and yet satisfied too the exacting requirements of "real literature", something very few novelists ever do'.

By Daphne du Maurier

Fiction
The Loving Spirit
I'll Never Be Young Again
Julius
Jamaica Inn
Rebecca
Frenchman's Creek
Hungry Hill
The King's General
The Parasites
My Cousin Rachel
Mary Anne
The Scapegoat
Castle Dor
The Glass-Blowers
The Flight of the Falcon
The House on the Strand
Rule Britannia
The Rendezvous and other stories
The Breaking Point: Short Stories
The Doll: Short Stories

Non-fiction
Gerald: A Portrait
The Du Mauriers
The Infernal World of Branwell Brontë
Golden Lads: A Study of Anthony Bacon, Francis,
and their Friends
The Winding Stair: Francis Bacon, His Rise and Fall
Myself When Young
The Rebecca Notebook and Other Memories
Vanishing Cornwall

THE BIRDS AND OTHER STORIES

Daphne du Maurier

with an Introduction
by David Thomson

virago

VIRAGO

Published by Virago Press 2004
Reprinted 2006, 2007 (twice), 2009 (twice), 2010, 2011 (twice), 2012, 2013 (twice)

First published in Great Britain
as *The Apple Tree* by Victor Gollancz Ltd in 1952

Copyright © The Estate of Daphne du Maurier 1952
Introduction copyright © David Thomson 2004

David Thomson asserts his right to be identified as the author
of the Introduction to this Work in accordance with the
Copyright, Designs and Patents Act 1988.

All rights reserved.
No part of this publication may be reproduced, stored in a
retrieval system, or transmitted, in any form or by any means, without
the prior permission in writing of the publisher, nor be otherwise circulated
in any form of binding or cover other than that in which it is published
and without a similar condition including this condition being
imposed on the subsequent purchaser.

A CIP catalogue record for this book
is available from the British Library.

ISBN 978-1-84408-087-8

Typeset by Palimpsest Book Production Limited,
Polmont, Stirlingshire
Printed and bound in Great Britain by
Clays Ltd, St Ives plc

Papers used by Virago are from well-managed forests
and other responsible sources.

MIX
Paper from
responsible sources
FSC   FSC® C104740

GREENWICH
LIBRARIES

BL

3 8028 02135310 4	
Askews & Holts	02-May-2014
AF	£8.99
4287002	

Introduction

Du Maurier, Hitchcock and
Holding an Audience

There's no doubt about the fondness that existed between Daphne du Maurier and Alfred Hitchcock – or between the writer and the movies as a whole. They were good to each other, and du Maurier's books inspired several more films than those made by Hitchcock. There was *Frenchman's Creek* (1944), with Joan Fontaine as Dona St Columb and Arturo De Cordova as her Frenchman; *My Cousin Rachel* (1952), with Olivia de Havilland and the young Richard Burton; and the story that inspired Nicolas Roeg's *Don't Look Now*. Throw in the Hitchcock trio – *Jamaica Inn*, *Rebecca* and *The Birds* – and you have a group where all but one picture did well at the box office, and du Maurier's sales bloomed all over the world.

Still, a serious writer needs to be wary of the movies – don't look for too many thanks, and keep away from the shooting if you're sensible, because writers' feelings are seldom spared. *Jamaica Inn*, the first du Maurier novel filmed, was significantly altered to make a star part for Charles Laughton. Far better that the author of *Frenchman's Creek* not hear the exasperation of Mitchell Leisen, who was obliged to direct the film. When asked whether his attention to colour, clothes and decor had lost sight of 'story values', he exploded: 'You tell me what the story values were in *Frenchman's Creek* and I'll answer that. She falls in love with a pirate, leaves her husband and comes back in time not to get caught. That's all. It's as dull as dishwater and it was a lousy picture. It was one of those things, either I did it or I got suspended and my agent didn't want me to take a suspension. I should have but I didn't.'

Well, you may say, that's what happens when a picture turns out badly. But then consider what Alfred Hitchcock had to say when Francois Truffaut asked him how many times he had read 'The Birds' as he pondered how to make that picture: 'What I do is to read a story only once, and if I like the basic idea, I just forget all about the book and start to create cinema. Today I would be unable to tell you the story of Daphne du Maurier's 'The Birds'. I read it only once, and very quickly at that. An author takes three or four years to write a fine novel; it's his whole life. Then other people take it over completely.'

Lovers of reading, and of Ms du Maurier, need not be alarmed. What we face here is the natural hostility, or trepidation, between novelists and those film-makers who elect to translate them to the screen. Once upon a time, many movie directors began as would-be novelists (I exclude Alfred Hitchcock from that company) and they failed. It wasn't that they couldn't write quite well for a few days at a time. It wasn't that they couldn't summon up good story material. Their problem was the stamina and the solitude, the way in which a writer of fiction for the page may nurse a world, an intrigue and a group of characters for a year, or much more, persevering in the loneliness. Film-making, by contrast, is communal and collaborative. You never know when an actor will improve a line or when the cameraman will suggest a movement you never thought of. But above all (and here Hitchcock was the leader of the pack), film-makers believe in 'visual storytelling' – in short they reckon that one packed moment on screen may deliver ten pages of a book.

And that's necessary, for novels are often three hundred pages or more, and the general working estimate is that, whereas a page of script equals a minute of screen time, a rich page from a novel sometimes requires twenty minutes in the movie. Indeed, when Hitchcock came to prepare *Rebecca* for the screen, he even worked it out that he was going to have to get into the 'backstory' (the events that have occurred before the book begins). He thought he was going to have to put Rebecca de Winter into the film! There's another valuable lesson that affects both narrative media:

that until the last moment, the novelist or the film director is wrestling with problems. I daresay there was a time when Daphne du Maurier herself took it for granted that, if the book was called *Rebecca*, why she had to be a living presence.

Then came the blessed moment when insight struck – of course not, she says, if Rebecca stays a ghost she can haunt the book; and if Rebecca is simply an atmosphere that explains why the second Mrs de Winter, the 'I' character is so intimidated, so threatened. Indeed, as Hitchcock might have reasoned: the 'I' character is just the eye that sees the whole thing!

You might then conclude, well, why should film-makers bother with books if they intend to tell every story visually? The answer is commerce. In the short history of the movies, producers have taken the prior success of a novel, a play or even a story very seriously. It helps them feel confident; it encourages them to believe that there is an audience primed for the film. In turn, that fosters the large fallacy: that there is a natural and true way of translating novels to the screen.

The point to hang on to is there in Hitchcock's rather brusque treatment of du Maurier's original version of 'The Birds' – 'if I like the basic idea'. Movie people have a simple test when it comes to possible projects. They may ask for a written synopsis, a treatment, or even a script. Yet, in truth, many movie people do not read easily, and film scripts – if you've tried it – are somewhere between prose and a blueprint. So film people say to a writer, 'Just tell me the story – in words, as if we were sitting at the same fireplace on a cold night. And if I'm hooked, if I want to know what happens next, if the hair starts to go up on the back of my neck, then we may be on to something.'

Alfred Hitchcock was very well disposed to Daphne du Maurier. For she was the daughter of Sir Gerald du Maurier, perhaps the leading actor-manager in the London of the early twentieth century, a handsome man, and a very accomplished actor in romance and melodrama. The two men had worked together on a picture called *Lord Camber's Ladies* (1932), produced by Hitchcock, and actually directed by Benn W. Levy, which starred du Maurier and Gertrude Lawrence. It proved to be more than a regular professional relationship, for Hitchcock and du Maurier discovered that they had a shared hobby: elaborate practical jokes. It has been said that if only, instead of *Lord Camber's Ladies*, we had the movie of these escapades – of bodies found in dressing-room cupboards; of immense emergency calls that required fools' errands; and the everyday booby-trapping of the prop in the picture.

So it was quite natural that Hitchcock should follow the emerging career of Gerald's daughter, Daphne (born in 1907), who was coming into her own by the mid 1930s. That's how he came to make the movie of *Jamaica Inn*, a project dominated by Charles Laughton's desire to play the villain, Sir Humphrey Pengallan, thus cancelling out the clergyman rogue from the book. Once more, Hitch was not flattering about the material: it was 'an absurd thing to undertake', he said, with a story that made no sense. But the film was a hit, and it is worth asking why. *Jamaica Inn* may have problems of logic or tidiness, but it has immense atmosphere, a wild setting (the Cornish coast) and a very strong clash between young and innocent characters and some who are older, darker and far more wicked. The story has a hook. We want to know what happens next.

Du Maurier wrote romances, and she liked to have innocent young heroines. But the romance often veers towards something more like horror – I note that in introducing *Jamaica Inn* in this series, Sarah Dunant said that the bond between the young woman and her towering uncle (the real relationship in du Maurier's book) is like that between Hannibal Lecter and Clarice Starling.

At some time during the work on *Jamaica Inn*, Hitchcock got an advance look at Daphne's next book – *Rebecca*. Did he read it himself, or did he get his very shrewd wife, Alma, to analyse it? Who knows? But the Hitchcocks were mad for the book, and Hitchcock tried to purchase the screen rights directly. Du Maurier was uncertain, for there was word that Hollywood – with much more money – was also fascinated by the book. David O. Selznick was bidding, the man famous for having paid $50,000 for the screen rights to Margaret Mitchell's *Gone with the Wind*. Hitchcock could not compete at that level. But Selznick was interested in picking up Hitchcock, too. The negotiations were very complicated, but they ended with the decision whereby Alfred Hitchcock would go to Hollywood where his first production would be *Rebecca*.

That is not the end of the story. Having arrived in Hollywood, Hitchcock was alarmed by the overbearing manner of Selznick, and was determined to stay independent. So he took the du Maurier novel and turned it into a Hitchcock scenario with a vengeance. In short, he delivered a script that made Selznick howl in complaint. 'But, Hitch, you've ruined the book!'

I do not mean to say that the Hitchcock scenario would not have worked. But Selznick had learned one thing on *Gone with the Wind*: if in doubt stay faithful to the book, for millions of readers are prepared to be upset if you make a foolish change. So, bit by bit, and with fierce comic battles, the producer dragged his director back to the du Maurier story. Hitch was hurt, and he took a little more umbrage when in the casting for 'I', Anne Baxter, Loretta Young, Margaret Sullavan and Vivien Leigh were all set aside in favour of a relative unknown, Joan Fontaine, who happened to have caught Selznick's fancy at that time.

To the end of his days, Hitchcock protested that Selznick had interfered too much on *Rebecca*. But viewers of the film – for over sixty years now – have had a hard time picking a fight. They think Fontaine is perfect, and Olivier as Max. They feel they know Manderley, the house, and they see Judith Anderson as the incarnation of that great character, Mrs Danvers (one of du Maurier's finest dark creations). Rebecca is nowhere, yet everywhere. You want to know what happens next. And it won the Oscar for Best Picture – which, after *Gone with the Wind*, made two in a row for Selznick.

Hitchcock was set on a great Hollywood career. In the next twenty years, he would make *Spellbound*, *Notorious*, *Strangers on a Train*, *Rear Window*, *North by Northwest* and *Psycho* (his greatest hit of all). At that point, he was at a peak where he could do whatever he liked. And he remembered 'The Birds'. What had hooked him about it? Well, this story may answer that. Once determined to do *The Birds*, he looked around for a new screen-writer, and his eye fell on James Kennaway who had just had a great success adapting his own novel, *Tunes of Glory*. So Hitch sent word to Kennaway: read the book, think it over and then we'll meet and you are to tell me the story of our picture – how we'll do it.

So Kennaway struggled with the short story about a Cornish family and their response to a sudden, concerted and unexplained onslaught by all the birds in creation. I think I have the answer, said Kennaway. Yes? said Hitchcock. We film the story, Kennaway began, entirely through the eyes of the family. We never see a single bird. We hear them, but we only see and feel them as our characters feel them!

Ah! sighed Hitchcock. Well, thank you very much, Mr Kennaway, for your efforts. There will be a cheque in the mail. That partnership was over. Hitchcock had other ideas: he would switch the action from rural Cornwall to Marin County in California; the characters would be educated, smart, self-aware. But who cared why the birds attacked or what it meant or symbolized? Hitch just wanted to do every trick with real birds that the cinema was then capable of. He liked the idea because of the huge technical challenge it represented. He had – if you like – become a very artistic film director, not overly interested in why things happened. Whereas readers always treasure the story and its first grip; they judge a film by its ability to deliver that old thrill. I think they're right, and the best movies show how Daphne du Maurier could take ordinary nervousness and build it into . . . dread.

David Thomson
2004

Contents

The Birds

On December the third the wind changed overnight and it was winter. Until then the autumn had been mellow, soft. The leaves had lingered on the trees, golden red, and the hedgerows were still green. The earth was rich where the plough had turned it.

Nat Hocken, because of a war-time disability, had a pension and did not work full-time at the farm. He worked three days a week, and they gave him the lighter jobs: hedging, thatching, repairs to the farm buildings.

Although he was married, with children, his was a solitary disposition; he liked best to work alone. It pleased him when he was given a bank to build up, or a gate to mend at the far end of the peninsula, where the sea surrounded the farm land on either side. Then, at midday, he would pause and eat the pasty that his wife had baked for him, and sitting on the cliff's edge would watch the birds. Autumn was best for this, better than spring. In spring the birds flew inland, purposeful, intent; they knew where they were bound, the rhythm and ritual of their life brooked no delay. In autumn those that had not migrated overseas but remained to pass the winter were caught up in the same driving urge, but because migration was denied them followed a pattern of their own. Great flocks of them came to the peninsula, restless, uneasy, spending themselves in motion; now wheeling, circling in the sky, now settling to feed on the rich new-turned soil, but even when they fed it was as though they did so without hunger, without desire. Restlessness drove them to the skies again.

Black and white, jackdaw and gull, mingled in strange partnership, seeking some sort of liberation, never satisfied, never still.

Flocks of starlings, rustling like silk, flew to fresh pasture, driven by the same necessity of movement, and the smaller birds, the finches and the larks, scattered from tree to hedge as if compelled.

Nat watched them, and he watched the sea-birds too. Down in the bay they waited for the tide. They had more patience. Oyster-catchers, redshank, sanderling, and curlew watched by the water's edge; as the slow sea sucked at the shore and then withdrew, leaving the strip of seaweed bare and the shingle churned, the sea-birds raced and ran upon the beaches. Then that same impulse to flight seized upon them too. Crying, whistling, calling, they skimmed the placid sea and left the shore. Make haste, make speed, hurry and begone: yet where, and to what purpose? The restless urge of autumn, unsatisfying, sad, had put a spell upon them and they must flock, and wheel, and cry; they must spill themselves of motion before winter came.

Perhaps, thought Nat, munching his pasty by the cliff's edge, a message comes to the birds in autumn, like a warning. Winter is coming. Many of them perish. And like people who, apprehensive of death before their time, drive themselves to work or folly, the birds do likewise.

The birds had been more restless than ever this fall of the year, the agitation more marked because the days were still. As the tractor traced its path up and down the western hills, the figure of the farmer silhouetted on the driving-seat, the whole machine and the man upon it would be lost momentarily in the great cloud of wheeling, crying birds. There were many more than usual, Nat was sure of this. Always, in autumn, they followed the plough, but not in great flocks like these, nor with such clamour.

Nat remarked upon it, when hedging was finished for the day. 'Yes,' said the farmer, 'there are more birds about than usual; I've noticed it too. And daring, some of them, taking no notice of the tractor. One or two gulls came so close to my head this afternoon I thought they'd knock my cap off! As it was, I could scarcely see what I was doing, when they were overhead and I had the sun in my eyes. I have a notion the weather will change. It will be a hard winter. That's why the birds are restless.'

2

Nat, tramping home across the fields and down the lane to his cottage, saw the birds still flocking over the western hills, in the last glow of the sun. No wind, and the grey sea calm and full. Campion in bloom yet in the hedges, and the air mild. The farmer was right, though, and it was that night the weather turned. Nat's bedroom faced east. He woke just after two and heard the wind in the chimney. Not the storm and bluster of a sou'westerly gale, bringing the rain, but east wind, cold and dry. It sounded hollow in the chimney, and a loose slate rattled on the roof. Nat listened, and he coud hear the sea roaring in the bay. Even the air in the small bedroom had turned chill: a draught came under the skirting of the door, blowing upon the bed. Nat drew the blanket round him, leant closer to the back of his sleeping wife, and stayed wakeful, watchful, aware of misgiving without cause.

Then he heard the tapping on the window. There was no creeper on the cottage walls to break loose and scratch upon the pane. He listened, and the tapping continued until, irritated by the sound, Nat got out of bed and went to the window. He opened it, and as he did so something brushed his hand, jabbing at his knuckles, grazing the skin. Then he saw the flutter of the wings and it was gone, over the roof, behind the cottage.

It was a bird, what kind of bird he could not tell. The wind must have driven it to shelter on the sill.

He shut the window and went back to bed, but feeling his knuckles wet put his mouth to the scratch. The bird had drawn blood. Frightened, he supposed, and bewildered, the bird, seeking shelter, had stabbed at him in the darkness. Once more he settled himself to sleep.

Presently the tapping came again, this time more forceful, more insistent, and now his wife woke at the sound, and turning in the bed said to him, 'See to the window, Nat, it's rattling.'

'I've already seen to it,' he told her, 'there's some bird there, trying to get in. Can't you hear the wind? It's blowing from the east, driving the birds to shelter.'

'Send them away,' she said, 'I can't sleep with that noise.'

3

He went to the window for the second time, and now when he opened it there was not one bird upon the sill but half a dozen; they flew straight into his face, attacking him.

He shouted, striking out at them with his arms, scattering them; like the first one, they flew over the roof and disappeared. Quickly he let the window fall and latched it.

'Did you hear that?' he said. 'They went for me. Tried to peck my eyes.' He stood by the window, peering into the darkness, and could see nothing. His wife, heavy with sleep, murmured from the bed.

'I'm not making it up,' he said, angry at her suggestion. 'I tell you the birds were on the sill, trying to get into the room.'

Suddenly a frightened cry came from the room across the passage where the children slept.

'It's Jill,' said his wife, roused at the sound, sitting up in bed. 'Go to her, see what's the matter.'

Nat lit the candle, but when he opened the bedroom door to cross the passage the draught blew out the flame.

There came a second cry of terror, this time from both children, and stumbling into their room he felt the beating of wings about him in the darkness. The window was wide open. Through it came the birds, hitting first the ceiling and the walls, then swerving in mid-flight, turning to the children in their beds.

'It's all right, I'm here,' shouted Nat, and the children flung themselves, screaming, upon him, while in the darkness the birds rose and dived and came for him again.

'What is it, Nat, what's happened?' his wife called from the further bedroom, and swiftly he pushed the children through the door to the passage and shut it upon them, so that he was alone now, in their bedroom, with the birds.

He seized a blanket from the nearest bed, and using it as a weapon flung it to right and left about him in the air. He felt the thud of bodies, heard the fluttering of wings, but they were not yet defeated, for again and again they returned to the assault, jabbing his hands, his head, the little stabbing beaks sharp as a pointed fork. The blanket became a weapon of defence; he wound

4

it about his head, and then in greater darkness beat at the birds with his bare hands. He dared not stumble to the door and open it, lest in doing so the birds should follow him.

How long he fought with them in the darkness he could not tell, but at last the beating of the wings about him lessened and then withdrew, and through the density of the blanket he was aware of light. He waited, listened; there was no sound except the fretful crying of one of the children from the bedroom beyond. The fluttering, the whirring of the wings had ceased.

He took the blanket from his head and stared about him. The cold grey morning light exposed the room. Dawn, and the open window, had called the living birds; the dead lay on the floor. Nat gazed at the little corpses, shocked and horrified. They were all small birds, none of any size; there must have been fifty of them lying there upon the floor. There were robins, finches, sparrows, blue tits, larks and bramblings, birds that by nature's law kept to their own flock and their own territory, and now, joining one with another in their urge for battle, had destroyed themselves against the bedroom walls, or in the strife had been destroyed by him. Some had lost feathers in the fight, others had blood, his blood, upon their beaks.

Sickened, Nat went to the window and stared out across his patch of garden to the fields.

It was bitter cold, and the ground had all the hard black look of frost. Not white frost, to shine in the morning sun, but the black frost that the east wind brings. The sea, fiercer now with the turning tide, white-capped and steep, broke harshly in the bay. Of the birds there was no sign. Not a sparrow chattered in the hedge beyond the garden gate, no early missel-thrush or blackbird pecked on the grass for worms. There was no sound at all but the east wind and the sea.

Nat shut the window and the door of the small bedroom, and went back across the passage to his own. His wife sat up in bed, one child asleep beside her, the smaller in her arms, his face bandaged. The curtains were tightly drawn across the window, the candles lit. Her face looked garish in the yellow light. She shook her head for silence.

'He's sleeping now,' she whispered, 'but only just. Something must have cut him, there was blood at the corner of his eyes. Jill said it was the birds. She said she woke up, and the birds were in the room.'

His wife looked up at Nat, searching his face for confirmation. She looked terrified, bewildered, and he did not want her to know that he was also shaken, dazed almost, by the events of the past few hours.

'There are birds in there,' he said, 'dead birds, nearly fifty of them. Robins, wrens, all the little birds from hereabouts. It's as though a madness seized them, with the east wind.' He sat down on the bed beside his wife, and held her hand. 'It's the weather,' he said, 'it must be that, it's the hard weather. They aren't the birds, maybe, from here around. They've been driven down, from up country.'

'But Nat,' whispered his wife, 'it's only this night that the weather turned. There's been no snow to drive them. And they can't be hungry yet. There's food for them, out there, in the fields.'

'It's the weather,' repeated Nat. 'I tell you, it's the weather.'

His face too was drawn and tired, like hers. They stared at one another for a while without speaking.

'I'll go downstairs and make a cup of tea,' he said.

The sight of the kitchen reassured him. The cups and saucers, neatly stacked upon the dresser, the table and chairs, his wife's roll of knitting on her basket chair, the children's toys in a corner cupboard.

He knelt down, raked out the old embers and relit the fire. The glowing sticks brought normality, the steaming kettle and the brown teapot comfort and security. He drank his tea, carried a cup up to his wife. Then he washed in the scullery, and, putting on his boots, opened the back door.

The sky was hard and leaden, and the brown hills that had gleamed in the sun the day before looked dark and bare. The east wind, like a razor, stripped the trees, and the leaves, crackling and dry, shivered and scattered with the wind's blast. Nat stubbed the earth with his boot. It was frozen hard. He had never known a change so swift and sudden. Black winter had descended in a single night.

The children were awake now. Jill was chattering upstairs and young Johnny crying once again. Nat heard his wife's voice, soothing, comforting. Presently they came down. He had breakfast ready for them, and the routine of the day began.

'Did you drive away the birds?' asked Jill, restored to calm because of the kitchen fire, because of day, because of breakfast.

'Yes, they've all gone now,' said Nat. 'It was the east wind brought them in. They were frightened and lost, they wanted shelter.'

'They tried to peck us,' said Jill. 'They went for Johnny's eyes.'

'Fright made them do that,' said Nat. 'They didn't know where they were, in the dark bedroom.'

'I hope they won't come again,' said Jill. 'Perhaps if we put bread for them outside the window they will eat that and fly away.'

She finished her breakfast and then went for her coat and hood, her school books and her satchel. Nat said nothing, but his wife looked at him across the table. A silent message passed between them.

'I'll walk with her to the bus,' he said, 'I don't go to the farm today.'

And while the child was washing in the scullery he said to his wife, 'Keep all the windows closed, and the doors too. Just to be on the safe side. I'll go to the farm. Find out if they heard anything in the night.' Then he walked with his small daughter up the lane. She seemed to have forgotten her experience of the night before. She danced ahead of him, chasing the leaves, her face whipped with the cold and rosy under the pixie hood.

'Is it going to snow, Dad?' she said. 'It's cold enough.'

He glanced up at the bleak sky, felt the wind tear at his shoulders.

'No,' he said, 'it's not going to snow. This is a black winter, not a white one.'

All the while he searched the hedgerows for the birds, glanced over the top of them to the fields beyond, looked to the small wood above the farm where the rooks and jackdaws gathered. He saw none.

The other children waited by the bus-stop, muffled, hooded like Jill, the faces white and pinched with cold.

Jill ran to them, waving. 'My Dad says it won't snow,' she called, 'it's going to be a black winter.'

She said nothing of the birds. She began to push and struggle with another little girl. The bus came ambling up the hill. Nat saw her on to it, then turned and walked back towards the farm. It was not his day for work, but he wanted to satisfy himself that all was well. Jim, the cowman, was clattering in the yard.

'Boss around?' asked Nat.

'Gone to market,' said Jim. 'It's Tuesday, isn't it?'

He clumped off round the corner of a shed. He had no time for Nat. Nat was said to be superior. Read books, and the like. Nat had forgotten it was Tuesday. This showed how the events of the preceding night had shaken him. He went to the back door of the farm-house and heard Mrs Trigg singing in the kitchen, the wireless making a background to her song.

'Are you there, missus?' called out Nat.

She came to the door, beaming, broad, a good-tempered woman.

'Hullo, Mr Hocken,' she said. 'Can you tell me where this cold is coming from? Is it Russia? I've never seen such a change. And it's going on, the wireless says. Something to do with the Arctic circle.'

'We didn't turn on the wireless this morning,' said Nat. 'Fact is, we had trouble in the night.'

'Kiddies poorly?'

'No . . .' He hardly knew how to explain it. Now, in daylight, the battle of the birds would sound absurd.

He tried to tell Mrs Trigg what had happened, but he could

8

see from her eyes that she thought his story was the result of a nightmare.

'Sure they were real birds,' she said, smiling, 'with proper feathers and all? Not the funny-shaped kind, that the men see after closing hours on a Saturday night?'

'Mrs Trigg,' he said, 'there are fifty dead birds, robins, wrens, and such, lying low on the floor of the children's bedroom. They went for me; they tried to go for young Johnny's eyes.'

Mrs Trigg stared at him doubtfully.

'Well there, now,' she answered, 'I suppose the weather brought them. Once in the bedroom, they wouldn't know where they were to. Foreign birds maybe, from that Arctic circle.'

'No,' said Nat, 'they were the birds you see about here every day.'

'Funny thing,' said Mrs Trigg, 'no explaining it, really. You ought to write up and ask the *Guardian*. They'd have some answer for it. Well, I must be getting on.'

She nodded, smiled, and went back into the kitchen.

Nat, dissatisfied, turned to the farm-gate. Had it not been for those corpses on the bedroom floor, which he must now collect and bury somewhere, he would have considered the tale exaggeration too.

Jim was standing by the gate.

'Had any trouble with the birds?' asked Nat.

'Birds? What birds?'

'We got them up our place last night. Scores of them, came in the children's bedroom. Quite savage they were.'

'Oh?' It took time for anything to penetrate Jim's head. 'Never heard of birds acting savage,' he said at length. 'They get tame, like, sometimes. I've seen them come to the windows for crumbs.'

'These birds last night weren't tame.'

'No? Cold maybe. Hungry. You put out some crumbs.'

Jim was no more interested than Mrs Trigg had been. It was, Nat thought, like air-raids in the war. No one down this end of the country knew what the Plymouth folk had seen and suffered. You had to endure something yourself before it touched you.

9

He walked back along the lane and crossed the stile to his cottage. He found his wife in the kitchen with young Johnny.

'See anyone?' she asked.

'Mrs Trigg and Jim,' he answered. 'I don't think they believed me. Anyway, nothing wrong up there.'

'You might take the birds away,' she said. 'I daren't go into the room to make the beds until you do. I'm scared.'

'Nothing to scare you now,' said Nat. 'They're dead, aren't they?'

He went up with a sack and dropped the stiff bodies into it, one by one. Yes, there were fifty of them, all told. Just the ordinary common birds of the hedgerow, nothing as large even as a thrush. It must have been fright that made them act the way they did. Blue tits, wrens, it was incredible to think of the power of their small beaks, jabbing at his face and hands the night before. He took the sack out into the garden and was faced now with a fresh problem. The ground was too hard to dig. It was frozen solid, yet no snow had fallen, nothing had happened in the past hours but the coming of the east wind. It was unnatural, queer. The weather prophets must be right. The change was something connected with the Arctic circle.

The wind seemed to cut him to the bone as he stood there, uncertainly, holding the sack. He could see the white-capped seas breaking down under in the bay. He decided to take the birds to the shore and bury them.

When he reached the beach below the headland he could scarcely stand, the force of the east wind was so strong. It hurt to draw breath, and his bare hands were blue. Never had he known such cold, not in all the bad winters he could remember. It was low tide. He crunched his way over the shingle to the softer sand and then, his back to the wind, ground a pit in the sand with his heel. He meant to drop the birds into it, but as he opened up the sack the force of the wind carried them, lifted them, as though in flight again, and they were blown away from him along the beach, tossed like feathers, spread and scattered, the bodies of the fifty frozen birds. There was something ugly in

10

the sight. He did not like it. The dead birds were swept away from him by the wind.

'The tide will take them when it turns,' he said to himself.

He looked out to sea and watched the crested breakers, combing green. They rose stiffly, curled, and broke again, and because it was ebb tide the roar was distant, more remote, lacking the sound and thunder of the flood.

Then he saw them. The gulls. Out there, riding the seas.

What he had thought at first to be the white caps of the waves were gulls. Hundreds, thousands, tens of thousands . . . They rose and fell in the trough of the seas, heads to the wind, like a mighty fleet at anchor, waiting on the tide. To eastward, and to the west, the gulls were there. They stretched as far as his eye could reach, in close formation, line upon line. Had the sea been still they would have covered the bay like a white cloud, head to head, body packed to body. Only the east wind, whipping the sea to breakers, hid them from the shore.

Nat turned, and leaving the beach climbed the steep path home. Someone should know of this. Someone should be told. Something was happening, because of the east wind and the weather, that he did not understand. He wondered if he should go to the call-box by the bus-stop and ring up the police. Yet what could they do? What could anyone do? Tens and thousands of gulls riding the sea there, in the bay, because of storm, because of hunger. The police would think him mad, or drunk, or take the statement from him with great calm. 'Thank you. Yes, the matter has already been reported. The hard weather is driving the birds inland in great numbers.' Nat looked about him. Still no sign of any other bird. Perhaps the cold had sent them all from up country? As he drew near to the cottage his wife came to meet him, at the door. She called to him, excited. 'Nat,' she said, 'it's on the wireless. They've just read out a special news bulletin. I've written it down.'

'What's on the wireless?' he said.

'About the birds,' she said. 'It's not only here, it's everywhere. In London, all over the country. Something has happened to the birds.'

11

Together they went into the kitchen. He read the piece of paper lying on the table.

'Statement from the Home Office at eleven a.m. today. Reports from all over the country are coming in hourly about the vast quantity of birds flocking above towns, villages, and outlying districts, causing obstruction and damage and even attacking individuals. It is thought that the Arctic air stream, at present covering the British Isles, is causing birds to migrate south in immense numbers, and that intense hunger may drive these birds to attack human beings. Householders are warned to see to their windows, doors, and chimneys, and to take reasonable precautions for the safety of their children. A further statement will be issued later.'

A kind of excitement seized Nat; he looked at his wife in triumph.

'There you are,' he said, 'let's hope they'll hear that at the farm. Mrs Trigg will know it wasn't any story. It's true. All over the country. I've been telling myself all morning there's something wrong. And just now, down on the beach, I looked out to sea and there are gulls, thousands of them, tens of thousands, you couldn't put a pin between their heads, and they're all out there, riding on the sea, waiting.'

'What are they waiting for, Nat?' she asked.

He stared at her, then looked down again at the piece of paper.

'I don't know,' he said slowly. 'It says here the birds are hungry.'

He went over to the drawer where he kept his hammer and tools.

'What are you going to do, Nat?'

'See to the windows and the chimneys too, like they tell you.'

'You think they would break in, with the windows shut? Those sparrows and robins and such? Why, how could they?'

He did not answer. He was not thinking of the robins and the sparrows. He was thinking of the gulls . . .

He went upstairs and worked there the rest of the morning, boarding the windows of the bedrooms, filling up the chimney bases. Good job it was his free day and he was not working at the farm. It reminded him of the old days, at the beginning of

12

the war. He was not married then, and he had made all the blackout boards for his mother's house in Plymouth. Made the shelter too. Not that it had been of any use, when the moment came. He wondered if they would take these precautions up at the farm. He doubted it. Too easy-going, Harry Trigg and his missus. Maybe they'd laugh at the whole thing. Go off to a dance or a whist drive.

'Dinner's ready.' She called him, from the kitchen.

'All right. Coming down.'

He was pleased with his handiwork. The frames fitted nicely over the little panes and at the base of the chimneys.

When dinner was over and his wife was washing up, Nat switched on the one o'clock news. The same announcement was repeated, the one which she had taken down during the morning, but the news bulletin enlarged upon it. 'The flocks of birds have caused dislocation in all areas,' read the announcer, 'and in London the sky was so dense at ten o'clock this morning that it seemed as if the city was covered by a vast black cloud.

'The birds settled on roof-tops, on window ledges and on chimneys. The species included blackbird, thrush, the common house-sparrow, and, as might be expected in the metropolis, a vast quantity of pigeons and starlings, and that frequenter of the London river, the black-headed gull. The sight has been so unusual that traffic came to a standstill in many thoroughfares, work was abandoned in shops and offices, and the streets and pavements were crowded with people standing about to watch the birds.'

Various incidents were recounted, the suspected reason of cold and hunger stated again, and warnings to householders repeated. The announcer's voice was smooth and suave. Nat had the impression that this man, in particular, treated the whole business as he would an elaborate joke. There would be others like him, hundreds of them, who did not know what it was to struggle in darkness with a flock of birds. There would be parties tonight in London, like the ones they gave on election nights. People standing about, shouting and laughing, getting drunk. 'Come and watch the birds!'

Nat switched off the wireless. He got up and started work on the kitchen windows. His wife watched him, young Johnny at her heels.

'What, boards for down here too?' she said. 'Why, I'll have to light up before three o'clock. I see no call for boards down here.'

'Better be sure than sorry,' answered Nat. 'I'm not going to take any chances.'

'What they ought to do,' she said, 'is to call the army out and shoot the birds. That would soon scare them off.'

'Let them try,' said Nat. 'How'd they set about it?'

'They have the army to the docks,' she answered, 'when the dockers strike. The soldiers go down and unload the ships.'

'Yes,' said Nat, 'and the population of London is eight million or more. Think of all the buildings, all the flats, and houses. Do you think they've enough soldiers to go round shooting birds from every roof?'

'I don't know. But something should be done. They ought to do something.'

Nat thought to himself that 'they' were no doubt considering the problem at that very moment, but whatever 'they' decided to do in London and the big cities would not help the people here, three hundred miles away. Each householder must look after his own.

'How are we off for food?' he said.

'Now, Nat, whatever next?'

'Never mind. What have you got in the larder?'

'It's shopping day tomorrow, you know that. I don't keep uncooked food hanging about, it goes off. Butcher doesn't call till the day after. But I can bring back something when I go in tomorrow.'

Nat did not want to scare her. He thought it possible that she might not go to town tomorrow. He looked in the larder for himself, and in the cupboard where she kept her tins. They would do, for a couple of days. Bread was low.

'What about the baker?'

'He comes tomorrow too.'

14

He saw she had flour. If the baker did not call she had enough to bake one loaf.

'We'd be better off in the old days,' he said, 'when the women baked twice a week, and had pilchards salted, and there was food for a family to last a siege, if need be.'

'I've tried the children with tinned fish, they don't like it,' she said.

Nat went on hammering the boards across the kitchen windows. Candles. They were low in candles too. That must be another thing she meant to buy tomorrow. Well, it could not be helped. They must go early to bed tonight. That was, if . . .

He got up and went out of the back door and stood in the garden, looking down towards the sea. There had been no sun all day, and now, at barely three o'clock, a kind of darkness had already come, the sky sullen, heavy, colourless like salt. He could hear the vicious sea drumming on the rocks. He walked down the path, half-way to the beach. And then he stopped. He could see the tide had turned. The rock that had shown in mid-morning was now covered, but it was not the sea that held his eyes. The gulls had risen. They were circling, hundreds of them, thousands of them, lifting their wings against the wind. It was the gulls that made the darkening of the sky. And they were silent. They made not a sound. They just went on soaring and circling, rising, falling, trying their strength against the wind.

Nat turned. He ran up the path, back to the cottage.

'I'm going for Jill,' he said. 'I'll wait for her, at the bus-stop.'

'What's the matter?' asked his wife. 'You've gone quite white.'

'Keep Johnny inside,' he said. 'Keep the door shut. Light up now, and draw the curtains.'

'It's only just gone three,' she said.

'Never mind. Do what I tell you.'

He looked inside the toolshed, outside the back door. Nothing there of much use. A spade was too heavy, and a fork no good. He took the hoe. It was the only possible tool, and light enough to carry.

He started walking up the lane to the bus-stop, and now and again glanced back over his shoulder.

The gulls had risen higher now, their circles were broader, wider, they were spreading out in huge formation across the sky.

He hurried on; although he knew the bus would not come to the top of the hill before four o'clock he had to hurry. He passed no one on the way. He was glad of this. No time to stop and chatter.

At the top of the hill he waited. He was much too soon. There was half an hour still to go. The east wind came whipping across the fields from the higher ground. He stamped his feet and blew upon his hands. In the distance he could see the clay hills, white and clean, against the heavy pallor of the sky. Something black rose from behind them, like a smudge at first, then widening, becoming deeper, and the smudge became a cloud, and the cloud divided again into five other clouds, spreading north, east, south and west, and they were not clouds at all; they were birds. He watched them travel across the sky, and as one section passed overhead, within two or three hundred feet of him, he knew from their speed, they were bound inland, up country, they had no business with the people here on the peninsula. They were rooks, crows, jackdaws, magpies, jays, all birds that usually preyed upon the smaller species; but this afternoon they were bound on some other mission.

'They've been given the towns,' thought Nat, 'they know what they have to do. We don't matter so much here. The gulls will serve for us. The others go to the towns.'

He went to the call-box, stepped inside and lifted the receiver. The exchange would do. They would pass the message on.

'I'm speaking from Highway,' he said, 'by the bus-stop. I want to report large formations of birds travelling up country. The gulls are also forming in the bay.'

'All right,' answered the voice, laconic, weary.

'You'll be sure and pass this message on to the proper quarter?'

'Yes . . . yes . . .' Impatient now, fed-up. The buzzing note resumed.

16

'She's another,' thought Nat, 'she doesn't care. Maybe she's had to answer calls all day. She hopes to go to the pictures tonight. She'll squeeze some fellow's hand, and point up at the sky, and say "Look at all them birds!" She doesn't care.'

The bus came lumbering up the hill. Jill climbed out and three or four other children. The bus went on towards the town.

'What's the hoe for, Dad?'

They crowded around him, laughing, pointing.

'I just brought it along,' he said. 'Come on now, let's get home. It's cold, no hanging about. Here, you. I'll watch you across the fields, see how fast you can run.'

He was speaking to Jill's companions who came from different families, living in the council houses. A short cut would take them to the cottages.

'We want to play a bit in the lane,' said one of them.

'No, you don't. You go off home, or I'll tell your mammy.'

They whispered to one another, round-eyed, then scuttled off across the fields. Jill stared at her father, her mouth sullen.

'We always play in the lane,' she said.

'Not tonight, you don't,' he said. 'Come on now, no dawdling.'

He could see the gulls now, circling the fields, coming in towards the land. Still silent. Still no sound.

'Look, Dad, look over there, look at all the gulls.'

'Yes. Hurry, now.'

'Where are they flying to? Where are they going?'

'Up country, I dare say. Where it's warmer.'

He seized her hand and dragged her after him along the lane.

'Don't go so fast. I can't keep up.'

The gulls were copying the rooks and crows. They were spreading out in formation across the sky. They headed, in bands of thousands, to the four compass points.

'Dad, what is it? What are the gulls doing?'

They were not intent upon their flight, as the crows, as the jackdaws had been. They still circled overhead. Nor did they fly so high. It was as though they waited upon some signal. As though some decision had yet to be given. The order was not clear.

17

'Do you want me to carry you, Jill? Here, come pick-a-back.'

This way he might put on speed; but he was wrong. Jill was heavy. She kept slipping. And she was crying too. His sense of urgency, of fear, had communicated itself to the child.

'I wish the gulls would go away. I don't like them. They're coming closer to the lane.'

He put her down again. He started running, swinging Jill after him. As they went past the farm turning he saw the farmer backing his car out of the garage. Nat called to him.

'Can you give us a lift?' he said.

'What's that?'

Mr Trigg turned in the driving seat and stared at them. Then a smile came to his cheerful, rubicund face.

'It looks as though we're in for some fun,' he said. 'Have you seen the gulls? Jim and I are going to take a crack at them. Everyone's gone bird crazy, talking of nothing else. I hear you were troubled in the night. Want a gun?'

Nat shook his head.

The small car was packed. There was just room for Jill, if she crouched on top of petrol tins on the back seat.

'I don't want a gun,' said Nat, 'but I'd be obliged if you'd run Jill home. She's scared of the birds.'

He spoke briefly. He did not want to talk in front of Jill.

'OK,' said the farmer, 'I'll take her home. Why don't you stop behind and join the shooting match? We'll make the feathers fly.'

Jill climbed in, and turning the car the driver sped up the lane. Nat followed after. Trigg must be crazy. What use was a gun against a sky of birds?

Now Nat was not responsible for Jill he had time to look about him. The birds were circling still, above the fields. Mostly herring gull, but the black-headed gull amongst them. Usually they kept apart. Now they were united. Some bond had brought them together. It was the black-backed gull that attacked the smaller birds, and even new-born lambs, so he'd heard. He'd never seen it done. He remembered this now, though, looking above him in the sky. They were coming in towards the farm. They

18

were circling lower in the sky, and the black-backed gulls were to the front, the black-backed gulls were leading. The farm, then, was their target. They were making for the farm.

Nat increased his pace towards his own cottage. He saw the farmer's car turn and come back along the lane. It drew up beside him with a jerk.

'The kid has run inside,' said the farmer. 'Your wife was watching for her. Well, what do you make of it? They're saying in town the Russians have done it. The Russians have poisoned the birds.'

'How could they do that?' asked Nat.

'Don't ask me. You know how stories get around. Will you join my shooting match?'

'No, I'll get along home. The wife will be worried else.'

'My missus says if you could eat gull, there'd be some sense in it,' said Trigg, 'we'd have roast gull, baked gull, and pickle 'em into the bargain. You wait until I let off a few barrels into the brutes. That'll scare 'em.'

'Have you boarded your windows?' asked Nat.

'No. Lot of nonsense. They like to scare you on the wireless. I've had more to do today than to go round boarding up my windows.'

'I'd board them now, if I were you.'

'Garn. You're windy. Like to come to our place to sleep?'

'No, thanks all the same.'

'All right. See you in the morning. Give you a gull breakfast.'

The farmer grinned and turned his car to the farm entrance.

Nat hurried on. Past the little wood, past the old barn, and then across the stile to the remaining field.

As he jumped the stile he heard the whirr of wings. A black-backed gull dived down at him from the sky, missed, swerved in flight, and rose to dive again. In a moment it was joined by others, six, seven, a dozen, black-backed and herring mixed. Nat dropped his hoe. The hoe was useless. Covering his head with his arms he ran towards the cottage. They kept coming at him from the air, silent save for the beating wings. The

19

terrible, fluttering wings. He could feel the blood on his hands, his wrists, his neck. Each stab of a swooping beak tore his flesh. If only he could keep them from his eyes. Nothing else mattered. He must keep them from his eyes. They had not learnt yet how to cling to a shoulder, how to rip clothing, how to dive in mass upon the head, upon the body. But with each dive, with each attack, they became bolder. And they had no thought for themselves. When they dived low and missed, they crashed, bruised and broken, on the ground. As Nat ran he stumbled, kicking their spent bodies in front of him.

He found the door, he hammered upon it with his bleeding hands. Because of the boarded windows no light shone. Everything was dark.

'Let me in,' he shouted, 'it's Nat. Let me in.'

He shouted loud to make himself heard above the whirr of the gulls' wings.

Then he saw the gannet, poised for the dive, above him in the sky. The gulls circled, retired, soared, one with another, against the wind. Only the gannet remained. One single gannet, above him in the sky. The wings folded suddenly to its body. It dropped like a stone. Nat screamed, and the door opened. He stumbled across the threshold, and his wife threw her weight against the door.

They heard the thud of the gannet as it fell.

His wife dressed his wounds. They were not deep. The backs of his hands had suffered most, and his wrists. Had he not worn a cap they would have reached his head. As to the gannet . . . the gannet could have split his skull.

The children were crying, of course. They had seen the blood on their father's hands.

'It's all right now,' he told them. 'I'm not hurt. Just a few scratches. You play with Johnny, Jill. Mammy will wash these cuts.'

He half shut the door to the scullery, so that they could not see. His wife was ashen. She began running water from the sink.

'I saw them overhead,' she whispered. 'They began collecting just as Jill ran in with Mr Trigg. I shut the door fast, and it jammed. That's why I couldn't open it at once, when you came.'

'Thank God they waited for me,' he said. 'Jill would have fallen at once. One bird alone would have done it.'

Furtively, so as not to alarm the children, they whispered together, as she bandaged his hands and the back of his neck.

'They're flying inland,' he said, 'thousands of them. Rooks, crows, all the bigger birds. I saw them from the bus-stop. They're making for the towns.'

'But what can they do, Nat?'

'They'll attack. Go for everyone out in the streets. Then they'll try the windows, the chimneys.'

'Why don't the authorities do something? Why don't they get the army, get machine-guns, anything?'

'There's been no time. Nobody's prepared. We'll hear what they have to say on the six o'clock news.'

Nat went back into the kitchen, followed by his wife. Johnny was playing quietly on the floor. Only Jill looked anxious.

'I can hear the birds,' she said. 'Listen, Dad.'

Nat listened. Muffled sounds came from the windows, from the door. Wings brushing the surface, sliding, scraping, seeking a way of entry. The sound of many bodies, pressed together, shuffling on the sills. Now and again came a thud, a crash, as some bird dived and fell. 'Some of them will kill themselves that way,' he thought, 'but not enough. Never enough.'

'All right,' he said aloud, 'I've got boards over the windows, Jill. The birds can't get in.'

He went and examined all the windows. His work had been thorough. Every gap was closed. He would make extra certain, however. He found wedges, pieces of old tin, strips of wood and metal, and fastened them at the sides to reinforce the boards. His hammering helped to deafen the sound of the birds, the shuffling, the tapping, and more ominous – he did not want his wife or the children to hear it – the splinter of cracked glass.

'Turn on the wireless,' he said, 'let's have the wireless.'

This would drown the sound also. He went upstairs to the bedrooms and reinforced the windows there. Now he could hear the birds on the roof, the scraping of claws, a sliding, jostling sound.

He decided they must sleep in the kitchen, keep up the fire, bring down the mattresses and lay them out on the floor. He was afraid of the bedroom chimneys. The boards he had placed at the chimney bases might give way. In the kitchen they would be safe, because of the fire. He would have to make a joke of it. Pretend to the children they were playing at camp. If the worst happened, and the birds forced an entry down the bedroom chimneys, it would be hours, days perhaps, before they could break down the doors. The birds would be imprisoned in the bedrooms. They could do no harm there. Crowded together, they would stifle and die.

He began to bring the mattresses downstairs. At sight of them his wife's eyes widened in apprehension. She thought the birds had already broken in upstairs.

'All right,' he said cheerfully, 'we'll all sleep together in the kitchen tonight. More cosy here by the fire. Then we shan't be worried by those silly old birds tapping at the windows.'

He made the children help him rearrange the furniture, and he took the precaution of moving the dresser, with his wife's help, across the window. It fitted well. It was an added safeguard. The mattresses could now be lain, one beside the other, against the wall where the dresser had stood.

'We're safe enough now,' he thought, 'we're snug and tight, like an air-raid shelter. We can hold out. It's just the food that worries me. Food, and coal for the fire. We've enough for two or three days, not more. By that time . . .'

No use thinking ahead as far as that. And they'd be giving directions on the wireless. People would be told what to do. And now, in the midst of many problems, he realized that it was dance music only coming over the air. Not Children's Hour, as it should have been. He glanced at the dial. Yes, they were on the Home Service all right. Dance records. He switched to the Light programme. He knew the reason. The usual programmes had been abandoned. This only happened at exceptional times. Elections, and such. He tried to remember if it had happened in the war, during the heavy raids on London. But of course. The BBC was not stationed in London during the war. The programmes were broadcast from other, temporary quarters. 'We're better off here,' he thought, 'we're better off here in the kitchen, with the windows and the doors boarded, than they are up in the towns. Thank God we're not in the towns.'

At six o'clock the records ceased. The time signal was given. No matter if it scared the children, he must hear the news. There was a pause after the pips. Then the announcer spoke. His voice was solemn, grave. Quite different from midday.

'This is London,' he said. 'A National Emergency was proclaimed at four o'clock this afternoon. Measures are being taken to safeguard the lives and property of the population, but it must be understood that these are not easy to effect immediately, owing to the unforeseen and unparalleled nature of the present crisis. Every householder must take precautions to his own building, and where several people live together, as in flats and apartments, they must unite to do the utmost they can to prevent entry. It is absolutely imperative that every individual stays indoors tonight, and that no one at all remains on the streets, or roads, or anywhere without doors. The birds, in vast numbers, are attacking anyone on sight, and have already begun an assault upon buildings; but these, with due care, should be impenetrable. The population is asked to remain calm, and not to panic. Owing to the exceptional nature of the emergency, there will be no further transmission from any broadcasting station until seven a.m. tomorrow.'

They played the National Anthem. Nothing more happened. Nat switched off the set. He looked at his wife. She stared back at him.

'What's it mean?' said Jill. 'What did the news say?'

'There won't be any more programmes tonight,' said Nat. 'There's been a breakdown at the BBC.'

'Is it the birds?' asked Jill. 'Have the birds done it?'

'No,' said Nat, 'it's just that everyone's very busy, and then of course they have to get rid of the birds, messing everything up, in the towns. Well, we can manage without the wireless for one evening.'

'I wish we had a gramophone,' said Jill, 'that would be better than nothing.'

She had her face turned to the dresser, backed against the windows. Try as they did to ignore it, they were all aware of the shuffling, the stabbing, the persistent beating and sweeping of wings.

'We'll have supper early,' suggested Nat, 'something for a treat. Ask Mammy. Toasted cheese, eh? Something we all like?'

He winked and nodded at his wife. He wanted the look of dread, of apprehension, to go from Jill's face.

He helped with the supper, whistling, singing, making as much clatter as he could, and it seemed to him that the shuffling and the tapping were not so intense as they had been at first. Presently he went up to the bedrooms and listened, and he no longer heard the jostling for place upon the roof.

'They've got reasoning powers,' he thought, 'they know it's hard to break in here. They'll try elsewhere. They won't waste their time with us.'

Supper passed without incident, and then, when they were clearing away, they heard a new sound, droning, familiar, a sound they all knew and understood.

His wife looked up at him, her face alight. 'It's planes,' she said, 'they're sending out planes after the birds. That's what I said they ought to do, all along. That will get them. Isn't that gun-fire? Can't you hear guns?'

It might be gun-fire, out at sea. Nat could not tell. Big naval guns might have an effect upon the gulls out at sea, but the gulls were inland now. The guns couldn't shell the shore, because of the population.

'It's good, isn't it,' said his wife, 'to hear the planes?'

And Jill, catching her enthusiasm, jumped up and down with

24

Johnny. 'The planes will get the birds. The planes will shoot them.'

Just then they heard a crash about two miles distant, followed by a second, then a third. The droning became more distant, passed away out to sea.

'What was that?' asked his wife. 'Were they dropping bombs on the birds?'

'I don't know,' answered Nat, 'I don't think so.'

He did not want to tell her that the sound they had heard was the crashing of aircraft. It was, he had no doubt, a venture on the part of the authorities to send out reconnaissance forces, but they might have known the venture was suicidal. What could aircraft do against birds that flung themselves to death against propeller and fuselage, but hurtle to the ground themselves? This was being tried now, he supposed, over the whole country. And at a cost. Someone high up had lost his head.

'Where have the planes gone, Dad?' asked Jill.

'Back to base,' he said. 'Come on, now, time to tuck down for bed.'

It kept his wife occupied, undressing the children before the fire, seeing to the bedding, one thing and another, while he went round the cottage again, making sure that nothing had worked loose. There was no further drone of aircraft, and the naval guns had ceased. 'Waste of life and effort,' Nat said to himself. 'We can't destroy enough of them that way. Cost too heavy. There's always gas. Maybe they'll try spraying with gas, mustard gas. We'll be warned first, of course, if they do. There's one thing, the best brains of the country will be on to it tonight.'

Somehow the thought reassured him. He had a picture of scientists, naturalists, technicians, and all those chaps they called the back-room boys, summoned to a council; they'd be working on the problem now. This was not a job for the government, for the chiefs-of-staff — they would merely carry out the orders of the scientists.

'They'll have to be ruthless,' he thought. 'Where the trouble's worst they'll have to risk more lives, if they use gas. All the live-stock, too, and the soil — all contaminated. As long as everyone

25

doesn't panic. That's the trouble. People panicking, losing their heads. The BBC was right to warn us of that.'

Upstairs in the bedrooms all was quiet. No further scraping and stabbing at the windows. A lull in battle. Forces regrouping. Wasn't that what they called it, in the old war-time bulletins? The wind hadn't dropped, though. He could still hear it, roaring in the chimneys. And the sea breaking down on the shore. Then he remembered the tide. The tide would be on the turn. Maybe the lull in battle was because of the tide. There was some law the birds obeyed, and it was all to do with the east wind and the tide.

He glanced at his watch. Nearly eight o'clock. It must have gone high water an hour ago. That explained the lull: the birds attacked with the flood tide. It might not work that way inland, up country, but it seemed as if it was so this way on the coast. He reckoned the time limit in his head. They had six hours to go, without attack. When the tide turned again, around one-twenty in the morning, the birds would come back . . .

There were two things he could do. The first to rest, with his wife and the children, and all of them snatch what sleep they could, until the small hours. The second to go out, see how they were faring at the farm, see if the telephone was still working there, so that they might get news from the exchange.

He called softly to his wife, who had just settled the children. She came half-way up the stairs and he whispered to her.

'You're not to go,' she said at once, 'you're not to go and leave me alone with the children. I can't stand it.'

Her voice rose hysterically. He hushed her, calmed her.

'All right,' he said, 'all right. I'll wait till morning. And we'll get the wireless bulletin then too, at seven. But in the morning, when the tide ebbs again, I'll try for the farm, and they may let us have bread and potatoes, and milk too.'

His mind was busy again, planning against emergency. They would not have milked, of course, this evening. The cows would be standing by the gate, waiting in the yard, with the household inside, battened behind boards, as they were here at the cottage.

26

That is, if they had time to take precautions. He thought of the farmer, Trigg, smiling at him from the car. There would have been no shooting party, not tonight.

The children were asleep. His wife, still clothed, was sitting on her mattress. She watched him, her eyes nervous.

'What are you going to do?' she whispered.

He shook his head for silence. Softly, stealthily, he opened the back door and looked outside.

It was pitch dark. The wind was blowing harder than ever, coming in steady gusts, icy, from the sea. He kicked at the step outside the door. It was heaped with birds. There were dead birds everywhere. Under the windows, against the walls. These were the suicides, the divers, the ones with broken necks. Wherever he looked he saw dead birds. No trace of the living. The living had flown seaward with the turn of the tide. The gulls would be riding the seas now, as they had done in the forenoon.

In the far distance, on the hill where the tractor had been two days before, something was burning. One of the aircraft that had crashed; the fire, fanned by the wind, had set light to a stack.

He looked at the bodies of the birds, and he had a notion that if he heaped them, one upon the other, on the window sills they would make added protection for the next attack. Not much, perhaps, but something. The bodies would have to be clawed at, pecked, and dragged aside, before the living birds gained purchase on the sills and attacked the panes. He set to work in the darkness. It was queer; he hated touching them. The bodies were still warm and bloody. The blood matted their feathers. He felt his stomach turn, but he went on with his work. He noticed, grimly, that every window-pane was shattered. Only the boards had kept the birds from breaking in. He stuffed the cracked panes with the bleeding bodies of the birds.

When he had finished he went back into the cottage. He barricaded the kitchen door, made it doubly secure. He took off his bandages, sticky with the birds' blood, not with his own cuts, and put on fresh plaster.

His wife had made him cocoa and he drank it thirstily. He was very tired.

'All right,' he said, smiling, 'don't worry. We'll get through.'

He lay down on his mattress and closed his eyes. He slept at once. He dreamt uneasily, because through his dreams there ran a thread of something forgotten. Some piece of work, neglected, that he should have done. Some precaution that he had known well but had not taken, and he could not put a name to it in his dreams. It was connected in some way with the burning aircraft and the stack upon the hill. He went on sleeping, though; he did not awake. It was his wife shaking his shoulder that awoke him finally.

'They've begun,' she sobbed, 'they've started this last hour, I can't listen to it any longer, alone. There's something smelling bad too, something burning.'

Then he remembered. He had forgotten to make up the fire. It was smouldering, nearly out. He got up swiftly and lit the lamp. The hammering had started at the windows and the doors, but it was not that he minded now. It was the smell of singed feathers. The smell filled the kitchen. He knew at once what it was. The birds were coming down the chimney, squeezing their way down to the kitchen range.

He got sticks and paper and put them on the embers, then reached for the can of paraffin.

'Stand back,' he shouted to his wife, 'we've got to risk this.'

He threw the paraffin on to the fire. The flame roared up the pipe, and down upon the fire fell the scorched, blackened bodies of the birds.

The children woke, crying, 'What is it?' said Jill. 'What's happened?'

Nat had no time to answer. He was raking the bodies from the chimney, clawing them out on to the floor. The flames still roared, and the danger of the chimney catching fire was one he had to take. The flames would send away the living birds from the chimney top. The lower joint was the difficulty, though. This was choked with the smouldering helpless bodies of the birds

28

caught by fire. He scarcely heeded the attack on the windows and the door: let them beat their wings, break their beaks, lose their lives, in the attempt to force an entry into his home. They would not break in. He thanked God he had one of the old cottages, with small windows, stout walls. Not like the new council houses. Heaven help them up the lane, in the new council houses.

'Stop crying,' he called to the children. 'There's nothing to be afraid of, stop crying.'

He went on raking at the burning, smouldering bodies as they fell into the fire.

'This'll fetch them,' he said to himself, 'the draught and the flames together. We're all right, as long as the chimney doesn't catch. I ought to be shot for this. It's all my fault. Last thing I should have made up the fire. I knew there was something.'

Amid the scratching and tearing at the window boards came the sudden homely striking of the kitchen clock. Three a.m. A little more than four hours yet to go. He could not be sure of the exact time of high water. He reckoned it would not turn much before half past seven, twenty to eight.

'Light up the primus,' he said to his wife. 'Make us some tea, and the kids some cocoa. No use sitting around doing nothing.'

That was the line. Keep her busy, and the children too. Move about, eat, drink; always best to be on the go.

He waited by the range. The flames were dying. But no more blackened bodies fell from the chimney. He thrust his poker up as far as it could go and found nothing. It was clear. The chimney was clear. He wiped the sweat from his forehead.

'Come on now, Jill,' he said, 'bring me some more sticks. We'll have a good fire going directly.' She wouldn't come near him, though. She was staring at the heaped singed bodies of the birds.

'Never mind them,' he said, 'we'll put those in the passage when I've got the fire steady.'

The danger of the chimney was over. It could not happen again, not if the fire was kept burning day and night.

'I'll have to get more fuel from the farm tomorrow,' he thought.

'This will never last. I'll manage, though. I can do all that with the ebb tide. It can be worked, fetching what we need, when the tide's turned. We've just got to adapt ourselves, that's all.'

They drank tea and cocoa and ate slices of bread and Bovril. Only half a loaf left, Nat noticed. Never mind though, they'd get by.

'Stop it,' said young Johnny, pointing to the windows with his spoon, 'stop it, you old birds.'

'That's right,' said Nat, smiling, 'we don't want the old beggars, do we? Had enough of 'em.'

They began to cheer when they heard the thud of the suicide birds.

'There's another, Dad,' cried Jill, 'he's done for.'

'He's had it,' said Nat, 'there he goes, the blighter.'

This was the way to face up to it. This was the spirit. If they could keep this up, hang on like this until seven, when the first news bulletin came through, they would not have done too badly.

'Give us a fag,' he said to his wife. 'A bit of a smoke will clear away the smell of the scorched feathers.'

'There's only two left in the packet,' she said. 'I was going to buy you some from the Co-op.'

'I'll have one,' he said, 't'other will keep for a rainy day.'

No sense trying to make the children rest. There was no rest to be got while the tapping and the scratching went on at the windows. He sat with one arm round his wife and the other round Jill, with Johnny on his mother's lap and the blankets heaped about them on the mattress.

'You can't help admiring the beggars,' he said, 'they've got persistence. You'd think they'd tire of the game, but not a bit of it.'

Admiration was hard to sustain. The tapping went on and on and a new rasping note struck Nat's ear, as though a sharper beak than any hitherto had come to take over from its fellows. He tried to remember the names of birds, he tried to think which species would go for this particular job. It was not the tap of the woodpecker. That would be light and frequent. This was more serious, because if it continued long the wood would splinter as the glass had done. Then he remembered the hawks. Could the hawks have taken over from the gulls? Were there buzzards now upon the sills, using talons as well as beaks? Hawks, buzzards, kestrels, falcons – he had forgotten the birds of prey. He had forgotten the gripping power of the birds of prey. Three hours to go, and while they waited the sound of the splintering wood, the talons tearing at the wood.

Nat looked about him, seeing what furniture he could destroy to fortify the door. The windows were safe, because of the dresser. He was not certain of the door. He went upstairs, but when he reached the landing he paused and listened. There was a soft patter on the floor of the children's bedroom. The birds had broken through . . . He put his ear to the door. No mistake. He could hear the rustle of wings, and the light patter as they searched the floor. The other bedroom was still clear. He went into it and began bringing out the furniture, to pile at the head of the stairs should the door of the children's bedroom go. It was a preparation. It might never be needed. He could not stack the furniture against the door, because it opened inward. The only possible thing was to have it at the top of the stairs.

'Come down, Nat, what are you doing?' called his wife.

'I won't be long,' he shouted. 'Just making everything ship-shape up here.'

He did not want her to come; he did not want her to hear the pattering of the feet in the children's bedroom, the brushing of those wings against the door.

At five-thirty he suggested breakfast, bacon and fried bread, if only to stop the growing look of panic in his wife's eyes and to calm the fretful children. She did not know about the birds upstairs. The bedroom, luckily, was not over the kitchen. Had it been so she could not have failed to hear the sound of them, up there, tapping the boards. And the silly, senseless thud of the suicide birds, the death-and-glory boys, who flew into the bedroom, smashing their heads against the walls. He knew them of old, the herring gulls. They had no brains. The black-backs

31

were different, they knew what they were doing. So did the buzzards, the hawks . . .

He found himself watching the clock, gazing at the hands that went so slowly round the dial. If his theory was not correct, if the attack did not cease with the turn of the tide, he knew they were beaten. They could not continue through the long day without air, without rest, without more fuel, without . . . his mind raced. He knew there were so many things they needed to withstand siege. They were not fully prepared. They were not ready. It might be that it would be safer in the towns after all. If he could get a message through, on the farm telephone, to his cousin, only a short journey by train up country they might be able to hire a car. That would be quicker — hire a car between tides . . .

His wife's voice, calling his name, drove away the sudden, desperate desire for sleep.

'What is it? What now?' he said sharply.

'The wireless,' said his wife. 'I've been watching the clock. It's nearly seven.'

'Don't twist the knob,' he said, impatient for the first time, 'it's on the Home where it is. They'll speak from the Home.'

They waited. The kitchen clock struck seven. There was no sound. No chimes, no music. They waited until a quarter past, switching to the Light. The result was the same. No news bulletin came through.

'We've heard wrong,' he said, 'they won't be broadcasting until eight o'clock.'

They left it switched on, and Nat thought of the battery, wondered how much power was left in it. It was generally recharged when his wife went shopping in the town. If the battery failed they would not hear the instructions.

'It's getting light,' whispered his wife, 'I can't see it, but I can feel it. And the birds aren't hammering so loud.'

She was right. The rasping, tearing sound grew fainter every moment. So did the shuffling, the jostling for place upon the step, upon the sills. The tide was on the turn. By eight there was no sound at all. Only the wind. The children, lulled at last by the stillness, fell asleep. At half past eight Nat switched the wireless off.

'What are you doing? We'll miss the news,' said his wife.

'There isn't going to be any news,' said Nat. 'We've got to depend upon ourselves.'

He went to the door and slowly pulled away the barricades. He drew the bolts, and kicking the bodies from the step outside the door breathed the cold air. He had six working hours before him, and he knew he must reserve his strength for the right things, not waste it in any way. Food, and light, and fuel; these were the necessary things. If he could get them in sufficiency, they could endure another night.

He stepped into the garden, and as he did so he saw the living birds. The gulls had gone to ride the sea, as they had done before; they sought sea food, and the buoyancy of the tide, before they returned to the attack. Not so the land birds. They waited and watched. Nat saw them, on the hedgerows, on the soil, crowded in the trees, outside in the field, line upon line of birds, all still, doing nothing.

He went to the end of his small garden. The birds did not move. They went on watching him.

'I've got to get food,' said Nat to himself, 'I've got to go to the farm to find food.'

He went back to the cottage. He saw to the windows and the doors. He went upstairs and opened the children's bedroom. It was empty, except for the dead birds on the floor. The living were out there, in the garden, in the fields. He went downstairs.

'I'm going to the farm,' he said.

His wife clung to him. She had seen the living birds from the open door.

'Take us with you,' she begged, 'we can't stay here alone. I'd rather die than stay here alone.'

He considered the matter. He nodded.

'Come on, then,' he said, 'bring baskets, and Johnny's pram. We can load up the pram.'

33

They dressed against the biting wind, wore gloves and scarves. His wife put Johnny in the pram. Nat took Jill's hand.

'The birds,' she whimpered, 'they're all out there, in the fields.'

'They won't hurt us,' he said, 'not in the light.'

They started walking across the field towards the stile, and the birds did not move. They waited, their heads turned to the wind.

When they reached the turning to the farm, Nat stopped and told his wife to wait in the shelter of the hedge with the two children.

'But I want to see Mrs Trigg,' she protested. 'There are lots of things we can borrow, if they went to market yesterday; not only bread, and . . .'

'Wait here,' Nat interrupted. 'I'll be back in a moment.'

The cows were lowing, moving restlessly in the yard, and he could see a gap in the fence where the sheep had knocked their way through, to roam unchecked in the front garden before the farm-house. No smoke came from the chimneys. He was filled with misgivings. He did not want his wife or the children to go down to the farm.

'Don't jib now,' said Nat, harshly, 'do what I say.'

She withdrew with the pram into the hedge, screening herself and the children from the wind.

He went down alone to the farm. He pushed his way through the herd of bellowing cows, which turned this way and that, distressed, their udders full. He saw the car standing by the gate, not put away in the garage. The windows of the farm-house were smashed. There were many dead gulls lying in the yard and around the house. The living birds perched on the group of trees behind the farm and on the roof of the house. They were quite still. They watched him.

Jim's body lay in the yard . . . what was left of it. When the birds had finished, the cows had trampled him. His gun was beside him. The door of the house was shut and bolted, but as the windows were smashed it was easy to lift them and climb through. Trigg's body was close to the telephone. He must have

34

been trying to get through to the exchange when the birds came for him. The receiver was hanging loose, the instrument torn from the wall. No sign of Mrs Trigg. She would be upstairs. Was it any use going up? Sickened, Nat knew what he would find.

'Thank God,' he said to himself, 'there were no children.'

He forced himself to climb the stairs, but half-way he turned and descended again. He could see her legs, protruding from the open bedroom door. Beside her were the bodies of the black-backed gulls, and an umbrella, broken.

'It's no use,' thought Nat, 'doing anything. I've only got five hours, less than that. The Triggs would understand. I must load up with what I can find.'

He tramped back to his wife and children.

'I'm going to fill up the car with stuff,' he said. 'I'll put coal in it, and paraffin for the primus. We'll take it home and return for a fresh load.'

'What about the Triggs?' asked his wife.

'They must have gone to friends,' he said.

'Shall I come and help you, then?'

'No; there's a mess down there. Cows and sheep all over the place. Wait, I'll get the car. You can sit in it.'

Clumsily he backed the car out of the yard and into the lane. His wife and the children could not see Jim's body from there.

'Stay here,' he said, 'never mind the pram. The pram can be fetched later. I'm going to load the car.'

Her eyes watched his all the time. He believed she under-stood, otherwise she would have suggested helping him to find the bread and groceries.

They made three journeys altogether, backwards and forwards between their cottage and the farm, before he was satisfied they had everything they needed. It was surprising, once he started thinking, how many things were necessary. Almost the most important of all was planking for the windows. He had to go round searching for timber. He wanted to renew the boards on all the windows at the cottage. Candles, paraffin, nails, tinned stuff; the list was endless. Besides all that, he milked three of the cows. The rest, poor brutes, would have to go on bellowing.

On the final journey he drove the car to the bus-stop, got out, and went to the telephone box. He waited a few minutes, jangling the receiver. No good, though. The line was dead. He climbed on to a bank and looked over the countryside, but there was no sign of life at all, nothing in the fields but the waiting, watching birds. Some of them slept – he could see the beaks tucked into the feathers.

'You'd think they'd be feeding,' he said to himself, 'not just standing in that way.'

Then he remembered. They were gorged with food. They had eaten their fill during the night. That was why they did not move this morning . . .

No smoke came from the chimneys of the council houses. He thought of the children who had run across the fields the night before.

'I should have known,' he thought, 'I ought to have taken them home with me.'

He lifted his face to the sky. It was colourless and grey. The bare trees on the landscape looked bent and blackened by the east wind. The cold did not affect the living birds, waiting out there in the fields.

'This is the time they ought to get them,' said Nat, 'they're a sitting target now. They must be doing this all over the country. Why don't our aircraft take off now and spray them with mustard gas? What are all our chaps doing? They must know, they must see for themselves.'

He went back to the car and got into the driver's seat.

'Go quickly past that second gate,' whispered his wife. 'The postman's lying there. I don't want Jill to see.'

He accelerated. The little Morris bumped and rattled along the lane. The children shrieked with laughter.

'Up-a-down, up-a-down,' shouted young Johnny.

It was a quarter to one by the time they reached the cottage. Only an hour to go.

'Better have cold dinner,' said Nat. 'Hot up something for

yourself and the children, some of that soup. I've no time to eat now. I've got to unload all this stuff.'

He got everything inside the cottage. It could be sorted later. Give them all something to do during the long hours ahead. First he must see to the windows and the doors.

He went round the cottage methodically, testing every window, every door. He climbed on to the roof also, and fixed boards across every chimney, except the kitchen. The cold was so intense he could hardly bear it, but the job had to be done. Now and again he would look up, searching the sky for aircraft. None came. As he worked he cursed the inefficiency of the authorities.

'It's always the same,' he muttered, 'they always let us down. Muddle, muddle, from the start. No plan, no real organization. And we don't matter, down here. That's what it is. The people up country have priority. They're using gas up there, no doubt, and all the aircraft. We've got to wait and take what comes.'

He paused, his work on the bedroom chimney finished, and looked out to sea. Something was moving out there. Something grey and white amongst the breakers.

'Good old Navy,' he said, 'they never let us down. They're coming down channel, they're turning in the bay.'

He waited, straining his eyes, watering in the wind, towards the sea. He was wrong, though. It was not ships. The Navy was not there. The gulls were rising from the sea. The massed flocks in the fields, with ruffled feathers, rose in formation from the ground, and wing to wing soared upwards to the sky.

The tide had turned again.

Nat climbed down the ladder and went inside the kitchen. The family were at dinner. It was a little after two. He bolted the door, put up the barricade, and lit the lamp.

'It's night-time,' said young Johnny.

His wife had switched on the wireless once again, but no sound came from it.

'I've been all round the dial,' she said, 'foreign stations, and that lot. I can't get anything.'

37

'Maybe they have the same trouble,' he said, 'maybe it's the same right through Europe.'

She poured out a plateful of the Triggs' soup, cut him a large slice of the Triggs' bread, and spread their dripping upon it.

They ate in silence. A piece of the dripping ran down young Johnny's chin and fell on to the table.

'Manners, Johnny,' said Jill, 'you should learn to wipe your mouth.'

The tapping began at the windows, at the door. The rustling, the jostling, the pushing for position on the sills. The first thud of the suicide gulls upon the step.

'Won't America do something?' said his wife. 'They've always been our allies, haven't they? Surely America will do something?'

Nat did not answer. The boards were strong against the windows, and on the chimneys too. The cottage was filled with stores, with fuel, with all they needed for the next few days. When he had finished dinner he would put the stuff away, stack it neatly, get everything shipshape, handy-like. His wife could help him, and the children too. They'd tire themselves out, between now and a quarter to nine, when the tide would ebb; then he'd tuck them down on their mattresses, see that they slept good and sound until three in the morning.

He had a new scheme for the windows, which was to fix barbed wire in front of the boards. He had brought a great roll of it from the farm. The nuisance was, he'd have to work at this in the dark, when the lull came between nine and three. Pity he had not thought of it before. Still, as long as the wife slept, and the kids, that was the main thing.

The smaller birds were at the window now. He recognized the light tap-tapping of their beaks, and the soft brush of their wings. The hawks ignored the windows. They concentrated their attack upon the door. Nat listened to the tearing sound of splintering wood, and wondered how many million years of memory were stored in those little brains, behind the stabbing beaks, the piercing eyes, now giving them this instinct to destroy mankind with all the deft precision of machines.

'I'll smoke that last fag,' he said to his wife. 'Stupid of me, it was the one thing I forgot to bring back from the farm.'

He reached for it, switched on the silent wireless. He threw the empty packet on the fire, and watched it burn.

Monte Verità

They told me afterwards they had found nothing. No trace of anyone, living or dead. Maddened by anger, and I believe by fear, they had succeeded at last in breaking into those forbidden walls, dreaded and shunned through countless years – to be met by silence. Frustrated, bewildered, frightened, driven to fury at the sight of those empty cells, that bare court, the valley people resorted to the primitive methods that have served so many peasants through so many centuries: fire and destruction.

It was the only answer, I suppose, to something they did not understand. Then, their anger spent, they must have realized that nothing of any purpose had been destroyed. The smouldering and blackened walls that met their eyes in the starry, frozen dawn had cheated them in the end.

Search parties were sent out, of course. The more experienced climbers amongst them, undaunted by the bare rock of the mountain summit, covered the whole ridge, from north to south, from east to west, with no result.

And that is the end of the story. Nothing more is known.

Two men from the village helped me to carry Victor's body to the valley, and he was buried at the foot of Monte Verità. I think I envied him, at peace there. He had kept his dream.

As to myself, my old life claimed me again. The second war churned up the world once more. Today, approaching seventy, I have few illusions; yet often I think of Monte Verità and wonder what could have been the final answer.

I have three theories, but none of them may be true.

The first, and the most fantastic, is that Victor was right, after all, to hold to his belief that the inhabitants of Monte Verità *had* reached some strange state of immortality which gave them power when the hour of need arrived, so that, like the prophets of old, they vanished into the heavens. The ancient Greeks believed this of their gods, the Jews believed it of Elijah, the Christians of their Founder. Throughout the long history of religious superstition and credulity runs this ever-recurrent conviction that some persons attain such holiness and power that death can be overcome. This faith is strong in eastern countries, and in Africa; it is only to our sophisticated western eyes that the disappearance of things tangible, of persons of flesh and blood, seems impossible.

Religious teachers disagree when they try to show the difference between good and evil: what is a miracle to one becomes black magic to another. The good prophets have been stoned, but so have the witch-doctors. Blasphemy in one age becomes holy utterance in the next, and this day's heresy is tomorrow's credo.

I am no great thinker, and never have been. But this I do know, from my old climbing days: that in the mountains we come closest to whatever Being it is that rules our destiny. The great utterances of old were given from the mountain tops: it was always to the hills that the prophets climbed. The saints, the messiahs, were gathered to their fathers in the clouds. It is credible to me, in my more solemn moods, that the hand of magic reached down that night to Monte Verità and plucked those souls to safety.

Remember, I myself saw the full moon shining upon that mountain. I also, at midday, saw the sun. What I saw and heard and felt was not of this world. I think of the rock-face, with the moon upon it; I hear the chanting from the forbidden walls; I see the crevasse, cupped like a chalice between the twin peaks of the mountain; I hear the laughter; I see the bare bronzed arms outstretched to the sun.

When I remember these things, I believe in immortality . . .

Then – and this is perhaps because my climbing days are over, and the magic of the mountains loses its grip over old memories, as it does over old limbs – I remind myself that the eyes I looked into that last day on Monte Verità were the eyes of a living, breathing person, and the hands I touched were flesh.

Even the spoken words belonged to a human being. 'Please do not concern yourself with us. We know what we must do.' And then that final, tragic word, 'Let Victor keep his dream.'

So my second theory comes into being, and I see nightfall, and the stars, and the courage of that soul which chose the wisest way for itself and for the others; and while I returned to Victor, and the people from the valley gathered themselves together for the assault, the little band of believers, the last company of those seekers after Truth, climbed to that crevasse, between the peaks, and so were lost.

My third theory is one that comes to me in moods more cynical, more lonely, when, having dined well with friends who mean little to me, I take myself home to my apartment in New York. Looking from the window at the fantastic light and colour of my glittering fairy-world of fact that holds no tenderness, no quietude, I long suddenly for peace, for understanding. Then, I tell myself, perhaps the inhabitants of Monte Verità had long prepared themselves against departure, and when the moment came it found them ready, neither for immortality nor for death, but for the world of men and women. In stealth, in secret, they came down into the valley unobserved, and, mingling with the people, went their separate ways. I wonder, looking down from my apartment into the hub and hustle of my world, if some of them wander there, in the crowded streets and subways, and whether, if I went out and searched the passing faces, I should find such a one and have my answer.

Sometimes, when travelling, I have fancied to myself, in coming upon a stranger, that there is something exceptional in the turn of a head, in the expression of an eye, that is at once compelling and strange. I want to speak, and hold such a person instantly in conversation, but – possibly it is my fancy – it is as though some instinct warns them. A momentary pause, a hesitation, and they are gone. It might be in a train, or in some crowded thoroughfare, and for one brief moment I am aware of someone with more than earthly beauty and human grace, and I want to stretch out my hand and say, swiftly, softly, 'Were you among those I saw on Monte Verità?' But there is never time. They vanish, they are gone, and I am alone again, with my third theory still unproven.

As I grow older – nearly seventy, as I have said, and memory shortens with the lengthening years – the story of Monte Verità becomes more dim to me, and more improbable, and because of this I have a great urge to write it down before memory fails me altogether. It may be that someone reading it will have the love of mountains that I had once, and so bring his own under-standing to the tale, his own interpretation.

One word of warning. There are many mountain peaks in Europe, and countless numbers may bear the name of Monte Verità. They can be found in Switzerland, in France, in Spain, in Italy, in the Tyrol. I prefer to give no precise locality to mine. In these days, after two world wars, no mountain seems inaccessible. All can be climbed. None, with due caution, need be dangerous. My Monte Verità was never shunned because of difficulties of height, of ice and snow. The track leading to the summit could be followed by anyone of sure and certain step, even in late autumn. No common danger kept the climber back, but awe and fear.

I have little doubt that today my Monte Verità has been plotted upon the map with all the others. There may be resting camps near the summit, even an hotel in the little village on the eastern slopes, and the tourist lifted to the twin peaks by electric cable. Even so, I like to think there can be no final desecration, that at midnight, when the full moon rises, the mountain face is still inviolate, unchanged, and that in winter, when snow and ice, great wind and drifting cloud make the climb impassable to man, the rock-face of Monte Verità, her twin peaks lifted to the sun, stares down in silence and compassion upon a blinded world.

We were boys together, Victor and I. We were both at Marlborough, and went up to Cambridge the same year. In those

43

days I was his greatest friend, and if we did not see so much of each other after we left the Varsity it was only because we moved in rather different worlds: my work took me much abroad, while he was busily employed running his own estate up in Shropshire. When we saw each other, we resumed our friendship without any sense of having grown apart.

My work was absorbing, so was his; but we had money enough, and leisure too, to indulge in our favourite pastime, which was climbing. The modern expert, with his equipment and his scientific training, would think our expeditions amateur in the extreme – I am talking of the idyllic days before the First World War – and, looking back on them, I suppose they were just that. Certainly there was nothing professional about the two young men who used to cling with the hands and feet to those projecting rocks in Cumberland and Wales, and later, when some experience was gained, tried the more hazardous ascents in southern Europe.

In time we became less foolhardy and more weather-wise, and learnt to treat our mountains with respect – not as an enemy to be conquered, but as an ally to be won. We used to climb, Victor and I, from no desire for danger or because we wanted to add mountain peaks to our repertoire of achievement. We climbed from desire, because we loved the thing we won.

The moods of a mountain can be more varying, more swiftly-changing, than any woman's, bringing joy, and fear, and also great repose. The urge to climb will never be explained. In olden days, perhaps, it was a wish to reach the stars. Today, anyone so minded can buy a seat on a plane and feel himself master of the skies. Even so, he will not have rock under his feet, or air upon his face; nor will he know the silence that comes only on the hills.

The best hours of my life were spent, when I was young, upon the mountains. That urge to spill all energy, all thought, to be as nothing, blotted against the sky – we called it mountain-fever, Victor and I. He used to recover from the experience more quickly than I did. He would look about him, methodical, careful, planning the descent, while I was lost in wonder, locked in a

44

dream I could not understand. Endurance had been tested, the summit was ours, but something indefinable waited to be won. Always it was denied to me, the experience I desired, and something seemed to tell me the fault was in myself. But they were good days. The finest I have known . . .

One summer, shortly after I returned to London from a business trip to Canada, a letter arrived from Victor, written in tremendous spirits. He was engaged to be married. He was, in fact, to be married very soon. She was the loveliest girl he had ever seen, and would I be his best man? I wrote back, as one does on these occasions, expressing myself delighted and wishing him all the happiness in the world. A confirmed bachelor myself, I considered him yet another good friend lost, the best of all, bogged down in domesticity.

The bride-to-be was Welsh and lived just over the border from Victor's place in Shropshire. 'And would you believe it,' said Victor in a second letter, 'she has never as much as set foot on Snowdon! I am going to take her education in hand.' I could imagine nothing I should dislike more than trailing an inexperienced girl after me on any mountain.

A third letter announced Victor's arrival in London, and hers too, in all the bustle and preparation of the wedding. I invited both of them to luncheon. I don't know what I expected. Someone small, I think, and dark and stocky, with handsome eyes. Certainly not the beauty that came forward, putting out her hand to me and saying, 'I am Anna.'

In those days, before the First World War, young women did not use make-up. Anna was free of lipstick, and her gold hair was rolled in great coils over her ears. I remember staring at her, at her incredible beauty, and Victor laughed, very pleased, and said, 'What did I tell you?' We sat down to lunch, and the three of us were soon at ease and chatting comfortably. A certain reserve was part of her charm, but because she knew I was Victor's greatest friend I felt myself accepted, and liked into the bargain.

Victor certainly was lucky, I said to myself, and any doubt I might have felt about the marriage went on sight of her. Inevitably, with Victor and myself, the conversation turned to mountains, and to climbing, before lunch was half-way through.

'So you are going to marry a man whose hobby is climbing mountains,' I said to her, 'and you've never even gone up your own Snowdon.'

'No,' she said, 'no, I never have.'

Some hesitation in her voice made me wonder. A little frown had come between those two very perfect eyes.

'Why?' I asked. 'It's almost criminal to be Welsh, and know nothing of your highest mountain.'

Victor interrupted. 'Anna is scared,' he said. 'Every time I suggest an expedition she thinks out an excuse.'

She turned to him swiftly. 'No, Victor,' she said, 'it's not that. You just don't understand. I'm not afraid of climbing.'

'What is it, then?' he said.

He put out his hand and held hers on the table. I could see how devoted he was to her, and how happy they were likely to become. She looked across at me, feeling me, as it were, with her eyes, and suddenly I knew instinctively what she was going to say.

'Mountains are very demanding,' she said. 'You have to give everything. It's wiser, for someone like myself, to keep away.'

I understood what she meant, at least I thought then that I did; but because Victor was in love with her, and she was in love with him, it seemed to me that nothing could be better than the fact that they might share the same hobby, once her initial awe was overcome.

'But that's splendid,' I said, 'you've got just the right approach to mountain climbing. Of course you have to give everything, but together you can achieve that. Victor won't let you attempt anything beyond you. He's more cautious than I am.'

Anna smiled, and then withdrew her hand from Victor's on the table.

'You are both very obstinate,' she said, 'and you neither of you understand. I was born in the hills. I know what I mean.'

And then some mutual friend of Victor's and my own came up to the table to be introduced, and there was no more talk of mountains.

They were married about six weeks later, and I have never seen a lovelier bride than Anna. Victor was pale with nerves, I remember well, and I thought what a responsibility lay on his shoulders, to make this girl happy for all time.

I saw much of her during the six weeks of their engagement, and, though Victor never realized it for one instant, came to love her as much as he did. It was not her natural charm, nor yet her beauty, but a strange blending of both, a kind of inner radiance, that drew me to her. My only fear for their future was that Victor might be a little too boisterous, too light-hearted and cheerful – his was a very open, simple nature – and that she might withdraw into herself because of it. Certainly they made a handsome pair as they drove off after the reception – given by an elderly aunt of Anna's, for her parents were dead – and I sentimentally looked forward to staying with them in Shropshire, and being godfather to the first child.

Business took me away shortly after the wedding, and it was not until the following December that I heard from Victor, asking me down for Christmas. I accepted gladly.

They had then been married about eight months. Victor looked fit and very happy, and Anna, it seemed to me, more beautiful than ever. It was hard to take my eyes off her. They gave me a great welcome, and I settled down to a peaceful week in Victor's fine old home, which I knew well from previous visits. The marriage was almost definitely a success, that I could tell from the first. And if there appeared to be no heir on the way, there was plenty of time for that.

We walked about the estate, shot a little, read in the evenings, and were a most contented trio.

I noticed that Victor had adapted himself to Anna's quieter personality, though quiet, perhaps, is hardly the right definition for her gift of stillness. This stillness – for there is no other word for it – came from some depth within her and put a spell upon the whole house. It had always been a pleasant place in which to stay, with its lofty rambling rooms and mullioned windows; but now the peaceful atmosphere was somehow intensified and deepened, and it was as though every room had become impregnated with a strange brooding silence, to my mind quite remarkable, and much more than merely restful, as it had been before.

It is odd, but looking back to that Christmas week I can recollect nothing of the traditional festivity itself. I don't remember what we ate or drank, or whether we set foot inside the church, which surely we must have done, with Victor as the local squire. I can only remember the quite indescribable peace of the evenings, when the shutters had been fastened and we sat before the fire in the great hall. My business trip must have tired me more than I realized, for sitting there, in Victor and Anna's home, I had no desire to do anything but relax and give myself up to this blessed, healing silence.

The other change that had come upon the house, which I did not fully take in until I had been there a few days, was that it was much barer than it had been before. The multiple odds and ends, and the collection of furniture handed down from Victor's forebears, seemed to have disappeared. The big rooms were now sparse and the great hall, where we sat, had nothing in it but a long refectory table and the chairs before the open fire. It seemed very right that it should be so, yet, thinking about it, it was an odd change for a woman to make. The usual habit of a bride is to buy new curtains and carpets, to bring the feminine touch into a bachelor house. I ventured to remark upon it to Victor.

'Oh yes,' he said, looking about him vaguely, 'we have cleared out a lot of stuff. It was Anna's idea. She doesn't believe in possessions, you know. No, we didn't have a sale, or anything like that. We gave them all away.'

The spare room allotted to me was the one I had always used in the past, and this was pretty much as it had been before. And I had the same old comforts – cans of hot water, early tea, biscuits by my bed, cigarette box filled, all the touches of a thoughtful hostess.

Yet once, passing down the long corridor to the stair-head, I noticed that the door of Anna's room, which was usually closed, was open; and knowing it to have been Victor's mother's room in former days, with a fine old four-poster bed and several pieces of heavy solid furniture, all in keeping with the style of the house, ordinary curiosity made me glance over my shoulder as I passed the open door. The room was bare of furniture. There were no curtains to the windows, and no carpet on the floor. The wooden boards were plain. There was a table and a chair, and a long trestle bed with no covering upon it but a blanket. The windows were wide open to the dusk, which was then falling. I turned away and walked down the stairs, and as I did so came face to face with Victor, who was ascending. He must have seen me glance into the room and I did not wish to appear furtive in any way.

'Forgive the trespass,' I said, 'but I happened to notice the room looked very different from your mother's day.'

'Yes,' he said briefly, 'Anna hates frills. Are you ready for dinner? She sent me to find you.'

And we went downstairs together without further conversation. Somehow I could not forget that bare sparse bedroom, comparing it with the soft luxury of my own, and I felt oddly inferior that Anna should consider me as someone who could not dispense with ease and elegance, which she, for some reason, did so well without.

That evening I watched her as we sat beside the fire. Victor had been called from the hall on some business, and she and I were alone for a few moments. As usual I felt the still, soothing peace of her presence come upon me with the silence; I was wrapped about with it, enfolded, as it were, and it was unlike anything I knew in my ordinary humdrum life; this stillness came out of her, yet from another world. I wanted to tell her about it but could not find the words. At last I said, 'You have done something to this house. I don't understand it.'

'Don't you?' she said. 'I think you do. We are both in search of the same thing, after all.'

For some reason I felt afraid. The stillness was with us just the same, but intensified, almost overpowering.

'I am not aware,' I said, 'that I am in search of anything.'

My words fell foolishly on the air and were lost. My eyes, that had drifted to the fire, were drawn, as if compelled, to hers.

'Aren't you?' she said.

I remember being swept by a feeling of profound distress. I saw myself, for the first time, as a very worthless, very trivial human being, travelling here and there about the world to no purpose, doing unnecessary business with other human beings as worthless as myself, and to no other end but that we should be fed and clothed and housed in adequate comfort until death.

I thought of my own small house in Westminster, chosen after long deliberation and furnished with great care. I saw my books, my pictures, my collection of china, and the two good servants who waited upon me and kept the house spotless always, in preparation for my return. Up to this moment my house and all it held had given me great pleasure. Now I was not sure that it had any value.

'What would you suggest?' I heard myself saying to Anna. 'Should I sell everything I have and give up my work? What then?'

Thinking back on the brief conversation that passed between us, nothing that she said warranted this sudden question on my part. She implied that I was in search of something, and instead of answering her directly, yes or no, I asked her if I must give up all I had? The significance of this did not strike me at the time. All I knew then was that I was profoundly moved, and whereas a few moments before I had been at peace, I was now troubled.

'Your answer may not be the same as mine,' she said, 'and anyway, I am not certain of my own, as yet. One day I shall know.'

Surely, I thought to myself in looking upon her, she has the answer now, with her beauty, her serenity, her understanding. What more can she possibly achieve, unless it is that up to the present she lacks children, and so feels unfulfilled?

Victor came back into the hall, and it seemed to me his presence brought solidity and warmth to the atmosphere; there was something familiar and comfortable about his old smoking jacket worn with his evening trousers.

'It's freezing hard,' he said. 'I went outside to see. The thermometer is down to thirty. Lovely night, though. Full moon.' He drew up his chair before the fire and smiled affectionately at Anna. 'Almost as cold as the night we spent on Snowdon,' he said. 'Heavens above, I shan't forget that in a hurry.' And turning to me with a laugh he added, 'I never told you, did I, that Anna condescended to come climbing with me after all?'

'No,' I said, astonished. 'I thought she had set herself against it.'

I looked across at Anna, and I noticed that her eyes had grown strangely blank, without expression. I felt instinctively that the subject brought up by Victor was one she would not have chosen. Victor, insensitive to this, went prattling on.

'She's a dark horse,' he said. 'She knows just as much about climbing mountains as you or I. In fact, she was ahead of me the whole time, and I lost her.'

He continued, half-laughing, half-serious, giving me every detail of the climb, which seemed hazardous in the extreme, as they had left it much too late in the year.

It seemed that the weather, which had promised well in the morning for their start, had turned by mid-afternoon, bringing thunder and lightning and finally a blizzard; so that darkness overtook them in the descent, and they were forced to spend the night in the open.

'The thing I shall never understand,' said Victor, 'is how I came to miss her. One moment she was by my side, and the next she had gone. I can tell you I had a very bad three hours, in pitch darkness and half a gale.'

Anna never said a word while he told the story. It was as

51

though she withdrew herself completely. She sat in her chair, motionless. I felt uneasy, anxious. I wanted Victor to stop.

'Anyway,' I said, to hasten him, 'you got down all right, and none the worse for it.'

'Yes,' he said ruefully, 'at about five in the morning, thoroughly wet and thoroughly frightened. Anna came up to me out of the mist not even damp, surprised that I was angry. Said she had been sheltered by a piece of rock. It was a wonder she had not broken her neck. Next time we go mountain climbing, I've told her that she can be the guide.'

'Perhaps,' I said, with a glance at Anna, 'there won't be a next time. Once was enough.'

'Not a bit of it,' said Victor cheerfully, 'we are all set, you know, to go off next summer. The Alps, or the Dolomites, or the Pyrenees, we haven't decided yet on the objective. You had better come with us and we'll have a proper expedition.'

I shook my head, regretfully.

'I only wish I could,' I said, 'but it's impossible. I must be in New York by May and shan't be home again until September.'

'Oh, that's a long way ahead,' said Victor, 'anything may happen by May. We'll talk of it again, nearer the time.'

Still Anna said no word, and I wondered why Victor saw nothing strange in her reticence. Suddenly she said good night and went upstairs. It was obvious to me that all this chatter of mountain climbing had been unwelcome to her. I felt an urge to attack Victor on the subject.

'Look here,' I said, 'do think twice about this holiday in the mountains. I am pretty sure Anna isn't for it.'

'Not for it?' said Victor, surprised. 'Why, it was her idea entirely.'

I stared at him.

'Are you sure?' I asked.

'Of course I'm sure. I tell you, old fellow, she's crazy about mountains. She had a fetish about them. It's her Welsh blood, I suppose. I was being light-hearted just now about that night on Snowdon, but between ourselves I was quite amazed at her courage and her endurance. I don't mind admitting that what

52

with the blizzard, and being frightened for her, I was dead beat by morning; but she came out of that mist like a spirit from another world. I've never seen her like it. She went down that blasted mountain as if she had spent the night on Olympus, while I limped behind her like a child. She is a very remarkable person: you realize that, don't you?'

'Yes,' I said slowly, 'I do agree. Anna is very remarkable.'

Shortly afterwards we went upstairs to bed, and as I undressed and put on my pyjamas, which had been left to warm for me before the fire, and noticed the thermos flask of hot milk on the bedside table, in case I should be wakeful, and padded about the thick carpeted room in my soft slippers, I thought once again of that strange bare room where Anna slept, and of the narrow trestle bed. In a futile, unnecessary gesture, I threw aside the heavy satin quilt that lay on top of my blankets, and before getting into bed opened my windows wide.

I was restless, though, and could not sleep. My fire sank low and the cold air penetrated the room. I heard my old worn travelling clock race round the hours through the night. At four I could stand it no longer and remembered the thermos of milk with gratitude. Before drinking it I decided to pamper myself still further and close the window.

I climbed out of bed and, shivering, went across the room to do so. Victor was right. A white frost covered the ground. The moon was full. I stood for a moment by the open window, and from the trees in shadow I saw a figure come and stand below me on the lawn. Not furtive, as a trespasser, not creeping, as a thief. Whoever it was stood motionless, as though in meditation, with face uplifted to the moon.

Then I perceived that it was Anna. She wore a dressing-gown, with a cord about it, and her hair was loose on her shoulders. She made no sound as she stood there on the frosty lawn, and I saw, with a shock of horror, that her feet were bare. I stood watching, my hand on the curtain, and suddenly I felt that I was looking upon something intimate and secret, which concerned me not. So I shut my window and returned to bed. Instinct told me that I must say nothing of what I had seen to Victor, or to Anna herself; and because of this I was filled with disquiet, almost with apprehension.

Next morning the sun shone and we were out about the grounds with the dogs, Anna and Victor both so normal and cheerful that I told myself I had been overwrought the previous night. If Anna chose to walk bare-foot in the small hours it was her business, and I had behaved ill in spying upon her. The rest of my visit passed without incident; we were all three happy and content, and I was very loath to leave them.

I saw them again for a brief moment, some months later, before I left for America. I had gone into the Map House, in St James's, to buy myself some half-dozen books to read on that long thrash across the Atlantic – a journey one took with certain qualms in those days, the *Titanic* tragedy still fresh in memory – and there were Victor and Anna, poring over maps, which they had spread out over every available space.

There was no chance of a real meeting. I had engagements for the rest of the day, and so had they, so it was hail and farewell.

'You find us,' said Victor, 'getting busy about the summer holiday. The itinerary is planned. Change your mind and join us.'

'Impossible,' I said. 'All being well, I should be home by September. I'll get in touch with you directly I return. Well, where are you making for?'

'Anna's choice,' said Victor. 'She's been thinking this out for weeks, and she's hit on a spot that looks completely inaccessible. Anyway, it's somewhere you and I have never climbed.'

He pointed down to the large-scale map in front of them. I followed his finger to a point that Anna had already marked with a tiny cross.

'Monte Verità,' I read.

I looked up and saw that Anna's eyes were upon me.

'Completely unknown territory, as far as I'm concerned,' I said. 'Be sure and have advice first, before setting forth. Get hold of local guides, and so on. What made you choose that particular ridge of mountains?'

54

Anna smiled, and I felt a sense of shame, of inferiority beside her.

'The Mountain of Truth,' she said. 'Come with us, do.'

I shook my head and went off upon my journey.

During the months that followed I thought of them both, and envied them too. They were climbing, and I was hemmed in, not by the mountains that I loved but by hard business. Often I wished I had the courage to throw my work aside, turn my back on the civilized world and its dubious delights, and go seeking after truth with my two friends. Only convention deterred me, the sense that I was making a successful career for myself, which it would be folly to cut short. The pattern of my life was set. It was too late to change.

I returned to England in September, and I was surprised, in going through the great pile of letters that awaited me, to have nothing from Victor. He had promised to write and give me news of all they had seen and done. They were not on the telephone, so I could not get in touch with them direct, but I made a note to write to Victor as soon as I had sorted out my business mail.

A couple of days later, coming out of my club, I ran into a man, a mutual friend of ours, who detained me a moment to ask some question about my journey, and then, just as I was going down the steps, called over his shoulder, 'I say, what a tragedy about poor Victor. Are you going to see him?'

'What do you mean? What tragedy?' I asked. 'Has there been an accident?'

'He's terribly ill in a nursing-home, here in London,' came the answer. 'Nervous breakdown. You know his wife has left him?'

'Good God, no,' I exclaimed.

'Oh, yes. That's the cause of all the trouble. He's gone quite to pieces. You know he was devoted to her.'

I was stunned. I stood staring at the fellow, my face blank.

'Do you mean,' I said, 'that she has gone off with somebody else?'

'I don't know. I assume so. No one can get anything out of

55

Victor. Anyway, there he has been for several weeks, with this breakdown.'

I asked for the address of the nursing-home, and at once, without further delay, jumped into a cab and was driven there.

At first I was told, on making inquiry, that Victor was seeing no visitors, but I took out my card and scribbled a line across the back. Surely he would not refuse to see me? A nurse came, and I was taken upstairs to a room on the first floor.

I was horrified, when she opened the door, to see the haggard face that looked up at me from the chair beside the gas-fire, so frail he was, so altered.

'My dear old boy,' I said, going towards him, 'I only heard five minutes ago that you were here.'

The nurse closed the door and left us together.

To my distress Victor's eyes filled with tears.

'It's all right,' I said, 'don't mind me. You know I shall understand.'

He seemed unable to speak. He just sat there, hunched in his dressing-gown, the tears running down his cheeks. I had never felt more helpless. He pointed to a chair, and I drew it up beside him. I waited. If he did not want to tell me what had happened I would not press him. I only wanted to comfort him, to be of some assistance.

At last he spoke, and I hardly recognized his voice.

'Anna's gone,' he said. 'Did you know that? She's gone.'

I nodded. I put my hand on his knee, as though he were a small boy again and not a man past thirty, of my own age.

'I know,' I said gently, 'but it will be all right. She will come back again. You are sure to get her back.'

He shook his head. I had never seen such despair, and such complete conviction.

'Oh no,' he said, 'she will never come back. I know her too well. She's found what she wants.'

It was pitiful to see how completely he had given in to what had happened. Victor, usually so strong, so well-balanced.

'Who is it?' I said. 'Where did she meet this other fellow?'

56

Victor stared at me, bewildered.

'What do you mean?' he said. 'She hasn't met anyone. It's not that at all. If it were, that would be easy . . .'

He paused, spreading out his hands in a hopeless gesture. And suddenly he broke down again, but this time not with weakness but with a more fearful sort of stifled rage, the impotent, useless rage of a man who fights against something stronger than himself. 'It was the mountain that got her,' he said, 'that God-damned mountain, Monte Verità. There's a sect there, a closed order, they shut themselves up for life — there, on that mountain. I never dreamed there could be such a thing. I never knew. And she's there. On that damned mountain. On Monte Verità . . .'

I sat there with him in the nursing-home all afternoon, and little by little had the whole story from him.

The journey itself, Victor said, had been pleasant and uneventful. Eventually they reached the centre from which they proposed to explore the terrain immediately below Monte Verità, and here they met with difficulties. The country was unknown to Victor, and the people seemed morose and unfriendly, very different, he said, to the sort of folk who had welcomed us in the past. They spoke in a patois hard to understand, and they lacked intelligence.

'At least, that's how they struck me,' said Victor. 'They were very rough and somehow undeveloped, the sort of people who might have stepped out of a former century. You know how, when we climbed together, the people could not do enough to help us, and we always managed to find guides. Here, it was different. When Anna and I tried to find out the best approach to Monte Verità, they would not tell us. They just stared at us in a stupid sort of way, and shrugged their shoulders. They had no guides, one fellow said; the mountain was — savage, unexplored.'

Victor paused, and looked at me with that same expression of despair.

'You see,' he said, 'that's when I made my mistake. I should

57

have realized the expedition was a failure – to that particular spot at any rate – and suggested to Anna that we turned back and tackled something else, something nearer to civilization anyhow, where the people were more helpful and the country more familiar. But you know how it is. You get a stubborn feeling inside you, on the mountains, and any opposition somehow rouses you.

'And Monte Verità itself . . .' he broke off and stared in front of him. It was as though he was looking upon it again in his own mind. 'I've never been one for lyrical description, you know that,' he said. 'On our finest climbs I was always the practical one and you the poet. For sheer beauty, I have never seen anything like Monte Verità. We have climbed many higher peaks, you and I, and far more dangerous ones, too; but this was somehow . . . sublime.'

After a few moments' silence he continued talking. 'I said to Anna, "What shall we do?", and she answered me without hesitation, "We must go on." I did not argue, I knew perfectly well that would be her wish. The place had put a spell on both of us.'

They left the valley, and began the ascent.

'It was a wonderful day,' said Victor, 'hardly a breath of wind, and not a cloud in the sky. Scorching sun, you know how it can be, cut the air clean and cold. I chaffed Anna about that other climb, up Snowdon, and made her promise not to leave me behind this time. She was wearing an open shirt, and a brief kilted skirt, and her hair was loose. She looked . . . quite beautiful.'

As he talked, slowly, quietly, I had the impression that it must surely be an accident that had happened, but that his mind, unhinged by tragedy, baulked at Anna's death. It must be so. Anna had fallen. He had seen her fall and had been powerless to help her. He had then returned, broken in mind and spirit, telling himself she still lived on Monte Verità.

'We came to a village an hour before sundown,' said Victor. 'The climb had taken us all day. We were still about three hours from the peak itself, or so I judged. The village consisted of some dozen dwellings or so, huddled together. And as we walked towards the first one, a curious thing happened.'

He paused and stared in front of him.

'Anna was a little ahead of me,' he said, 'moving swiftly with those long strides of hers, you know how she does. I saw two or three men, with some children and goats, come on to the track from a piece of pasture land to the right of us. Anna raised her hand in salute, and at sight of her the men started, as if terrified, and snatching up the children ran to the nearest group of hovels, as if all the fiends in hell were after them. I heard them bolt the doors and shutter the windows. It was the most extraordinary thing. The goats went scattering down the track, equally scared.'

Victor said he had made some joke to Anna about a charming welcome, and that she seemed upset; she did not know what she could have done to frighten them. Victor went to the first hut and knocked upon the door.

Nothing happened at all, but he could hear whispers inside and a child crying. Then he lost patience and began to shout. This had effect, and after a moment one of the shutters was removed and a man's face appeared at the gap and stared at him. Victor, by way of encouragement, nodded and smiled. Slowly the man withdrew the whole of the shutter and Victor spoke to him. At first the man shook his head, then he seemed to change his mind and came and unbolted the door. He stood in the entrance, peering nervously about him, and, ignoring Victor, looked at Anna. He shook his head violently and, speaking very quickly and quite unintelligibly, pointed towards the summit of Monte Verità. Then from the shadows of the small room came an elderly man, leaning on two sticks, who motioned aside the terrified children and moved past them to the door. He, at least, spoke a language that was not entirely patois.

'Who is that woman?' he asked. 'What does she want with us?'

Victor explained that Anna was his wife, that they had come

from the valley to climb the mountain, that they were tourists on holiday, and they would be glad of shelter for the night. He said the old man stared away from him to Anna.

'She is your wife?' he said. 'She is not from Monte Verità?'

'She is my wife,' repeated Victor. 'We come from England. We are in this country on holiday. We have never been here before.'

The old man turned to the younger and they muttered together for a few moments. Then the younger man went back inside the house, and there was further talk from the interior. A woman appeared, even more frightened than the younger man. She was literally trembling, Victor said, as she looked out of the doorway towards Anna. It was Anna who disturbed them.

'She is my wife,' said Victor again, 'we come from the valley.'

Finally the old man made a gesture of consent, of understanding.

'I believe you,' he said. 'You are welcome to come inside. If you are from the valley, that is all right. We have to be careful.'

Victor beckoned to Anna, and slowly she came up the track and stood beside Victor, on the threshold of the house. Even now the woman looked at her with timidity, and she and the children backed away.

The old man motioned his visitors inside. The living-room was bare but clean, and there was a fire burning.

'We have food,' said Victor, unshouldering his pack, 'and mattresses too. We don't want to be a nuisance. But if we could eat here, and sleep on the floor, it will do very well indeed.'

The old man nodded. 'I am satisfied,' he said, 'I believe you.'

Then he withdrew with his family.

Victor said he and Anna were both puzzled at their reception, and could not understand why the fact of their being married, and coming from the valley, should have gained them admittance, after that first odd show of terror. They ate, and unrolled their packs, and then the old man appeared again with milk for them, and cheese. The woman remained behind, but the younger man, out of curiosity, accompanied the elder.

Victor thanked the old fellow for his hospitality, and said that now they would sleep, and in the morning, soon after sunrise, they would climb to the summit of the mountain.

'Is the way easy?' he asked.

'It is not difficult,' came the reply. 'I would offer to send someone with you, but no one cares to go.'

His manner was diffident, and Victor said he glanced again at Anna.

'Your wife will be all right in the house here,' he said. 'We will take care of her.'

'My wife will climb with me,' said Victor. 'She won't want to stay behind.'

A look of anxiety came into the old man's face.

'It is better that your wife does not go up Monte Verità,' he said. 'It will be dangerous.'

'Why is it dangerous for me to go up to Monte Verità?' asked Anna.

The old man looked at her, his anxiety deepening.

'For girls,' he said, 'for women, it is dangerous.'

'But how?' asked Anna. 'Why? You told my husband the path is easy.'

'It is not the path that is dangerous,' he answered; 'my son can set you on the path. It is because of the . . .' and Victor said he used a word that neither he nor Anna understood, but that it sounded like *sacerdotessa*, or *sacerdozio*.

'That's priestess, or priesthood,' said Victor. 'It can't be that. I wonder what on earth he means?'

The old man, anxious and distressed, looked from one to the other of them.

'It is safe for you to climb Monte Verità, and to descend again,' he repeated to Victor, 'but not for your wife. They have great power, the *sacerdotesse*. Here in the village we are always in fear for our young girls, for our women.'

Victor said the whole thing sounded like an African travel tale, where a tribe of wild men pounced out of the jungle and carried off the female population into captivity.

'I don't know what he's talking about,' he said to Anna, 'but

I suppose they are riddled with some sort of superstition, which will appeal to you, with your Welsh blood.'

He laughed, he told me, making light of it, and then, being confoundedly sleepy, arranged their mattresses in front of the fire. Bidding the old man good evening, he and Anna settled themselves for the night.

He slept soundly, in the profound sleep that comes after climbing, and woke suddenly, just before daybreak, to the sound of a cock crowing in the village outside.

He turned over on his side to see if Anna was awake.

The mattress was thrown back, and bare. Anna had gone . . .

No one was yet astir in the house, Victor said, and the only sound was the cock crowing. He got up and put on his shoes and coat, went to the door and stepped outside.

It was the cold, still moment that comes just before sunrise. The last few stars were paling in the sky. Clouds hid the valley, some thousands of feet below. Only here, near the summit of the mountain, was it clear.

At first Victor felt no misgiving. He knew by this time that Anna was capable of looking after herself, and was as sure-footed as he – more so, possibly. She would take no foolish risks, and anyway the old man had told them that the climb was not dangerous. He felt hurt, though, that she had not waited for him. It was breaking the promise that they should always climb together. And he had no idea how much of a start she had in front of him. The only thing he could do was to follow her as swiftly as he could.

He went back into the room to collect their rations for the day – she had not thought of that. Their packs they could fetch later, for the descent, and they would probably have to accept hospitality here for another night.

His movements must have roused his host, for suddenly the old man appeared from the inner room and stood beside him. His eyes fell on Anna's empty mattress, then he searched Victor's eyes, almost in accusation.

'My wife has gone on ahead,' Victor said. 'I am going to follow her.'

The old man looked very grave. He went to the open door and stood there, staring away from the village, up the mountain.

'It was wrong to let her go,' he said, 'you should not have permitted it.' He appeared very distressed, Victor said, and shook his head to and fro, murmuring to himself.

'It's all right,' said Victor. 'I shall soon catch her up, and we shall probably be back again, soon after midday.'

He put his hand on the old fellow's arm, to reassure him.

'I fear very much that it will be too late,' said the old man. 'She will go to them, and once she is with them she will not come back.'

Once again he used the word *sacerdotesse*, the power of the *sacerdotesse*, and his manner, his state of apprehension, now communicated itself to Victor, so that he too felt a sense of urgency, and of fear.

'Do you mean that there are living people at the top of Monte Verità?' he said. 'People who may attack her, and harm her bodily?'

The old man began to talk rapidly, and it was difficult to make any sense out of the torrent of words that now sprang from him. No, he said, the *sacerdotesse* would not hurt her, they hurt no one; it was that they would take her to become one of them. Anna would go to them, she could not help herself, the power was so strong. Twenty, thirty years ago, the old man said, his daughter had gone to them: he had never seen her again. Other young women from the village, and from down below, in the valley, were called by the *sacerdotesse*. Once they were called they had to go, no one could keep them back. No one saw them again. Never, never. It had been so for many years, in his father's time, his father's father's time, before that, even.

It was not known now when the *sacerdotesse* first came to Monte Verità. No man living had set eyes upon them. They lived there, enclosed, behind their walls, but with power, he kept insisting, with magic. 'Some say they have this from God, some from the Devil,' he said, 'but we do not know, we cannot tell. It is rumoured that the *sacerdotesse* on Monte Verità never grow old, they stay for ever young and beautiful, and that it is from the moon they draw their power. It is the moon they worship, and the sun.'

Victor gathered little from this wild talk. It must all be legend, superstition.

The old man shook his head and looked towards the mountain track. 'I saw it in her eyes last night,' he said, 'I was afraid of it. She had the eyes they have, when they are called. I have seen it before. With my own daughter, with others.'

By now the rest of the family had woken and had come by turn into the room. They seemed to sense what had happened. The younger man, and the woman, even the children, looked at Victor with anxiety and a strange sort of compassion. He said the atmosphere filled him not so much with alarm as with anger and irritation. It made him think of cats, and broomsticks, and sixteenth-century witchcraft.

The mist was breaking slowly, down in the valley, and the clouds were going. The soft glow in the sky, beyond the range of mountains to the eastward, heralded the rising sun.

The old man said something to the younger, and pointed with his stick.

'My son will put you on the track,' he said, 'he will come part of the way only. Further he does not care to go.'

Victor said he set off with all their eyes upon him; and not only from this first hut, but from the other dwellings in the little village, he was aware of faces looking from drawn shutters, and faces peering from half-open doors. The whole village was astir now and intent upon watching him, held by a fearful fascination.

His guide made no attempt to talk to him. He walked ahead, his shoulders bent, his eyes on the ground. Victor felt that he went only on command of the old man, his father.

The track was rough and stony, broken in many places, and was, Victor judged, part of an old water-course that would be impassable when the rains came. Now, in full summer, it was easy enough to climb. Verdure, thorn, and scrub they left behind them, after climbing steadily for an hour, and the summit of the mountain pierced the sky directly above their heads, split into two like a divided hand. From the depths of the valley, and from the village even, this division could not be seen; the two peaks seemed as one.

The sun had risen with them as they climbed, and now shone in full upon the south-eastern face, turning it to coral. Great banks of clouds, soft and rolling, hid the world below. Victor's guide stopped suddenly and pointed ahead, where a jutting lip of rock wound in a razor's edge and curved southward out of sight.

'Monte Verità,' he said, and then repeated it again, 'Monte Verità.'

Then he turned swiftly and began scrambling back along the way that they had come.

Victor called to him, but the man did not answer; he did not even bother to turn his head. In a moment he was out of sight. There was nothing for it but to go on alone, round the lip of the escarpment, Victor said, and trust that he found Anna waiting for him on the further side.

It took him another half-hour to encircle the projecting shoulder of the mountain, and with every step he took his anxiety deepened, because now, on the southward side, there was no gradual incline – the mountain face was sheer. Soon further progress would be impossible.

'Then,' Victor said, 'I came out through a sort of gully-way, over a ridge about three hundred feet only from the summit; and I saw it, the monastery, built out of the rock between the two peaks, absolutely bare and naked; a steep rock wall enclosing it, a drop of a thousand feet beneath the wall to the next ridge, and above, nothing but the sky and the twin peaks of Monte Verità.'

It was true, then. Victor had not lost his mind. The place existed. There had been no accident. He sat there, in his chair by the gas-fire, in the nursing-home; and this had happened, it was not fantasy, born out of tragedy.

He seemed calm, now that he had told me so much. A great

part of the strain had gone, his hands no longer trembled. He looked more like the old Victor, and his voice was steady.

'It must have been centuries old,' he said, after a moment or two. 'God knows how long it must have taken to build, hewn out of the rock-face like that. I have never seen anything more stark and savage, nor, in a strange way, more beautiful. It seemed to hang there, suspended, between the mountain and the sky. There were many long narrow slits, for light and air. No real windows, in the sense we know them. There was a tower, looking west, with a sheer drop below. The great wall encircled the whole place, making it impregnable, like a fortress. I could see no way of entrance. There was no sign of life. No sign of anyone. I stood there staring at the place, and the narrow window slits stared back at me. There was nothing I could do but wait there until Anna showed herself. Because now, you see, I was convinced the old man had been right, and I knew what must have happened. The inhabitants had seen Anna, from behind those slit windows, and had called to her. She was with them now, inside. She must see me, standing outside the wall, and presently would come out to me. So I waited there, all day . . .'

His words were simple. Just a plain statement of fact. Any husband might have waited thus for a wife who had, during their holiday, ventured forth one morning to call upon friends. He sat down, and later ate his lunch, and watched the rolling banks of cloud that hid the world below move, and disperse, and form again; and the sun, in all its summer strength, beat down upon the unprotected face of Monte Verità, on the tower and the narrow window-slits, and the great encircling wall, from whence came no movement and no sound.

'I sat there all the day,' said Victor, 'but she did not come. The force of the sun was blinding, scorching, and I had to go back to the gully-way for shelter. There, lying under the shadow of a projecting rock, I could still watch that tower and those window slits. You and I in the past have known silence on the mountains, but nothing like the silence beneath those twin peaks of Monte Verità.

'The hours dragged by and I went on waiting. Gradually it grew cooler, and then, as my anxiety increased, time raced instead. The sun went too fast into the west. The colour of the rock-face was changing. There was no longer any glare. I began to panic then. I went to the wall and shouted. I felt along the wall with my hands, but there was no entrance, there was nothing. My voice echoed back to me, again and again. I looked up, and all I could see were those blind slits of windows. I began to doubt everything, the old man's story, all that he had said. This place was uninhabited, no one had lived there for a thousand years. It was something built long ago in time, and now deserted. And Anna had never come to it at all. She had fallen, on that narrow lip-way where the track ended and the man had left me. She must have fallen into the sheer depths where the southern shoulder of the mountain ridge began. And this is what had happened to the other women who had come this way, the old man's daughter, the girls from the valleys; they had all fallen, none of them had ever reached the ultimate rock-face, here between the peaks.'

The suspense would have been easier to bear if the first strain and sign of breakdown had come back into Victor's voice. As it was, sitting there in the London nursing-home, the room imper-sonal and plain, the routine bottles of medicines and pills on the table by his side, and the sound of traffic coming from Wigmore Street, his voice took on a steady monotonous quality, like a clock ticking; it would have been more natural had he turned suddenly, and screamed.

'Yet I dared not go back,' he said, 'unless she came. I was compelled to go on waiting there, beneath the wall. The clouds banked up towards me and turned grey. All the warning evening shadows that I knew too well crept into the sky. One moment the rock-face, and the wall, and the slit windows were golden; then, suddenly, the sun was gone. There was no dusk at all. It was cold, and it was night.'

Victor told me that he stayed there against the wall until daybreak. He did not sleep. He paced up and down to keep warm. When dawn came he was chilled and numb, faint, too, from want of food. He had brought with him only the rations for their midday meal.

Sense told him that to wait now, through another day, was madness. He must return to the village for food and drink, and if possible enlist the help of the men there to form a search-party. Reluctantly, when the sun rose, he left the rock-face. Silence enwrapped it still. He was certain now there was no life behind the walls.

He went back, round the shoulder of the mountain, to the track; and so down into the morning mist, and to the village.

Victor said they were waiting there for him. It was as though he was expected. The old man was standing at the entrance of his home, and gathered about him were neighbours, mostly men and children.

Victor's first question was, 'Has my wife returned?' Somehow, descending from the summit, hope had come to him again – that she had never climbed the mountain track, that she had walked another way, and had come back to the village by a different path. When he saw their faces his hope went.

'She will not come back,' said the old man, 'we told you she would not come back. She has gone to them, on Monte Verità.'

Victor had wisdom enough to ask for food and drink before entering into argument. They gave him this. They stood beside him, watching him with compassion. Victor said the greatest agony was the sight of Anna's pack, her mattress, her drinking bottle, her knife; the little personal possessions she had not taken with her.

When he had eaten they continued to stand there, waiting for him to speak. He told the old man everything. How he had waited all day, and through the night. How there was never a sound, or a sign of life, from those slit windows on the rock-face on Monte Verità. Now and again the old man translated what Victor said to the neighbours.

When Victor had finished the old man spoke.

'It is as I said. Your wife is there. She is with them.'

Victor, his nerves to pieces, shouted aloud.

'How can she be there? There is no one alive in that place. It's dead, it's empty. It's been dead for centuries.'

The old man leant forward and put his hand on Victor's shoulder. 'It is not dead. That is what many have said before. They went and waited, as you waited. Twenty-five years ago I did the same. This man here, my neighbour, waited three months, day after day, night after night, many years ago, when his wife was called. She never came back. No one who is called to Monte Verità returns.'

She had fallen, then. She had died. It was that after all. Victor told them this, he insisted upon it, he begged that they would go now, with him, and search the mountain for her body.

Gently, compassionately, the old man shook his head. 'In the past we did that too,' he said. 'There are those among us who climb with great skill, who know the mountain, every inch of it, and who have descended the southern side even, to the edge of the great glacier, beyond which no one can live. There are no bodies. Our women never fell. They were not there. They are in Monte Verità, with the *sacerdotesse*.'

It was hopeless, Victor said. It was no use to try argument. He knew that he must go down to the valley, and if he could not get help there go further yet, back to some part of the country that was familiar to him, where he could find guides who would be willing to return with him.

'My wife's body is somewhere on this mountain,' he said. 'I must find it. If your people won't help me, I will get others.'

The old man looked over his shoulder and spoke a name. From the little crowd of silent spectators came a child, a small girl of about nine years old. He laid his hand upon her head.

'This child,' he said to Victor, 'has seen and spoken with the *sacerdotesse*. Other children, in the past, have seen them too. Only to children, and then rarely, do they show themselves. She will tell you what she saw.'

The child began her recitation, in a high sing-song voice, her eyes fixed upon Victor; and he could tell, he said, that it was a tale she had repeated so many times, to the same listeners, that it was now a chant, a lesson learnt by heart. And it was all in patois. Not one word could Victor understand.

When she had finished the old man acted as interpreter; and from force of habit he too declaimed as the child had done, his tone taking that same sing-song quality.

'I was with my companions on Monte Verità. A storm came, and my companions ran away. I walked, and lost myself, and came to the place where the wall is, and the windows. I cried; I was afraid. She came out of the wall, the tall and splendid one, and another with her, also young and beautiful. They comforted me and I wanted to go inside the walls with them, when I heard the singing from the tower, but they told me it was forbidden. When I was thirteen years old I could return to live with them. They wore white raiment to the knees, their arms and legs were bare, the hair close to the head. They were more beautiful than the people of this world. They led me back from Monte Verità, down the track where I could find my way. Then they went from me. I have told all I know.'

The old man watched Victor's face when he had finished his recital. Victor said the faith that must have been put in the child's statement astounded him. It was obvious, he thought, that the child had fallen asleep, and dreamt, and translated her dream into reality.

'I am sorry,' he told his interpreter, 'but I can't believe the child's tale. It is imagination.'

Once again the child was called and spoken to, and she at once ran out of the house and disappeared.

'They gave her a circlet of stones on Monte Verità,' said the old man. 'Her parents keep it locked up, in case of evil. She has gone to ask for it, to show you.'

In a few moments the child returned, and she put into Victor's hand a girdle, small enough to encompass a narrow waist, or else to hang about the neck. The stones, which looked like quartz, were cut and shaped by hand, fitting into one another in hollowed grooves. The craftsmanship was fine, even exquisitely done. It was

70

not the rude handiwork of peasants, done of a winter's evening, to pass the time. In silence Victor handed the circlet back to the child.

'She may have found it on the mountain side,' he said.

'We do not work thus,' answered the old man, 'nor the people in the valley, nor even in the cities of this country, where I have been. The child was given the circlet, as she has told us, by those who inhabit Monte Verità.'

Victor knew then that further argument was useless. Their obstinacy was too strong, and their superstition proof against all worldly sense. He asked if he might remain in the house another day and night.

'You are welcome to stay,' said the old man, 'until you know the truth.'

One by one the neighbours dispersed, the routine of the quiet day was resumed. It was as though nothing had happened. Victor went out again, this time towards the northern shoulder of the mountain. He had not gone far before he realized that this ridge was unclimbable, at any rate without skilled help and equipment. If Anna had gone that way she had found certain death.

He came back to the village, which, situated as it was on the eastern slopes, had already lost the sun. He went into the living-room, and saw that there was a meal there prepared for him, and his mattress lay on the floor before the hearth.

He was too exhausted to eat. He flung himself down on the mattress and slept. Next morning he rose early, and climbed once more to Monte Verità, and sat there all day. He waited, watching the slit windows, while the hot sun scorched the rock-face through the long hours and then sank down into the western sky; and nothing stirred, and no one came.

He thought of that other man from the village who some years ago had waited there three months, day after day, night after night; and Victor wondered what limitation time would put to his endurance, and whether he would equal the other in fortitude.

71

On the third day, at that moment of midday when the sun was strongest, he could bear the heat no longer and went to lie in the gully-way, in the shadow and blessed coolness of the projecting rock. Worn with the strain of watching, and with the despair that now filled his entire being, Victor slept.

He awoke with a start. The hands of his watch pointed to five o'clock, and it was already cold inside the gully. He climbed out and looked towards the rock-face, golden now in the setting sun. Then he saw her. She was standing beneath the wall, but on a ledge only a few feet in circumference, and below her the rock-face fell away sheer, a thousand feet or more.

She waited there, looking towards him, and he ran towards her shouting 'Anna . . . Anna . . .' And he said that he heard himself sobbing, and he thought his heart would burst.

When he drew closer he saw that he could not reach her. The great drop to the depths below divided them. She was a bare twelve feet away from him, and he could not touch her.

'I stood where I was, staring at her,' said Victor. 'I did not speak. Something seemed to choke my voice. I felt the tears running down my face. I was crying. I had made up my mind that she was dead, you see, that she had fallen. And she was there, she was alive. Ordinary words wouldn't come. I tried to say 'What has happened? Where have you been?' – but it wasn't any use. Because as I looked at her I knew in one moment, with terrible blinding certainty, that it was all true, what the old man had said, and the child; it wasn't imagination, it wasn't superstition. Though I saw no one but Anna, the whole place suddenly became alive. From behind those window slits above me there were God knows how many eyes, watching, looking down on me. I could feel the nearness of them, beyond those walls. And it was uncanny, and horrible, and real.'

Now the strain had come back into Victor's voice, now his hands trembled once again. He reached out for a glass of water and drank thirstily.

'She was not wearing her own clothes,' he said. 'She had a kind of shirt, like a tunic, to her knees, and round her waist a

72

circlet of stones, like the one the child had shown me. Nothing on her feet, and her arms bare. What frightened me most was that her hair was cut quite short, as short as yours or mine. It altered her strangely, made her look younger, but in some way terribly austere. Then she spoke to me. She said quite naturally, as if nothing had happened, "I want you to go back home, Victor darling. You mustn't worry about me any more.'"

Victor told me he could hardly credit it, at first, that she could stand there and say this to him. It reminded him of those so-called psychic messages that mediums give out to relatives at a spiritualistic séance. He could hardly trust himself to answer. He thought that perhaps she had been hypnotized and was speaking under suggestion.

'Why do you want me to go home?' he said, very gently, not wanting to damage her mind, which these people might have destroyed.

'It's the only thing to do,' she answered. And then, Victor said, she smiled, normally, happily, as if they were at home discussing plans. 'I'm all right, darling,' she said. 'This isn't madness, or hypno-tism, or any of the things you imagine it to be. They have fright-ened you in the village, and it's understandable. This thing is so much stronger than most people. But I must have always known it existed, somewhere; and I've been waiting all these years. When men go into monasteries, and women shut themselves up in convents, their relatives suffer very much, I know, but in time they come to bear it. I want you to do the same, Victor, please. I want you, if you can, to understand.'

She stood there, quite calm, quite peaceful, smiling down at him.

'You mean,' he said, 'you want to stay in this place always?'

'Yes,' she said, 'there can be no other life for me, any more, ever. You must believe this. I want you to go home, and live as you have always done, and look after the house and the estate, and if you fall in love with anyone to marry and be happy. Bless you for your love and kindness and devotion, darling, which I shall never forget. If I were dead, you would want to think of me at peace, in paradise. This place, to me, is paradise. And I would rather jump now, to those rocks hundreds of feet below me, than go back to the world from Monte Verità.'

Victor said he went on staring at her as she spoke, and he said there was a radiance about her there had never been before, even in their most contented days.

'You and I,' he said to me, 'have both read of transfiguration in the Bible. That is the only word I can use to describe her face. It was not hysteria, it was not emotion; it was just that. Something – out of this world of ours – had put its hand upon her. To plead with her was useless, to attempt force impossible. Anna, rather than go back to the world, would throw herself off the rock-face. I should achieve nothing.'

He said the feeling of utter helplessness was overwhelming, the knowledge that there was nothing he could do. It was as if he and she were standing on a dockway, and she was about to set foot in a ship, bound to an unknown destination, and the last few minutes were passing by before the ship's siren blew, warning him the gangways would be withdrawn and she must go.

He asked her if she had all she needed, if she would be given sufficient food, enough covering, and whether there were any facilities should she fall ill. He wanted to know if there was anything she wanted that he could send to her. And she smiled back at him, saying she had everything, within those walls, that she would ever need.

He said to her, 'I shall return every year, at this time, to ask you to come back. I shall never forget.'

She said, 'It will be harder for you if you do that. Like putting flowers on a grave. I would rather you stayed away.'

'I can't stay away,' he said, 'with the knowledge you are here, behind these walls.'

'I won't be able to come to you again,' she said, 'this is the last time you will see me. Remember, though, that I shall go on looking like this, always. That is part of the belief. Carry me with you.'

Then, Victor said, she asked him to go. She could not return inside the walls until he had gone. The sun was low in the sky and already the rock-face was in shadow.

Victor looked at Anna a long time; then he turned his back on her, standing by the ledge, and walked away from the wall towards the gully, without looking over his shoulder. When he came to the gully he waited there a few minutes, then looked out again towards the rock-face. Anna was no longer standing on the ledge. There was nothing there but the wall and the slit windows, and above, not yet in shadow, the twin peaks of Monte Verità.

I managed to spare half an hour or so, every day, to go and visit Victor in the nursing-home. Each day he appeared stronger, more himself. I spoke to the doctor attending him, to the matron and the nurses. They told me there was no question of a deranged mind; he came to them suffering from severe shock and nervous collapse. It had already done him immense good to see me and to talk to me. In a fortnight he was well enough to leave the nursing-home, and he came to stay with me in Westminster.

During those autumn evenings we went over all that had happened again and again. I questioned him more closely than I had done before. He denied that there had ever been anything abnormal about Anna. Theirs had been a normal, happy marriage. Her dislike of possessions, her spartan way of living, was, he agreed, unusual; but it had not struck him as peculiar – it was Anna. I told him of the night I had seen her standing with bare feet in the garden, on the frosted lawn. Yes, he said, that was the sort of thing she did. But she had a fastidiousness, a certain personal reticence, that he respected. He never intruded upon it.

I asked him how much he knew of her life before he married her. He told me there was very little to know. Her parents had died when she was young, and she had been brought up in Wales by an aunt. There was no peculiar background, no skeletons in the cupboard. Her upbringing had been entirely ordinary in every way.

'It's no use,' said Victor, 'you can't explain Anna. She is just herself, unique. You can't explain her any more than you can explain the sudden phenomenon of a musician, born to ordinary parents, or a poet, or a saint. There is no accounting for them. They just appear. It was my great fortune, praise God, to find her, just as it is my own personal hell, now, to have lost her. Somehow I shall continue living, as she expected me to do. And once a year I shall go back to Monte Verità.'

His acquiescence to the total break-up of his life astounded me. I felt that I could not have overcome my own despair, had the tragedy been mine. It seemed to me monstrous that an unknown sect, on a mountain side, could, in the space of a few days, have such power over a woman, a woman of intelligence and personality. It was understandable that ignorant peasant girls could be emotionally misled and their relatives, blinded by superstition, do nothing about it. I told Victor this. I told him that it should be possible, through the ordinary channels of our embassy, to approach the government of that country, to have a nationwide inquiry, to get the Press on to it, the backing of our own government. I told him I was prepared, myself, to set all this in motion. We were living in the twentieth century, not in the Middle Ages. A place like Monte Verità should not be permitted to exist. I would arouse the whole country with the story, create an international situation.

'But why,' said Victor quietly, 'to what end?'

'To get Anna back,' I said, 'and to free the rest. To prevent the break-up of other people's lives.'

'We don't,' said Victor, 'go about destroying monasteries or convents. There are hundreds of them, all over the world.'

'That is different,' I argued. 'They are organized bodies of religious people. They have existed for centuries.'

'I think, very probably, Monte Verità has too.'

'How do they live, how do they eat, what happens when they fall ill, when they die?'

'I don't know. I try not to think about it. All I cling to is that Anna said she had found what she was searching for, that she was happy. I'm not going to destroy that happiness.'

Then he looked at me, in a way half puzzled, half wise, and said, 'It's odd, your talking in this way. Because by rights you should understand Anna's feelings more than I do. You were always the one with mountain fever. You were the one, in old climbing days, to have your head in the clouds and quote to me —

> *The world is too much with us; late and soon,*
> *Getting and spending, we lay waste our powers.'*

I remember getting up and going over to the window and looking out over the foggy street, down to the embankment. I said nothing. His words had moved me very much. I could not answer them. And I knew, in the depths of my heart, why I hated the story of Monte Verità and wanted the place to be destroyed. It was because Anna had found her Truth, and I had not . . .

That conversation between Victor and myself made, if not a division in our friendship, at least a turning-point. We had reached a half-way mark in both our lives. He went back to his home in Shropshire, and later wrote to me that he intended making over the property to a young nephew, still at school, and during the next few years intended having the lad to stay with him in the holidays, to get him acquainted with the place. After that, he did not know. He would not commit himself to plans. My own future, at this time, was full with change. My work necessitated living in America for a period of two years.

Then, as it turned out, the whole tenor of the world became disrupted. The following year was 1914.

Victor was one of the first to join up. Perhaps he thought this would be his answer. Perhaps he thought he might be killed. I did not follow his example until my period in America was over. It was certainly not my answer, and I disliked every moment of my army years. I saw nothing of Victor during the whole of the war; we fought on different fronts, and did not even meet on leave. I did hear from him, once. And this is what he said:

In spite of everything, I have managed to get to Monte Verità each year, as I promised to do. I stayed a night with the old man in the village, and climbed on to the mountain top the following day. It looked exactly the same. Quite dead, and silent. I left a letter for Anna beneath the wall and sat there, all the day, looking at the place, feeling her near. I knew she would not come to me. The next day I went again, and was overjoyed to find a letter from her in return. If you can call it a letter. It was cut on flat stone, and I suppose this is the only method they have of communication. She said she was well, and strong, and very happy. She gave me her blessing, and you also. She told me never to be anxious for her. That was all. It was, as I told you at the nursing-home, like a spirit message from the dead. With this I have to be content, and am. If I survive this war, I shall probably go out and live somewhere in that country, so that I can be near her, even if I never see her again, or hear nothing of her but a few words scrawled on a stone once a year.

Good luck to yourself, old fellow. I wonder where you are.

Victor

When the Armistice came, and I got myself demobilized and set about the restoration of my normal life, one of the first things I did was to inquire for Victor. I wrote to him, in Shropshire. I had a courteous reply from the nephew. He had taken over the house and the estate. Victor had been wounded, but not badly. He had now left England and was somewhere abroad, either in Italy or Spain, the nephew was not sure which. But he believed his uncle had decided to live out there for good. If he had news of him, he would let me know. No further news came. As to myself, I decided I disliked post-war London and the people who lived there. I cut myself loose from home ties too, and went to America.

I did not see Victor again for nearly twenty years.

It was not chance that brought us together again. I am sure of that. These things are predestined. I have a theory that each man's life is like a pack of cards, and those we meet and sometimes love are shuffled with us. We find ourselves in the same suit, held by the hand of Fate. The game is played, we are discarded, and pass on. What combination of events brought me to Europe again at the age of fifty-five, two or three years before the Second World War, does not matter to this story. It so happened that I came.

I was flying from one capital city to another – the names of both are immaterial – and the aeroplane in which I travelled made a forced landing, luckily without loss of life, in desolate mountainous country. For two days the crew and passengers, myself amongst them, held no contact with the outer world. We camped in the partially wrecked machine and waited for rescue. This adventure made headlines in the world Press at the time, even taking precedence, for a few days, over the simmering European situation.

Hardship, for those forty-eight hours, was not acute. Luckily there were no women or children passengers travelling, so we men put the best face on it we could, and waited for rescue. We were confident that help would reach us before long. Our wireless had functioned until the moment of the forced landing, and the operator had given our position. It was all a matter of patience, and of keeping warm.

For my part, with my mission in Europe accomplished and no ties strong enough back in the States to believe myself anxiously awaited, this sudden plunging into the sort of country that years ago I had most passionately loved was a strange experience. I had become so much a man of cities, and a creature of comfort. The high pulse of American living, the pace, the vitality, the whole breathless energy of the New World, had combined to make me forget the ties that still bound me to the Old.

Now, looking about me in the desolation and the splendour, I knew what I had lacked all these years. I forgot my fellow-travellers, forgot the grey fuselage of the crippled plane – an anachronism, surely, amid the wilderness of centuries – and forgot too my grey hair, my heavy frame, and all the burden of my five-and-fifty years. I was a boy again, hopeful, eager, seeking an answer to eternity. Surely it was there, waiting, beyond the further peaks. I stood there, incongruous in my city clothes, and the mountain fever raced back into my blood.

I wanted to get away from the wrecked plane and the pinched faces of my companions; I wanted to forget the waste of the years between. What I would have given to be young again, a boy, and, reckless of the consequences, set forth towards those peaks and climb to glory. I knew how it would feel, up there on the higher mountains. The air keener and still more cold, the silence deeper. The strange burning quality of ice, the penetrating strength of the sun, and that moment when the heart misses a beat as the foot, momentarily slipping on the narrow ledge, seeks safety; the hand's clutch to the rope.

I gazed up at them, the mountains that I loved, and felt a traitor. I had betrayed them for baser things, for comfort, ease, security. When rescue came to me and to my fellow-travellers, I would make amends for the time that had been lost. There was no pressing hurry to return to the States. I would take a vacation, here in Europe, and go climbing once again. I would buy proper clothes, equipment, set myself to it. This decision taken, I felt light-hearted, irresponsible. Nothing seemed to matter any more. I returned to my little party, sheltering beside the plane, and laughed and joked through the remaining hours.

Help reached us on the second day. We had been certain of rescue when we had sighted an aeroplane, at dawn, hundreds of feet above us. The search party consisted of true mountaineers and guides, rough fellows but likeable. They had brought clothing, kit, and food for us, and were astonished, they admitted, that we were all in condition to make use of them. They had thought to find none of us alive.

They helped us down to the valley in easy stages, and it took us until the following day. We spent the night encamped on the north side of the great ridge of mountains that had seemed to us, beside the useless plane, so remote and so inaccessible. At daybreak we set forth again, a splendid clear day, and the whole of the valley below our camp lay plain to the eye. Eastward the mountain range ran sheer, and as far as I could judge impassable, to a snow-capped peak, or possibly two, that pierced the dazzling sky like the knuckles on a closed hand.

I said to the leader of the rescue expedition, just as we were starting out on the descent, 'I used to climb much, in old days, when I was young. I don't know this country at all. Do many expeditions come this way?'

He shook his head. He told me conditions were difficult. He and his companions came from some distance away. The people in the valley to the eastward there were backward and ignorant; there were few facilities for tourists or for strangers. If I cared about climbing he could take me to other places, where I should find good sport. It was already rather late in the year, though, for expeditions.

I went on looking at that eastward ridge, remote and strangely beautiful.

'What do they call them,' I said, 'those twin peaks, to the east?'

He answered, 'Monte Verità.'

I knew then what had brought me back to Europe . . .

We parted, my fellow-travellers and I, at a little town some twenty miles from the spot where the aeroplane had crashed. Transport took them on to the nearest railway line, and to civil-ization. I remained behind. I booked a room at the small hotel and deposited my luggage there. I bought myself strong boots, a pair of breeches, a jerkin, and a couple of shirts. Then I turned my back upon the town and climbed.

It was, as the guide had told me, late in the year for expeditions. Somehow I did not care. I was alone, and on the mountains once again. I had forgotten how healing solitude could be. The old strength came back to my legs and to my lungs, and the cold air bit into the whole of me. I could have shouted with delight, at fifty-five. Gone was the turmoil and the stress, the anxious stir of many millions; gone were the lights, and the vapid city smells. I had been mad to endure it for so long.

In a mood of exaltation I came to the valley that lies at the eastern foot of Monte Verità. It had not changed much, it seemed to me, from the description Victor gave of it, those many years ago before the war. The little town was small and primitive, the people dull and dour. There was a rough sort of inn – one could not grace it by the name of hotel – where I proposed to stay the night.

I was received with indifference, though not discourtesy. After supper I asked if the track was still passable to the summit of Monte Verità. My informant behind his bar – for bar and café were in one, and I ate there, being the only visitor – regarded me without interest as he drank the glass of wine I offered him.

'It is passable, I believe, as far as the village. Beyond that I do not know,' he said.

'Is there much coming and going between your people in the valley here and those in the village on the mountain?' I asked.

'Sometimes. Perhaps. Not at this time of year,' he answered.

'Do you ever have tourists here?'

'Few tourists. They go north. It is better in the north.'

'Is there any place in the village where I could sleep tomorrow night?'

'I do not know.'

I paused a moment, watching his heavy sullen face, then I said to him, 'And the *sacerdotesse*, do they still live on the rock-face on the summit of Monte Verità?'

He started. He turned his eyes full upon me, and leant over the bar. 'Who are you, then? What do you know of them?'

'Then they do exist still?' I said.

He watched me, suspicious. Much had happened to his country in the past twenty years, violence, revolution, hostility between father and son, and even this remote corner must have had its share. It may have been this that made reserve.

'There are stories,' he said, slowly. 'I prefer not to mix myself up in such matters. It is dangerous. One day there will be trouble.'

'Trouble for whom?'

'For those in the village, for those who may live on Monte Verità – I know nothing of them – for us here in the valley. I do not know. If I do not know, no harm can come to me.'

He finished his wine, and cleaned his glass, and wiped the bar with a cloth. He was anxious to be rid of me.

'At what time do you wish for your breakfast in the morning?' he said.

I told him seven, and went up to my room.

I opened the double windows and stood out on the narrow balcony. The little town was quiet. Few lights winked in the darkness. The night was clear and cold. The moon had risen and would be full tomorrow or the day after. It shone upon the dark mountain mass in front of me. I felt oddly moved, as though I had stepped back into the past. This room, where I should pass the night, might have been the same one where Victor and Anna slept, all those years ago, in the summer of 1913. Anna herself might have stood here, on the balcony, gazing up at Monte Verità, while Victor, unconscious of the tragedy so few hours distant, called to her from within.

And now, in their footsteps, I had come to Monte Verità.

The next morning I took my breakfast in the café-bar, and my landlord of the night before was absent. My coffee and bread were brought to me by a girl, perhaps his daughter. Her manner was quiet and courteous, and she wished me a pleasant day.

'I am going to climb,' I said, 'the weather seems set fair. Tell me, have you ever been to Monte Verità?'

Her eyes flickered away from mine instantly.

'No,' she said, 'no, I have never been away from the valley.'

My manner was matter-of-fact, and casual. I said something about friends of mine having been here, some while ago – I did not say how long – and that they had climbed to the summit, and had found the rock-face there, between the peaks, and had been much interested to learn about the sect who lived enclosed within the walls.

'Are they still there, do you know?' I asked, lighting a cigarette, elaborately at ease.

She glanced over her shoulder nervously, as though conscious that she might be overheard.

'It is said so,' she answered. 'My father does not discuss it before me. It is a forbidden subject to young people.'

I went on smoking my cigarette.

'I live in America,' I said, 'and I find that there, as in most places, when the young people get together there is nothing they like discussing so well as forbidden subjects.'

She smiled faintly but said nothing.

'I dare say you and your young friends often whisper together about what happens on Monte Verità,' I said.

I felt slightly ashamed of my duplicity, but I felt that this method of attack was the most likely one to produce information.

'Yes,' she said, 'that is true. But we say nothing out loud. But just lately . . .' Once again she glanced over her shoulder, and then resumed, her voice pitched lower, 'A girl I knew quite well, she was to marry shortly, she went away one day, she has not come back, and they are saying she has been called to Monte Verità.'

'No one saw her go?'

'No. She went by night. She left no word, nothing.'

'Could she not have gone somewhere quite different, to a large town, to one of the tourist centres?'

'It is believed not. Besides, just before, she had acted strangely. She had been heard talking in her sleep about Monte Verità.'

I waited for a moment, then continued my inquiry, still nonchalant, still casual.

'What is the fascination in Monte Verità?' I asked. 'The life there must be unbearably harsh, and even cruel?'

'Not to those who are called,' she said, shaking her head. 'They stay young always, they never grow old.'

'If nobody has ever seen them, how can you know?'

'It has always been so. That is the belief. That is why here, in the valley, they are hated and feared, and also envied. They have the secret of life, on Monte Verità.'

She looked out of the window towards the mountain. There was a wistful expression in her eyes.

'And you?' I said. 'Do you think you will ever be called?'

'I am not worthy,' she said. 'Also, I am afraid.'

She took away my coffee and offered me some fruit.

'And now,' she said, her voice still lower, 'since this last disappearance, there is likely to be trouble. The people are angry, here in the valley. Some of the men have climbed to the village and are trying to rouse them there, to get force of numbers, and then they will attack the rock. Our men will go wild. They will try to kill those who live there. Then there will be more trouble, we shall get the army here, there will be inquiries, punishments, shooting; it will all end badly. So it is not pleasant at the moment. Everyone goes about afraid. Everybody is whispering in secret.'

A footstep outside sent her swiftly behind the bar. She busied herself there, her head low, as her father came into the room.

He glanced at both of us, suspiciously. I put out my cigarette and rose from the table.

'So you are still intent to climb?' he asked me.

'Yes,' I said. 'I shall be back in a day or two.'

'It would be imprudent to stay there longer,' he said.

'You mean the weather will break?'

'The weather will break, yes. Also, it might not be safe.'

'In what way might it not be safe?'

'There may be disturbance. Things are unsettled just now. Men are out of temper. When they are out of temper, they lose their heads. And strangers, foreigners, can come to harm at such a time.

85

It would be better if you gave up your idea of climbing Monte Verità and turned northwards. There is no trouble there.'

'Thank you. But I have set my heart on climbing Monte Verità.'

He shrugged his shoulders. He looked away from me.

'As you will,' he said, 'it is not my affair.'

I walked out of the inn, down to the street, and crossing the little bridge above the mountain stream I set my face to the track through the valley that led me to the eastern face of Monte Verità.

At first the sounds from the valley were distinct. The barking of dogs, the tinkle of cow bells, the voices of men calling to one another, all these rose clearly to me in the still air. Then the blue smoke from the houses merged and became one misty haze, and the houses themselves took on a toy-town quality. The track wound above me and away, ever deeper into the heart of the mountain itself, until by midday the valley was lost in the depths and I had no other thought in my mind but to climb upwards, higher, always higher, win my way beyond that first ridge to the left, leave it behind me and gain the second, forget both in turn to achieve the third, steeper yet and overshadowed. My progress was slow, with untuned muscles and imperfect wind, but exhilaration of spirit kept me going and I was in no way tired, rather the reverse. I could have gone on for ever.

It was with a shock of surprise that I came finally upon the village, for I had pictured it at least another hour away. I must have climbed at a great pace, for it was barely four o'clock. The village wore a forlorn, almost deserted appearance, and I judged that today there were few remaining inhabitants. Some of the dwellings were boarded up, others fallen in and partly destroyed. Smoke came only from two or three of them, and I saw no one working in the pasture-land around. A few cows, lean-looking and unkempt, grazed by the side of the track, the jangling bells around their necks sounding hollow somehow in the still air. The place had a sombre, depressing effect, after the stimulation of the climb. If this was where I must spend the night I did not think much of it.

I went to the door of the first dwelling that had a thin wisp of smoke coming from the roof and knocked upon the door. It was opened, after some time, by a lad of about fourteen, who after one look at me called over his shoulder to somebody within. A man of about my own age, stupid-looking and heavy, came to the door. He said something to me in patois, then staring a moment, and realizing his mistake, he broke, even more haltingly than I, into the language of the country.

'You are the doctor from the valley?' he said to me.

'No,' I replied, 'I am a stranger on vacation, climbing in the district. I want a bed for the night, if you can give me one.'

His face fell. He did not reply directly to my request.

'We have someone here very sick,' he said, 'I do not know what to do. They said a doctor would come from the valley. You met no one?'

'I'm afraid not. No one climbed from the valley except myself. Who is ill? A child?'

The man shook his head. 'No, no, we have no children here.'

He went on looking at me, in a dazed, helpless sort of way, and I felt sorry for his trouble, but I did not see what I could do. I had no sort of medicines upon me but a first-aid packet and a small bottle of aspirin. The aspirin might be of use, if there was fever. I undid it from my pack and gave a handful to the man.

'These may help,' I said, 'if you care to try them.'

He beckoned me inside. 'Please to give them yourself,' he said.

I had some reluctance to step within and be faced with the grim spectacle of a dying relative, but plain humanity told me I could hardly do otherwise. I followed him into the living-room. There was a trestle bed against the wall and lying upon it, covered with two blankets, was a man, his eyes closed. He was pale and unshaven, and his features had that sharp pointed look about them that comes upon the face when near to death. I went close to the bed and gazed down upon him. He opened his eyes. For a moment we stared at one another, unbelieving. Then he put out his hand to me, and smiled. It was Victor . . .

'Thank God,' he said.

I was too much moved to speak. I saw him beckon to the fellow, who stood apart, and speak to him in the patois, and he must have told him we were friends, for some sort of light broke in the man's face and he withdrew. I went on standing by the trestle bed, with Victor's hand in mine.

'How long have you been like this?' I asked at length.

'Nearly five days,' he said. 'Touch of pleurisy; I've had it before. Rather worse this time. I'm getting old.'

Once again he smiled, and although I guessed him to be desperately ill, he was little changed, he was the same Victor still.

'You seem to have prospered,' he said to me, still smiling, 'you have all the sleek appearance of success.'

I asked him why he had never written, and what he had been doing with himself for twenty years.

'I cut myself adrift,' he said. 'I gather you did the same, but in a different way. I haven't been back to England since I left. What is it that you're holding there?'

I showed him the bottle of aspirin.

'I'm afraid that's no use to you,' I said. 'The best thing I can suggest is for me to stay here tonight, and then first thing in the morning get the chap here, and one or two others, to help me carry you down to the valley.'

He shook his head. 'Waste of time,' he said. 'I'm done for. I know that.'

'Nonsense. You need a doctor, proper nursing. That's impossible in this place.' I looked around the primitive living-room, dark and airless.

'Never mind about me,' he said. 'Someone else is more important.'

'Who?'

'Anna,' he said, and then as I answered nothing, at a loss for words, he added, 'She's still here, you know, on Monte Verità.'

'You mean,' I said, 'that she's in that place, enclosed, she's never left it?'

'That's why I'm here,' said Victor. 'I come every year, and have

88

done, since the beginning. I wrote and told you, surely, after the war? I live in a little fishing port all the year round, very isolated and quiet, and then come here once in twelve months. I left it later this year, because I had been ill.'

It was incredible. What an existence, all these years, without friends, without interests, enduring the long months until the time came for this hopeless annual pilgrimage.

'Have you ever seen her?' I asked.

'Never.'

'Do you write to her?'

'I bring a letter every year. I take it up with me and leave it beneath the wall, and then return the following day.'

'The letter gets taken?'

'Always. And in its place there is a slab of stone, with writing scrawled upon it. Never more than a few words. I take the stones away with me. I have them all down on the coast, where I live.'

It was heart-rending, his faith in her, his fidelity through the years.

'I've tried to study it,' he said, 'this religion, belief. It's very ancient, way back before Christianity. There are old books that hint at it. I've picked them up from time to time, and I've spoken to people, scholars, who have made a study of mysticism and the old rites of ancient Gaul, and the Druids; there's a strong link between all mountain folk of those times. In every instance that I have read there is this insistence on the power of the moon and the belief that the followers stay young and beautiful.'

'You talk, Victor, as if you believe that too,' I said.

'I do,' he answered. 'The children believe it, here in the village, the few that remain.'

Talking to me had tired him. He reached out for a pitcher of water that stood beside the bed.

'Look here,' I said, 'these aspirins can't hurt you, they can only help, if you have fever. And you might get some sleep.'

I made him swallow three, and drew the blankets closer round him.

89

'Are there any women in the house?' I asked.

'No,' he said, 'I've been puzzled about that, since I've been here this time. The village is pretty much deserted. All the women and children have shifted to the valley. There are about twenty men and boys left, all told.'

'Do you know when the women and children went?'

'I gather they left a few days before I came. This fellow here – he's the son of the old man who used to live here, who died many years ago – is such a fool that he never knows anything. He just looks vague if you question him. But he's competent, in his own way. He'll give you food, and find bedding for you, and the little chap is bright enough.'

Victor closed his eyes, and I hoped that he might sleep. I thought I knew why the women and children had left the village. It was since the girl from the valley had disappeared. They had been warned that trouble might come to Monte Verità. I did not dare tell Victor this. I wished I could persuade him to be carried down into the valley.

By this time it was quite dark, and I was hungry. I went through a sort of recess to the back. There was no one there but the boy. I asked him for something to eat and drink, and he understood. He brought me bread, and meat, and cheese, and I ate it in the living-room, with the boy watching me. Victor's eyes were still closed and I believed he slept.

'Will he get better?' asked the boy. He did not speak in patois.

'I think so,' I answered, 'if I can get help to carry him to a doctor in the valley.'

'I will help you,' said the boy, 'and two of my companions. We should go tomorrow. After that, it will be difficult.'

'Why?'

'There will be coming and going the day after. Men from the valley, much excitement, and my companions and I will join them.'

'What is going to happen?' He hesitated. He looked at me with quick bright eyes.

'I do not know,' he said. He slipped away, back to the recess. Victor's voice came from the trestle bed.

'What did the boy say?' he asked. 'Who is coming from the valley?'

'I don't know,' I said casually, 'some expedition, perhaps. But he has offered to help take you down the mountain tomorrow.'

'No expeditions ever come here,' said Victor, 'there must be some mistake.' He called to the boy, and when the lad reappeared spoke to him in the patois. The boy was ill at ease, and diffident; he seemed reluctant now to answer questions. Several times I heard the words Monte Verità repeated, both by him and Victor. Presently he went back to the inner room and left us alone.

'Did you understand any of that?' asked Victor.

'No,' I replied.

'I don't like it,' he said, 'there's something queer. I've felt it, since I've lain here these last few days. The men look furtive, odd. He tells me there's been some disturbance in the valley, and the people there are very angry. Did you hear anything about it?'

I did not know what to say. He was watching me closely.

'The fellow in the inn was not very forthcoming,' I said, 'but he did advise against coming to Monte Verità.'

'What reason did he give?'

'No particular reason. He just said there might be trouble.'

Victor was silent. I could feel him thinking there beside me.

'Have any of the women disappeared from the valley?' he said.

It was useless to lie. 'I heard something about a missing girl,' I told him, 'but I don't know if it's true.'

'It will be true. That is it, then.'

He said nothing for a long while, and I could not see his face – it was in shadow. The room was lit by a single lamp, giving a pallid glow.

'You must climb tomorrow and warn Anna at Monte Verità,' he said at last.

I think I had expected this. I asked him how it could be done.

'I can sketch the track for you,' he said, 'you can't go wrong. It's straight up the old water-course, heading south all the while. The rains haven't made it impassable yet. If you leave before dawn you'll have all day before you.'

'What happens when I get there?'

'You must leave a letter, as I do, and then come away. They won't fetch it while you are there. I will write, also. I shall tell Anna that I am ill here, and that you've suddenly appeared, after nearly twenty years. You know, I was thinking, just now, while you were talking to the boy, it's like a miracle. I have a strange sort of feeling Anna brought you here.'

His eyes were shining with that old boyish faith that I remembered.

'Perhaps,' I said. 'Either Anna, or what you used to call my mountain fever.'

'Isn't that the same thing?' he said to me.

We looked at one another in the silence of that small dark room, and then I turned away and called the boy to bring me bedding and a pillow. I would sleep the night on the floor by Victor's bed.

He was restless in the night, and breathed with difficulty. Several times I got up to him and gave him more aspirin and water. He sweated much, which might be a good thing or a bad, I did not know. The night seemed endless, and for myself, I barely slept at all. We were both awake when the first darkness paled.

'You should start now,' he said, and going to him I saw with apprehension that his skin had gone clammy cold. He was worse, I was certain, and much weaker.

'Tell Anna,' he said, 'that if the valley people come she and the others will be in great danger. I am sure of it.'

'I will write all that,' I said.

'She knows how much I love her. I tell her that always in my letters, but you could say so, once again. Wait in the gully. You may have to wait two hours, or even three, or longer still. Then go back to the wall and look for the answer on the slab of stone. It will be there.'

I touched his cold hand and went out into the chill morning air. Then, as I looked about me, I had my first misgiving. There was cloud everywhere. Not only beneath me, masking the track from the valley where I had come the night before, but here in the silent village, wreathing in mist the roofs of the huts, and also above me, where the path wound through scrub and disappeared upon the mountain side.

Softly, silently, the clouds touched my face and drifted past, never dissolving, never clearing. The moisture clung to my hair and to my hands, and I could taste it on my tongue. I looked this way and that, in the half light, wondering what I should do. All the old instinct of self-preservation told me to return. To set forth, in breaking weather, was madness, to my remembered mountain lore. Yet to stay there, in the village, with Victor's eyes upon me, hopeful, patient, was more than I could stand. He was dying, we both knew it. And I carried in my breast pocket his last letter to his wife.

I turned to the south, and still the clouds came travelling past, slowly, relentlessly, down from the summit of Monte Verità.

I began to climb . . .

Victor had told me that I should reach the summit in two hours. Less than that, with the rising sun behind me. I had also a guide, the rough sketch map that he had drawn.

In the first hour after leaving the village I realized my error. I should never see the sun that day. The clouds drove past me, vapour in my face, clammy and cold. They hid the winding water-course up which I had climbed five minutes since, down which already came the mountain springs, loosening the earth and stones.

By the time the contour changed, and I was free of roots and scrub and feeling my way upon bare rock, it was past midday. I was defeated. Worse still, I was lost. I turned back and could not find the water-course that had brought me so far. I approached another, but it ran north-east and had already broken for the season; a torrent of water washed away down the mountain-side. One false move, and the current would have borne me away, tearing my hands to pieces as I sought for a grip among the stones,

Gone was my exultation of the day before. I was no longer

in the thrall of mountain fever but held instead by the equally well-remembered sense of fear. It had happened in the past, many a time, the coming of cloud. Nothing renders a man so helpless, unless he can recognize every inch of the way by which he has come, and so descend. But I had been young in those days, trained, and climbing fit. Now I was a middle-aged city dweller, alone on a mountain I had never climbed before, and I was scared.

I sat down under the lee of a great boulder, away from the drifting cloud, and ate my lunch – the remainder of sandwiches packed at the valley inn – and waited. Then, still waiting, I got up and stamped about for warmth. The air was not penetrating yet but seeping cold, the moist chill cold that always comes with cloud.

I had this one hope, that with the coming of darkness, and with a fall in temperature, the cloud would lift. I remembered it would be full moon, a great point to my advantage, for cloud rarely lingers at these times, but tends to break up and dissolve. I welcomed, therefore, the coming of a sharper cold into the atmosphere. The air was perceptibly keener, and looking out towards the south, from which direction the cloud had drifted all the day, I could now see some ten feet ahead. Below me it was still as thick as ever. A wall of impenetrable mist hid the descent. I went on waiting. Above me, always to the south, the distance that I could see increased from a dozen feet to fifteen, from fifteen to twenty. The cloud was cloud no longer, but vapour only, thin, and vanishing; and suddenly the whole contour of the mountain came into view, not the summit as yet, but the great jutting shoulder, leaning south, and beyond it my first glimpse of the sky.

I looked at my watch again. It was a quarter to six. Night had fallen on Monte Verità.

Vapour came again, obscuring that clear patch of sky that I had seen, and then it drifted, and the sky was there once more. I left my place of shelter where I had been all day. For the second time I was faced with a decision. To climb, or to descend. Above

94

me, the way was clear. There was the shoulder of the mountain, described by Victor; I could even see the ridge along it running to the south, which was the way I should have taken twelve hours before. In two or three hours the moon would have risen and would give me all the light I needed to reach the rock-face of Monte Verità. I looked east, to the descent. The whole of it was hidden in the same wall of cloud. Until the cloud dissolved I should still be in the same position I had been all day, uncertain of direction, helpless in visibility that was never more than three feet.

I decided to go on, and to climb to the summit of the mountain with my message.

Now the cloud was beneath me my spirits revived. I studied the rough map drawn by Victor, and set out towards the southern shoulder. I was hungry, and would have given much to have back the sandwiches I had eaten at midday. A roll of bread was all that remained to me. That, and a packet of cigarettes. Cigarettes were not helpful to the wind, but at least they staved off the desire for food.

Now I could see the twin peaks themselves, clear and stark against the sky. And a new excitement came to me, as I looked up at them, for I knew that when I had rounded the shoulder and had come to the southern face of the mountain, I should have reached my journey's end.

I went on climbing; and I saw how the ridge narrowed and how the rock steepened, becoming more sheer as the southern slopes opened up to view, and then, over my shoulder, rose the first tip of the moon's great face, out of the misty vapour to the east. The sight of it stirred me to a new sense of isolation. It was as though I walked alone on the earth's rim, the universe below me and above. No one trod this empty discus but myself, and it spun its way through space to ultimate darkness.

As the moon rose, the man that climbed with it shrank to insignificance. I was no longer aware of personal identity. This shell, in which I had my being, moved forward without feeling, drawn to the summit of the mountain by some nameless force which seemed to hold suction from the moon itself. I was impelled, like the flow and ebb of tide upon water. I could not disobey the law that urged me on, any more than I could cease to breathe. This was not mountain fever in my blood, but mountain magic. It was not nervous energy that drove me, but the tug of the full moon.

The rock narrowed and closed above my head, making an arch, a gully, so that I had to stoop and feel my way; then I emerged from darkness into light, and there before me, silver-white, were the twin peaks and the rock face of Monte Verità.

For the first time in my life I looked on beauty bare. My mission was forgotten, my anxiety for Victor, my own fear of cloud that had clamped me through the day. This indeed was journey's end. This was fulfilment. Time did not matter. I had no thought of it. I stood there staring at the rock-face under the moon.

How long I remained motionless I do not know, nor do I remember when the change came to the tower and the walls; but suddenly the figures were there, that had not been before. They stood one behind the other on the walls, silhouetted against the sky, and they might have been stone images, carved from the rock itself, so still they were, so motionless.

I was too distant from them to see their faces or their shape. One stood alone, within the open tower; this one alone was shrouded, in a garment reaching from head to foot. Suddenly there came to my mind old tales of ancient days, of Druids, of slaughter, and of sacrifice. These people worshipped the moon, and the moon was full. Some victim was going to be flung to the depths below, and I would witness the act.

I had known fear in my life before, but never terror. Now it came upon me in full measure. I knelt down, in the shadow of the gully, for surely they must see me standing there, in the moon's path. I saw them raise their arms above their heads, and slowly a murmur came from them, low and indistinct at first, then swelling louder, breaking upon the silence that hitherto had been profound. The sound echoed from the rock-face, rose and fell upon the air, and I saw them one and all turn to the full moon. There was no sacrifice. No act of slaughter. This was their song of praise.

I hid there, in the shadows, with all the ignorance and shame of one who stumbles into a place of worship alien to his knowledge, while the chanting rang in my ears, unearthly, terrifying, yet beautiful in a way impossible to bear. I clasped my hands over my head, I shut my eyes, I bent low until my forehead touched the ground.

Then slowly, very slowly, the great hymn of praise faded in strength. It sank lower to a murmur, to a sigh. It hushed and died away. Silence came back to Monte Verità.

Still I dared not move. My hands covered my head. My face was to the ground. I am not ashamed of my terror. I was lost between two worlds. My own was gone, and I was not of theirs. I longed for the sanctuary of the drifting clouds again.

I waited, still upon my knees. Then furtive, creeping, I lifted up my head and looked towards the rock-face. The walls and the tower were bare. The figures had vanished. And a cloud, dark and ragged, hid the moon.

I stood up, but I did not move. I kept my eyes fixed upon the tower and the walls. Nothing stirred, now that the moon was masked. They might never have been, the figures and the chanting. Perhaps my own fear and imagination had created them.

I waited until the cloud that hid the moon's face passed away. Then I took courage and felt for the letters in my pocket. I do not know what Victor had written, but my own ran thus:

Dear Anna,

Some strange providence brought me to the village on Monte Verità. I found Victor there. He is desperately ill, and I think dying. If you have a message to send him, leave it beneath the wall. I will carry it to him. I must warn you also that I believe your community to be in danger. The people from the valley are frightened and angry because one of their women has disappeared. They

97

are likely to come to Monte Verità, and do damage.

In parting, I want to tell you that Victor has never stopped loving you and thinking about you.

And I signed my name at the bottom of the page.

I started walking towards the wall. As I drew close I could see the slit windows, described to me long ago by Victor, and it came to me that there might be eyes behind them, watching, that beyond each narrow opening there could be a figure, waiting.

I stooped and put the letters on the ground beneath the wall. As I did so, the wall before me swung back suddenly and opened. Arms stretched forth from the yawning gap and seized me, and I was flung to the ground, with hands about my throat.

The last thing I heard, before losing consciousness, was the sound of a boy, laughing.

I awoke with violence, jerked back into reality from some great depth of slumber, and I knew that a moment before I had not been alone. Someone had been beside me, kneeling, peering down into my sleeping face.

I sat up and looked about me, cold and numb. I was in a cell about ten foot long, and the daylight, ghostly pale, filtered through the narrow slit in the stone wall. I glanced at my watch. The hands pointed to a quarter to five. I must have lain unconscious for a little over four hours, and this was the false light that comes before dawn.

My first feeling now, on waking, was one of anger. I had been fooled. The people in the village below Monte Verità had lied to me, and to Victor too. The rough hands that had seized me, and the boy's laugh that I heard, these had belonged to the villagers themselves. That man, and his son, had preceded me up the mountain track, and had lain in wait for me. They knew a way of entry through the walls. They had fooled Victor through the years, and thought to fool me too. God alone knew their motive. It could not be robbery. We neither of us had anything but the clothes we wore. This cell into which they had thrust me was quite bare. No sign of human habitation, not even a board on which to lie. A strange thing, though – they had not bound me. And there was no door to the cell. The entry was open, a long slit, like the window, but large enough to permit the passage of a single form.

I sat waiting for the light to strengthen and for the feeling, too, to come back to my shoulders, arms and legs. My sense of caution told me this was wise. If I ventured through the opening now, I might in the dim light stumble, and fall, and be lost in some labyrinth of passage-way or stair.

My anger grew with the daylight, yet with it also a feeling of despair. I longed more than anything to get hold of the fellow and his son, threaten them both, fight them if necessary – I would not be thrown to the ground a second time unawares. But what if they had gone away and left me in this place, without means of exit? Supposing this, then, was the trick they played on strangers, and had done so through countless years, the old man before them, and others before him, luring the women from the valley too, and once inside these walls leaving the victims to star-vation and death? The uneasiness mounting in me would turn to panic if I thought too far ahead, and to calm myself I felt in my pocket for my cigarette case. The first few puffs steadied me, the smell and the taste of the smoke belonged to the world I knew.

Then I saw the frescoes. The growing light betrayed them to me. They covered the walls of the cell, and were drawn upon the ceiling too. Not the rough primitive efforts of uncultured peasants, nor yet the saintly scrawling of religious artists, deeply moved by faith. These frescoes had life and vigour, colour and intensity, and whether they told a story or not I did not know, but the motif was clearly worship of the moon. Some figures knelt, others stood; one and all had their arms up, raised to the full moon traced upon the ceiling. Yet in some strange fashion the eyes of the worshippers, drawn with uncanny skill, looked down upon me, not upwards to the moon. I smoked my ciga-rette and looked away, but all the time I felt their eyes fasten on me, as the daylight grew, and it was like being back outside the walls again, aware of silent watchers from behind the slit windows.

I got up, stamping on my cigarette, and it seemed to me that anything would be better than to remain there in the cell, alone with those figures on the painted walls. I moved to the opening, and as I did so I heard the laughter once again. Softer this time, as though subdued, but mocking and youthful still. That damned boy . . .

I plunged through the opening, cursing him and shouting. He might have a knife upon him but I didn't care. And there he was, flattened against the wall, waiting for me. I could see the gleam of his eyes, and I saw his close-cropped hair. I struck at his face, and missed. I heard him laughing as he slipped to one side. Then he wasn't alone any more; there was another just behind, and a third. They threw themselves upon me and I was borne to the ground as though I had no strength at all, and the first one knelt with his knee on my chest and his hands about my throat, and he was smiling at me.

I lay fighting for breath, and he relaxed his grip, and the three of them watched me, with that same mocking smile upon their lips. I saw then that none of them was the boy from the village, nor was the father there, and they did not have the faces of village people or of the valley people: their faces were like the painted frescoes on the wall.

Their eyes were heavy-lidded, slanting, without mercy, like the eyes I had seen once long ago on an Egyptian tomb, and on a vase long hidden and forgotten under the dust and rubble of a buried city. Each wore a tunic to his knees, with bare arms, bare legs and hair cropped close to the head, and there was a strange austere beauty about them, and a devilish grace as well. I tried to raise myself from the ground, but the one who had his hand upon my throat pressed me back, and I knew I was no match for him or his companions, and if they wanted to they could throw me from the walls down to the depths below Monte Verità. This was the end, then. It was only a matter of time, and Victor would die alone, back in the hut on the mountain-side.

'Go ahead,' I said, 'have done with it,' resigned, caring no longer. I expected the laughter again, mocking and youthful, and the sudden seizing of my body with their hands, and the savage thrusting of me through the slit window to darkness and to death. I closed my eyes, and with nerves taut braced myself for horror. Nothing happened. I felt the boy touch my lips. I opened my eyes and he was smiling still, and he had a cup in his hands, with milk in it, and he was urging me to drink, but he did not speak. I shook my head but his companions came and knelt behind me, supporting my shoulders and my back, and I began to drink, foolishly, gratefully, like a child. The fear went as they held me, and the horror too, and it was as though strength passed from their hands to mine, and not only to my hands but to the whole of me.

When I had finished drinking the first one took the cup from me and put it on the ground, then he placed his two hands on my heart, his fingers touching, and the feeling that came to me was something I had never experienced in my life before. It was as if the peace of God came upon me, quiet and strong, and, with the touch of hands, took from me all anxiety and fear, all the fatigue and terror of the preceding night; and my memory of the cloud and mist on the mountain, and Victor dying on his lonely bed, became suddenly things of no importance. They shrank into insignificance beside this feeling of strength and beauty that I knew now. If Victor died it would not matter. His body would be a shell lying there in the peasant hut, but his heart would be beating here, as mine was beating, and his mind would come to us too.

I say 'to us' because it seemed to me, sitting there in the narrow cell, that I had been accepted by my companions and made one of them. This, I thought to myself, still wondering but bewildered, happy, this is what I always hoped that death would be. The negation of all pain and all distress, and the centre of life flowing, not from the quibbling brain, but from the heart.

The boy took his hands from me, still smiling, but the feeling of strength, of power, was with me still. He rose to his feet and

I did the same, and I followed him and the two others through the gap in the cell. There was no honeycomb of twisting corridors, no dark cloisters, but a great open court on to which the cells all gave, and the fourth side of the court led upwards to the twin peaks of Monte Verità, ice-capped, beautiful, caught now in the rose light of the rising sun. Steps cut in the ice led to the summit, and now I knew the reason for the silence within the walls and in the court as well, for there were the other ones, ranged upon the steps, dressed in those same tunics with bare arms and legs, girdles about the waist, and the hair cropped close to the head.

We passed through the court and up the steps beside them. There was no sound: they did not speak to me or to one another, but they smiled as the first three had done; and their smile was neither courteous nor tender, as we know it in the world, but had a strange exulting quality, as if wisdom and triumph and passion were all blended into one. They were ageless, they were sexless, they were neither male nor female, old or young, but the beauty of their faces, and of their bodies too, was more stirring and exciting than anything I had ever seen or known, and with a sudden longing I wanted to be one of them, to be dressed as they were dressed, to love as they must love, to laugh and worship and be silent.

I looked down at my coat and shirt, my climbing breeches, my thick socks and shoes, and suddenly I hated and despised them. They were like grave clothes covering the dead, and I flung them off, in haste to have them gone, throwing them over my shoulder down to the court below; and I stood naked under the sun. I was without embarrassment or shame. I was quite unconscious how I looked and I did not care. All I knew was that I wanted to have done with the trappings of the world, and my clothes seemed to symbolize the self I had once been.

We climbed the steps and reached the summit, and now the whole world lay before us, without mist or cloud, the lesser peaks stretching away into infinity, and far below, concerning us not at all, hazy and green and still, were the valleys and the streams and the little sleeping towns. Then, turning from the world below, I saw that the twin peaks of Monte Verità were divided by a great crevasse, narrow yet impassable, and standing on the summit, gazing downwards, I realized with wonder, and with awe as well, that my eyes could not penetrate the depths. The ice-blue walls of the crevasse descended smooth and hard without a break to some great bottomless chasm, hidden for ever in the mountain heart. The sun that rose to bathe the peaks at midday would never touch the depths of that crevasse, nor would the rays of the full moon come to it, but it seemed to me, between the peaks, that the shape of it was like a chalice held between two hands.

Someone was standing there, dressed in white from head to foot, on the very brink of the chasm, and although I could not see her features, for the cowl of the white robe concealed them, the tall upright figure, with head thrown back and arms outstretched, caught at my heart with sudden tense excitement.

I knew it was Anna. I knew that no one else would stand in just that way. I forgot Victor, I forgot my mission, I forgot time and place and all the years between. I remembered only the stillness of her presence, the beauty of her face, and that quiet voice saying to me, 'We are both in search of the same thing, after all.' I knew then that I had loved her always, and that though she had met Victor first, and chosen him, and married him, the ties and ceremony of marriage concerned neither of us, and never had. Our minds had met and crossed and understood from the first moment when Victor introduced us in my club, and that queer, inexplicable bond of the heart, breaking through every barrier, every restraint, had kept us close to one another always, in spite of silence, absence, and long years of separation.

The mistake was mine from the beginning in letting her go alone to find her mountain. Had I gone with them, she and Victor, when they asked me that day in the Map House long ago, intuition would have told me what was in her mind and the spell would have come upon me as well. I would not have slept on in the hut, as Victor had slept, but would have woken and gone with her, and the years that I had wasted and thrown away, futile and mis-spent, would have been our years, Anna's and mine, shared here on the mountain, cut off from the world.

Once again I looked about me and at the faces of those who stood beside me, and I guessed dimly, with a sort of hunger near to pain, what ecstasy of love they knew, that I had never known. Their silence was not a vow, condemning them to darkness, but a peace that the mountain gave to them, merging their minds in tune. There was no need for speech, when a smile, a glance, conveyed a message and a thought; while laughter, triumphant always, sprang from the heart's centre, never to be suppressed. This was no closed order, gloomy, sepulchral, denying all that instinct gave the heart. Here Life was fulfilled, clamouring, intense, and the great heat of the sun seeped into the veins, becoming part of the blood stream, part of the living flesh; and the frozen air, merging with the direct rays of the sun, cleansed the body and the lungs, bringing power and strength – the power I had felt when the fingers touched my heart.

In the space of so short a while my values had all changed, and the self who had climbed the mountain through the mist, fearful, anxious and angry too, but a little while ago, seemed to exist no more. I was grey-haired, past middle age, a madman to the world's eyes if they could see me now, a laughing-stock, a fool; and I stood naked with the rest of them on Monte Verità and held up my arms to the sun. It rose now in the sky and shone upon us, and the blistering of my skin was pain and pleasure blended, and the heat drove through my heart and through my lungs.

I kept my eyes fixed on Anna, loving her with such intensity that I heard myself calling aloud, 'Anna . . . Anna . . .' And she knew that I was there, for she lifted her hand in signal. None of them minded, none of them cared. They laughed with me, they understood.

Then from the midst of us came a girl, walking. She was dressed in a simple village frock, with stockings and shoes, and her hair hung loose on her shoulders. I thought her hands were folded together, as though in prayer, but they were not. She held them to her heart, the fingers touching.

She went to the brink of the crevasse, where Anna stood. Last night, beneath the moon, I should have been gripped by fear, but not now. I had been accepted. I was one of them. For one instant, in its space of time above us in the sky, the sun's ray touched the lip of the crevasse, and the blue ice shone. We knelt with one accord, our faces to the sun, and I heard the hymn of praise.

'This,' I thought, 'was how men worshipped in the beginning, how they will worship in the end. Here is no creed, no saviour, and no deity. Only the sun, which gives us light and life. This is how it has always been, from the beginning of time.'

The sun's ray lifted and passed on, and then the girl, rising to her feet, threw off her stockings and her shoes and her dress also, and Anna, with a knife in her hand, cut off her hair, cropping it close above the ears. The girl stood before her, her hands upon her heart.

'Now she is free,' I thought. 'She won't go back to the valley again. Her parents will mourn her, and her young man too, and they'll never discover what she has found, here on Monte Verità. In the valley there would have been feasting and celebration, and then dancing at the wedding, and afterwards the turmoil of a brief romance turning to humdrum married life, the cares of her house, the cares of children, anxiety, fret, illness, trouble, the day-by-day routine of growing old. Now she is spared all that. Here, nothing once felt is lost. Love and beauty don't die or fade away. Living's hard, because Nature's hard, and Nature has no mercy; but it was this she wanted in the valley, it was for this she came. She will know everything here that she never knew before and would not have discovered, below there in the world. Passion and joy and laughter, the heat of the sun, the tug of the moon, love without emotion, sleep with no waking dream. And that's why they hate it, in the valley, that's why they're afraid of Monte Verità. Because here on the summit is something they don't possess and never will, so they are angry and envious and unhappy.'

Then Anna turned, and the girl who had thrown her sex away with her past life and her village clothes followed barefoot, bare armed, cropped-haired like the others; and she was radiant, smiling, and I knew that nothing would ever matter to her again.

They descended to the court, leaving me alone on the summit, and I felt like an outcast before the gates of heaven. My brief moment had come and gone. They belonged here, and I did not. I was a stranger from the world below.

I put on my clothes again, restored to a sanity I did not want, and remembering Victor and my mission I too went down the steps to the court, and looking upwards I saw that Anna was waiting for me in the tower above.

The others flattened themselves against the wall to let me pass, and I saw that Anna alone amongst them wore the long white robe and the cowl. The tower was lofty, open to the sky, and characteristically, with that same gesture I remembered when she used to sit on the low stool before the fire in the great hall, Anna sat down now, on the topmost step of the tower, one knee raised and elbow on that knee. Today was yesterday, today was six-and-twenty years ago, and we were alone once more in the manor house in Shropshire; and the peace she had brought to me then she brought me now. I wanted to kneel beside her and take her hand. Instead I went and stood beside the wall, my arms folded.

'So you found it at last,' she said. 'It took a little time.'

The voice was soft and still and quite unchanged.

'Did you bring me here?' I asked. 'Did you call me when the aircraft crashed?'

She laughed, and I had never been away from her. Time stood still on Monte Verità.

'I wanted you to come long before that,' she said, 'but you shut your mind away from me. It was like clamping down a receiver. It always took two to make a telephone call. Does it still?'

'It does,' I answered, 'and our more modern inventions need valves for contact. Not the mind, though.'

'Your mind has been a box for so many years,' she said. 'It was a pity – we could have shared so much. Victor had to tell me his thoughts in letters, which wouldn't have been necessary with you.'

It was then, I think, that the first hope came to me. I must feel my way towards it, though, with care.

'You've read his letter,' I asked, 'and mine as well? You know that he's dying?'

'Yes,' she said, 'he's been ill for many weeks. That's why I wanted you to be here at this time, so that you could be with him when he died. And it will be all right for him, now, when you go back to him and tell him that you've spoken to me. He'll be happy then.'

'Why not come yourself?'

'Better this way,' she said. 'Then he can keep his dream.'

His dream? What did she mean? They were not, then, all-powerful here on Monte Verità? She understood the danger in which they stood.

'Anna,' I said, 'I'll do what you want me to do. I'll return to Victor and be with him at the last. But time is very short. More important still is the fact that you and the others here are in great danger. Tomorrow, tonight even, the people from the valley are going to climb here to Monte Verità, and they'll break into this place and kill you. It's imperative that you get away before they come. If you have no means of saving yourselves, then you must allow me to do something to help you. We are not so far from civilization as to make that impossible. I can get down to the valley, find a telephone, get through to the police, to the army, to some authority in charge . . .'

My words trailed off, because although my plans were not clear in my own mind I wanted her to have confidence in me, to feel that she could trust me.

'The point is,' I told her, 'that life is going to be impossible for you here, from now on. If I can prevent the attack this time, which is doubtful, it will happen next week, next month. Your days of security are numbered. You've lived here shut away so long that you don't understand the state of the world as it is now. Even this country here is torn in two with suspicion, and the people in the valley aren't superstitious peasants any longer; they're armed with modern weapons, and they've got murder in their hearts. You won't stand a chance, you and the rest, here on Monte Verità.'

She did not answer. She sat there on the step, listening, a remote and silent figure in her white robe and cowl.

'Anna,' I said, 'Victor's dying. He may be already dead. When you leave here he can't help you, but I can. I've loved you always. No need to tell you that, you must have guessed it. You destroyed two men, you know, when you came to live on Monte Verità six-and-twenty years ago. But that doesn't matter any more. I've found you again. And there are still places far away, inaccessible to civilization, where we could live, you and I – and the others with you here, if they wished to come with us. I have money enough to arrange all that; you won't have to worry about anything.'

I saw myself discussing practicalities with consuls, embassies, going into the question of passports, papers, clothing.

I saw too, in my mind's eye, the map of the world. I ranged in thought from a ridge of mountains in South America to the Himalayas, from the Himalayas to Africa. Or the northern wastes of Canada were still vast and unexplored, and stretches of Greenland. And there were islands, innumerable, countless islands, where no man ever trod, visited only by sea-birds, washed by the lonely sea. Mountain or island, scrubby wilderness or desert, impenetrable forest or Arctic waste, I did not care which she chose; but I had been without sight of her for so long, and now all I wanted was to be with her always.

This was now possible, because Victor, who would have claimed her, was going to die. I was blunt. I was truthful. I told her this as well. And then I waited, to hear what she would say.

She laughed, that warm, much loved and well-remembered laugh, and I wanted to go to her and put my arms round her, because the laugh held so much life in it, and so much joy and promise.

'Well?' I said.

Then she got up from the step and came and stood beside me, very still.

'There was once a man,' she said, 'who went to the booking office at Waterloo and said to the clerk eagerly, hopefully, 'I want a ticket to Paradise. A single ticket. No return.' And when the clerk told him there was no such place the man picked up the ink-well and threw it in the clerk's face. The police were summoned, and took the man away and put him in prison. Isn't that what you're asking of me now, a ticket to Paradise? This is the mountain of truth, which is very different.'

I felt hurt, irritated even. She hadn't taken a word of my plans seriously and was making fun of me.

'What do you propose, then?' I asked. 'To wait here, behind these walls, for the people to come and break them down?'

'Don't worry about us,' she said. 'We know what we shall do.'

She spoke with indifference, as if the matter was of no importance, and in agony I saw the future, that I had begun to plan for us both, slip away from me.

'Then you do possess some secret?' I asked, almost in accusation. 'You can work some miracle, and save yourself and the others, too? What about me? Can't you take me with you?'

'You wouldn't want to come,' she said. She put her hand on my arm. 'It takes time, you know, to build a Monte Verità. It isn't just doing without clothes and worshipping the sun.'

'I realize that,' I told her. 'I'm prepared to begin all over again, to learn new values, to start from the beginning. I know that nothing I've done in the world is any use. Talent, hard work, success, all those things are meaningless. But if I could be with you . . .'

'How? With me?' she said.

And I did not know what to answer, because it would be too sudden and too direct, but I knew in my heart that what I wanted was everything that could be between a woman and a man; not at first, of course, but later, when we had found our other mountain, or our wilderness, or wherever it was we might go to hide

109

ourselves from the world. There was no need to rehearse all that now. The point was that I was prepared to follow her anywhere, if she would let me.

'I love you, and have always loved you. Isn't that enough?' I asked.

'No,' she said, 'not on Monte Verità.'

And she threw back her cowl and I saw her face.

I gazed at her in horror . . . I could not move, I could not speak. It was as though all feeling had been frozen. My heart was cold . . . One side of her face was eaten quite away, ravaged, terrible. The disease had come upon her brow, her cheek, her throat, blotching, searing the skin. The eyes that I had loved were blackened, sunk deep into the sockets.

'You see,' she said, 'it isn't Paradise.'

I think I turned away. I don't remember. I know I leant against the rock of the tower and stared down into the depths below, and saw nothing but the great bank of cloud that hid the world.

'It happened to others,' Anna said, 'but they died. If I survived longer, it was because I was hardier than they. Leprosy can come to anyone, even to the supposed immortals of Monte Verità. It hasn't really mattered, you know. I regret nothing. Long ago I remember telling you that those who go to the mountain must give everything. That's all there is to it. I no longer suffer, so there's no need to suffer for me.'

I said nothing. I felt the tears run down my face. I didn't bother to wipe them away.

'There are no illusions and no dreams on Monte Verità,' she said. 'They belong to the world, and you belong there too. If I've destroyed the fantasy you made of me, forgive me. You've lost the Anna you knew once, and found another one instead. Which you will remember longer rather depends upon yourself. Now go back to your world of men and women and build yourself a Monte Verità.'

Somewhere there was scrub and grass and stunted trees; some-where there was earth and stones and the sound of running water. Deep in the valley there were homes, where men lived with their women, reared their children. They had firelight, curling smoke and lighted windows. Somewhere there were roads, there were railways, there were cities. So many cities, so many streets. And all with crowded buildings, lighted windows. They were there, beneath the cloud, beneath Monte Verità.

'Don't be anxious or afraid,' said Anna, 'and as for the valley people, they can't harm us. One thing only . . .' She paused, and although I did not look at her I think she smiled. 'Let Victor keep his dream,' she said.

Then she took my hand, and we went down the steps of the tower together, and through the court and to the walls of the rock-face. They stood there watching us, those others, with their bare arms and legs, their close-cropped hair, and I saw too the little village girl, the proselyte, who had renounced the world and was now one of them. I saw her turn and look at Anna, and I saw the expression in her eyes; there was no horror there, no fear and no revulsion. One and all they looked at Anna with triumph, with exultation, with all knowledge and all under-standing. And I knew that what she felt and what she endured they felt also, and shared with her, and accepted. She was not alone.

They turned their eyes to me, and their expression changed; instead of love and knowledge I read compassion.

Anna did not say goodbye. She put her hand an instant on my shoulder. Then the wall opened, and she was gone from me. The sun was no longer overhead. It had started its journey in the western sky. The great white banks of cloud rolled upward from the world below. I turned my back on Monte Verità.

It was evening when I came to the village. The moon had not yet risen. Presently, within two hours or less, it would top the eastern ridge of the further mountains and give light to the whole sky. They were waiting, the people from the valley. There must have been three hundred or more, waiting there in groups beside the huts. All of them were armed, some with rifles, with grenades, others, more primitive, with picks and axes. They had kindled

111

fires, on the village track between the huts, and had brought provisions too. They stood or sat before the fires eating and drinking, smoking and talking. Some of them had dogs, held tightly on a leash.

The owner of the first hut stood by the door with his son. They too were armed. The boy had a pick and a knife thrust in his belt. The man watched me with his sullen, stupid face.

'Your friend is dead,' he said. 'He has been dead these many hours.'

I pushed past him and went into the living-room of the hut. Candles had been lit. One at the head of the bed, one at the foot. I bent over Victor and took his hand. The man had lied to me. Victor was breathing still. When he felt me touch his hand, he opened his eyes.

'Did you see her?' he asked.

'Yes,' I answered.

'Something told me you would,' he said. 'Lying here, I felt that it would happen. She's my wife, and I've loved her all these years, but you only have been allowed to see her. Too late, isn't it, to be jealous now?'

The candlelight was dim. He could not see the shadows by the door, nor hear the movement and the whispering without.

'Did you give her my letter?' he said.

'She has it,' I answered. 'She told you not to worry, not to be anxious. She is all right. Everything is well with her.'

Victor smiled. He let go my hand.

'So it's true,' he said, 'all the dreams I had of Monte Verità. She is happy and contented and she will never grow old, never lose her beauty. Tell me, her hair, her eyes, her smile – were they still the same?'

'Just the same,' I said. 'Anna will always be the most beautiful woman you or I have ever known.'

He did not answer. And as I waited there, beside him, I heard the sudden blowing of a horn, echoed by a second and a third. I heard the restless movement of the men outside in the village, as they shouldered their weapons, kicked out the fires and gath-

112

ered together for the climb. I heard the dogs barking and the men laughing, ready now, excited. When they had gone I went and stood alone in the deserted village, and I watched the full moon rising from the dark valley.

The Apple Tree

It was three months after she died that he first noticed the apple tree. He had known of its existence, of course, with the others, standing upon the lawn in front of the house, sloping upwards to the field beyond. Never before, though, had he been aware of this particular tree looking in any way different from its fellows, except that it was the third one on the left, a little apart from the rest and leaning more closely to the terrace.

It was a fine clear morning in early spring, and he was shaving by the open window. As he leant out to sniff the air, the lather on his face, the razor in his hand, his eye fell upon the apple tree. It was a trick of light, perhaps, something to do with the sun coming up over the woods, that happened to catch the tree at this particular moment; but the likeness was unmistakable.

He put his razor down on the window-ledge and stared. The tree was scraggy and of a depressing thinness, possessing none of the gnarled solidity of its companions. Its few branches, growing high up on the trunk like narrow shoulders on a tall body, spread themselves in martyred resignation, as though chilled by the fresh morning air. The roll of wire circling the tree, and reaching to about halfway up the trunk from the base, looked like a grey tweed skirt covering lean limbs; while the topmost branch, sticking up into the air above the ones below, yet sagging slightly, could have been a drooping head poked forward in an attitude of weariness.

How often he had seen Midge stand like this, dejected. No matter where it was, whether in the garden, or in the house, or even shopping in the town, she would take upon herself this same stooping posture, suggesting that life treated her hardly, that she had been singled out from her fellows to carry some impossible burden, but in spite of it would endure to the end without complaint. 'Midge, you look worn out, for heaven's sake sit down and take a rest!' But the words would be received with the inevitable shrug of the shoulder, the inevitable sigh, 'Someone has got to keep things going,' and straightening herself she would embark upon the dreary routine of unnecessary tasks she forced herself to do, day in, day out, through the interminable change-less years.

He went on staring at the apple tree. That martyred bent posi-tion, the stooping top, the weary branches, the few withered leaves that had not blown away with the wind and rain of the past winter and now shivered in the spring breeze like wispy hair; all of it protested soundlessly to the owner of the garden looking upon it, 'I am like this because of you, because of your neglect.'

He turned away from the window and went on shaving. It would not do to let his imagination run away with him and start building fancies in his mind just when he was settling at long last to freedom. He bathed and dressed and went down to break-fast. Egg and bacon were waiting for him on the hot-plate, and he carried the dish to the single place laid for him at the dining-table. *The Times*, folded smooth and new, was ready for him to read. When Midge was alive he had handed it to her first, from long custom, and when she gave it back to him after breakfast, to take with him to the study, the pages were always in the wrong order and folded crookedly, so that part of the pleasure of reading it was spoilt. The news, too, would be stale to him after she had read the worst of it aloud, which was a morning habit she used to take upon herself, always adding some derogatory remark of her own about what she read. The birth of a daughter to mutual friends would bring a click of the tongue, a little jerk of the head, 'Poor things, another girl,' or if a son, 'A boy can't be much fun to educate these days.' He used to think it psychological, because they themselves were childless, that she should so grudge the entry of new life into the world; but as time passed it became thus with all bright or joyous things, as though there was some fundamental blight upon good cheer.

'It says here that more people went on holiday this year than ever before. Let's hope they enjoyed themselves, that's all.' But no hope lay in her words, only disparagement. Then, having finished breakfast, she would push back her chair and sigh and say, 'Oh well . . .', leaving the sentence unfinished; but the sigh, the shrug of the shoulders, the slope of her long, thin back as she stooped to clear the dishes from the serving-table – thus sparing work for the daily maid – was all part of her long-term reproach, directed at him, that had marred their existence over a span of years.

Silent, punctilious, he would open the door for her to pass through to the kitchen quarters, and she would labour past him, stooping under the weight of the laden tray that there was no need for her to carry, and presently, through the half-open door, he would hear the swish of the running water from the pantry tap. He would return to his chair and sit down again, the crumpled *Times*, a smear of marmalade upon it, lying against the toast-rack; and once again, with monotonous insistence, the question hammered at his mind, 'What have I done?'

It was not as though she nagged. Nagging wives, like mothers-in-law, were chestnut jokes for music-halls. He could not remember Midge ever losing her temper or quarrelling. It was just that the undercurrent of reproach, mingled with suffering nobly borne, spoilt the atmosphere of his home and drove him to a sense of furtiveness and guilt.

Perhaps it would be raining and he, seeking sanctuary within his study, electric fire aglow, his after-breakfast pipe filling the small room with smoke, would settle down before his desk in a pretence of writing letters, but in reality to hide, to feel the snug security of four safe walls that were his alone. Then the door would open and Midge, struggling into a raincoat, her wide-brimmed felt hat pulled low over her brow, would pause and wrinkle her nose in distaste.

'Phew! What a fug.'

He said nothing, but moved slightly in his chair, covering with his arm the novel he had chosen from a shelf in idleness.

'Aren't you going into the town?' she asked him.

'I had not thought of doing so.'

'Oh! Oh, well, it doesn't matter.' She turned away again towards the door.

'Why, is there anything you want done?'

'It's only the fish for lunch. They don't deliver on Wednesdays. Still, I can go myself if you are busy. I only thought . . .'

She was out of the room without finishing her sentence.

'It's all right, Midge,' he called, 'I'll get the car and go and fetch it presently. No sense in getting wet.'

Thinking she had not heard he went out into the hall. She was standing by the open front door, the mizzling rain driving in upon her. She had a long flat basket over her arm and was drawing on a pair of gardening gloves.

'I'm bound to get wet in any case,' she said, 'so it doesn't make much odds. Look at those flowers, they all need staking. I'll go for the fish when I've finished seeing to them.'

Argument was useless. She had made up her mind. He shut the front door after her and sat down again in the study. Somehow the room no longer felt so snug, and a little later, raising his head to the window, he saw her hurry past, her raincoat not buttoned properly and flapping, little drips of water forming on the brim of her hat and the garden basket filled with limp michaelmas daisies already dead. His conscience pricking him, he bent down and turned out one bar of the electric fire.

Or yet again it would be spring, it would be summer. Strolling out hatless into the garden, his hands in his pockets, with no other purpose in his mind but to feel the sun upon his back and stare out upon the woods and fields and the slow winding river, he would hear, from the bedrooms above, the high-pitched whine of the Hoover slow down suddenly, gasp, and die. Midge called down to him as he stood there on the terrace.

'Were you going to do anything?' she said.

He was not. It was the smell of spring, of early summer, that had driven him out into the garden. It was the delicious knowledge that being retired now, no longer working in the City, time was a thing of no account, he could waste it as he pleased.

'No,' he said, 'not on such a lovely day. Why?'

'Oh, never mind,' she answered, 'it's only that the wretched drain under the kitchen window has gone wrong again. Completely plugged up and choked. No one ever sees to it, that's why. I'll have a go at it myself this afternoon.'

Her face vanished from the window. Once more there was a gasp, a rising groan of sound, and the Hoover warmed to its task again. What foolishness that such an interruption could damp the brightness of the day. Not the demand, nor the task itself – clearing a drain was in its own way a schoolboy piece of folly, playing with mud – but that wan face of hers looking out upon the sunlit terrace, the hand that went up wearily to push back a strand of falling hair, and the inevitable sigh before she turned from the window, the unspoken, 'I wish I had the time to stand and do nothing in the sun. Oh, well . . .'

He had ventured to ask once why so much cleaning of the house was necessary. Why there must be the incessant turning out of rooms. Why chairs must be lifted to stand upon other chairs, rugs rolled up and ornaments huddled together on a sheet of newspaper. And why, in particular, the sides of the upstairs corridor, on which no one ever trod, must be polished labori-ously by hand, Midge and the daily woman taking it in turns to crawl upon their knees the whole endless length of it, like slaves of bygone days.

Midge stared at him, not understanding.

'You'd be the first to complain,' she said, 'if the house was like a pigsty. You like your comforts.'

So they lived in different worlds, their minds not meeting. Had it been always so? He did not remember. They had been married nearly twenty-five years and were two people who, from force of habit, lived under the same roof.

When he had been in business, it seemed different. He had not noticed it so much. He came home to eat, to sleep, and to go up by train again in the morning. But when he retired he became aware of her forcibly, and day by day his sense of her resentment, of her disapproval, grew stronger.

Finally, in that last year before she died, he felt himself engulfed in it, so that he was led into every sort of petty deception to get away from her, making a pretence of going up to London to have his hair cut, to see the dentist, to lunch with an old business friend; and in reality he would be sitting by his club window, anonymous, at peace.

It was mercifully swift, the illness that took her from him. Influenza, followed by pneumonia, and she was dead within a week. He hardly knew how it happened, except that as usual she was overtired and caught a cold, and would not stay in bed. One evening, coming home by the late train from London, having sneaked into a cinema during the afternoon, finding release amongst the crowd of warm friendly people enjoying themselves – for it was a bitter December day – he found her bent over the furnace in the cellar, poking and thrusting at the lumps of coke.

She looked up at him, white with fatigue, her face drawn.

'Why, Midge, what on earth are you doing?' he said.

'It's the furnace,' she said, 'we've had trouble with it all day, it won't stay alight. We shall have to get the men to see it tomorrow. I really cannot manage this sort of thing myself.'

There was a streak of coal dust on her cheek. She let the stubby poker fall on the cellar floor. She began to cough, and as she did so winced with pain.

'You ought to be in bed,' he said, 'I never heard of such nonsense. What the dickens does it matter about the furnace?'

'I thought you would be home early,' she said, 'and then you might have known how to deal with it. It's been bitter all day, I can't think what you found to do with yourself in London.'

She climbed the cellar stairs slowly, her back bent, and when she reached the top she stood shivering and half closed her eyes.

'If you don't mind terribly,' she said, 'I'll get your supper right away, to have it done with. I don't want anything myself.'

'To hell with my supper,' he said, 'I can forage for myself. You go up to bed. I'll bring you a hot drink.'

'I tell you, I don't want anything,' she said. 'I can fill my

119

hot-water bottle myself. I only ask one thing of you. And that is to remember to turn out the lights everywhere, before you come up.' She turned into the hall, her shoulders sagging.

'Surely a glass of hot milk?' he began uncertainly, starting to take off his overcoat; and as he did so the torn half of the ten-and-sixpenny seat at the cinema fell from his pocket on to the floor. She saw it. She said nothing. She coughed again and began to drag herself upstairs.

The next morning her temperature was a hundred and three. The doctor came and said she had pneumonia. She asked if she might go to a private ward in the cottage hospital, because having a nurse in the house would make too much work. This was on the Tuesday morning. She went there right away, and they told him on the Friday evening that she was not likely to live through the night. He stood inside the room, after they told him, looking down at her in the high impersonal hospital bed, and his heart was wrung with pity, because surely they had given her too many pillows, she was propped too high, there could be no rest for her that way. He had brought some flowers, but there seemed no purpose now in giving them to the nurse to arrange, because Midge was too ill to look at them. In a sort of delicacy he put them on a table beside the screen, when the nurse was bending down to her.

'Is there anything she needs?' he said. 'I mean, I can easily . . .' He did not finish the sentence, he left it in the air, hoping the nurse would understand his intention, that he was ready to go off in the car, drive somewhere, fetch what was required.

The nurse shook her head. 'We will telephone you,' she said, 'if there is any change.'

What possible change could there be, he wondered, as he found himself outside the hospital? The white pinched face upon the pillows would not alter now, it belonged to no one.

Midge died in the early hours of Saturday morning.

He was not a religious man, he had no profound belief in immortality, but when the funeral was over, and Midge was buried, it distressed him to think of her poor lonely body lying

120

in that brand-new coffin with the brass handles: it seemed such a churlish thing to permit. Death should be different. It should be like bidding farewell to someone at a station before a long journey, but without the strain. There was something of indecency in this haste to bury underground the thing that but for ill-chance would be a living breathing person. In his distress he fancied he could hear Midge saying with a sigh, 'Oh, well . . .' as they lowered the coffin into the open grave.

He hoped with fervour that after all there might be a future in some unseen Paradise and that poor Midge, unaware of what they were doing to her mortal remains, walked somewhere in green fields. But who with, he wondered? Her parents had died in India many years ago; she would not have much in common with them now if they met her at the gates of Heaven. He had a sudden picture of her waiting her turn in a queue, rather far back, as was always her fate in queues, with that large shopping bag of woven straw which she took everywhere, and on her face that patient martyred look. As she passed through the turnstile into Paradise she looked at him, reproachfully.

These pictures, of the coffin and the queue, remained with him for about a week, fading a little day by day. Then he forgot her. Freedom was his, and the sunny empty house, the bright crisp winter. The routine he followed belonged to him alone. He never thought of Midge until the morning he looked out upon the apple tree.

Later that day he was taking a stroll round the garden, and he found himself drawn to the tree through curiosity. It had been stupid fancy after all. There was nothing singular about it. An apple tree like any other apple tree. He remembered then that it had always been a poorer tree than its fellows, was in fact more than half dead, and at one time there had been talk of chopping it down, but the talk came to nothing. Well, it would be something for him to do over the weekend. Axing a tree was healthy exercise, and apple wood smelt good. It would be a treat to have it burning on the fire.

Unfortunately wet weather set in for nearly a week after that

121

day, and he was unable to accomplish the task he had set himself. No sense in pottering out of doors this weather, and getting a chill into the bargain. He still noticed the tree from his bedroom window. It began to irritate him, humped there, straggling and thin, under the rain. The weather was not cold, and the rain that fell upon the garden was soft and gentle. None of the other trees wore this aspect of dejection. There was one young tree – only planted a few years back, he recalled quite well – growing to the right of the old one and standing straight and firm, the lithe young branches lifted to the sky, positively looking as if it enjoyed the rain. He peered through the window at it, and smiled. Now why the devil should he suddenly remember that incident, years back, during the war, with the girl who came to work on the land for a few months at the neighbouring farm? He did not suppose he had thought of her in months. Besides, there was nothing to it. At weekends he had helped them at the farm himself – war work of a sort – and she was always there, cheerful and pretty and smiling; she had dark curling hair, crisp and boyish, and a skin like a very young apple.

He looked forward to seeing her, Saturdays and Sundays; it was an antidote to the inevitable news bulletins put on throughout the day by Midge, and to ceaseless war talk. He liked looking at the child – she was scarcely more than that, nineteen or so – in her slim breeches and gay shirts; and when she smiled it was as though she embraced the world.

He never knew how it happened, and it was such a little thing; but one afternoon he was in the shed doing something to the tractor, bending over the engine, and she was beside him, close to his shoulder, and they were laughing together; and he turned round, to take a bit of waste to clean a plug, and suddenly she was in his arms and he was kissing her. It was a happy thing, spontaneous and free, and the girl so warm and jolly, with her fresh young mouth. Then they went on with the work of the tractor, but united now, in a kind of intimacy that brought gaiety to them both, and peace as well. When it was time for the girl to go and feed the pigs he followed her from the shed, his hand on her shoulder, a careless gesture that meant nothing really, a half caress; and as they came out into the yard he saw Midge standing there, staring at them.

'I've got to go in to a Red Cross meeting,' she said. 'I can't get the car to start. I called you. You didn't seem to hear.'

Her face was frozen. She was looking at the girl. At once guilt covered him. The girl said good evening cheerfully to Midge, and crossed the yard to the pigs.

He went with Midge to the car and managed to start it with the handle. Midge thanked him, her voice without expression. He found himself unable to meet her eyes. This, then, was adultery. This was sin. This was the second page in a Sunday newspaper – 'Husband Intimate with Land Girl in Shed. Wife Witnesses Act.' His hands were shaking when he got back to the house and he had to pour himself a drink. Nothing was ever said. Midge never mentioned the matter. Some craven instinct kept him from the farm the next weekend, and then he heard that the girl's mother had been taken ill and she had been called back home.

He never saw her again. Why, he wondered, should he remember her suddenly, on such a day, watching the rain falling on the apple trees? He must certainly make a point of cutting down the old dead tree, if only for the sake of bringing more sunshine to the little sturdy one; it hadn't a fair chance, growing there so close to the other.

On Friday afternoon he went round to the vegetable garden to find Willis, the jobbing gardener, who came three days a week, to pay him his wages. He wanted, too, to look in the toolshed and see if the axe and saw were in good condition. Willis kept everything neat and tidy there – this was Midge's training – and the axe and saw were hanging in their accustomed place upon the wall.

He paid Willis his money, and was turning away when the man suddenly said to him, 'Funny thing, sir, isn't it, about the old apple tree?'

The remark was so unexpected that it came as a shock. He felt himself change colour.

'Apple tree? What apple tree?' he said.

'Why, the one at the far end, near the terrace,' answered Willis. 'Been barren as long as I've worked here, and that's some years now. Never an apple from her, nor as much as a sprig of blossom. We were going to chop her up that cold winter, if you remember, and we never did. Well, she's taken on a new lease now. Haven't you noticed?' The gardener watched him smiling, a knowing look in his eye.

What did the fellow mean? It was not possible that he had been struck also by that fantastic freak resemblance – no, it was out of the question, indecent, blasphemous; besides, he had put it out of his own mind now, he had not thought of it again.

'I've noticed nothing,' he said, on the defensive.

Willis laughed. 'Come round to the terrace, sir,' he said, 'I'll show you.'

They went together to the sloping lawn, and when they came to the apple tree Willis put his hand up and pulled down a branch within reach. It creaked a little as he did so, as though stiff and unyielding, and Willis brushed away some of the dry lichen and revealed the spiky twigs. 'Look there, sir,' he said, 'she's growing buds. Look at them, feel them for yourself. There's life here yet, and plenty of it. Never known such a thing before. See this branch too.' He released the first, and leant up to reach another.

Willis was right. There were buds in plenty, but so small and brown that it seemed to him they scarcely deserved the name, they were more like blemishes upon the twig, dusty and dry. He put his hands in his pockets. He felt a queer distaste to touch them.

'I don't think they'll amount to much,' he said.

'I don't know, sir,' said Willis, 'I've got hopes. She's stood the winter, and if we get no more bad frosts there's no knowing what we'll see. It would be some joke to watch the old tree blossom. She'll bear fruit yet.' He patted the trunk with his open hand, in a gesture at once familiar and affectionate.

The owner of the apple tree turned away. For some reason he felt irritated with Willis. Anyone would think the damned tree lived. And now his plan to axe the tree, over the weekend, would come to nothing.

'It's taking the light from the young tree,' he said. 'Surely it would be more to the point if we did away with this one, and gave the little one more room?'

He moved across to the young tree and touched a limb. No lichen here. The branches smooth. Buds upon every twig, curling tight. He let go the branch and it sprang away from him, resilient.

'Do away with her, sir,' said Willis, 'while there's still life in her? Oh no, sir, I wouldn't do that. She's doing no harm to the young tree. I'd give the old tree one more chance. If she doesn't bear fruit, we'll have her down next winter.'

'All right, Willis,' he said, and walked swiftly away. Somehow he did not want to discuss the matter any more.

That night, when he went to bed, he opened the window wide as usual and drew back the curtains; he could not bear to wake up in the morning and find the room close. It was full moon, and the light shone down upon the terrace and the lawn above it, ghostly pale and still. No wind blew. A hush upon the place. He leant out, loving the silence. The moon shone full upon the little apple tree, the young one. There was a radiance about it in this light that gave it a fairy-tale quality. Small and lithe and slim, the young tree might have been a dancer, her arms upheld, poised ready on her toes for flight. Such a careless, happy grace about it. Brave young tree. Away to the left stood the other one, half of it in shadow still. Even the moonlight could not give it beauty. What in heaven's name was the matter with the thing that it had to stand there, humped and stooping, instead of looking upwards to the light? It marred the still quiet night, it spoilt the setting. He had been a fool to give way to Willis and agree to spare the tree. Those ridiculous buds would never blossom, and even if they did . . .

His thoughts wandered, and for the second time that week he found himself remembering the landgirl and her joyous smile. He wondered what had happened to her. Married probably, with a young family. Made some chap happy, no doubt. Oh, well . . . He smiled. Was he going to make use of that expression now? Poor Midge! Then he caught his breath and stood quite still, his hand upon the curtain. The apple tree, the one on the left, was no longer in shadow. The moon shone upon the withered branches, and they looked like skeleton's arms raised in supplication. Frozen arms, stiff and numb with pain. There was no wind, and the other trees were motionless; but there, in those topmost branches, something shivered and stirred, a breeze that came from nowhere and died away again. Suddenly a branch fell from the apple tree to the ground below. It was the near branch, with the small dark buds upon it, which he would not touch. No rustle, no breath of movement came from the other trees. He went on staring at the branch as it lay there on the grass, under the moon. It stretched across the shadow of the young tree close to it, pointing as though in accusation.

For the first time in his life that he could remember he drew the curtains over the window to shut out the light of the moon.

Willis was supposed to keep to the vegetable garden. He had never shown his face much round the front when Midge was alive. That was because Midge attended to the flowers. She even used to mow the grass, pushing the wretched machine up and down the slope, her back bent low over the handles.

It had been one of the tasks she set herself, like keeping the bedrooms swept and polished. Now Midge was no longer there to attend to the front garden and to tell him where he should work, Willis was always coming through to the front. The gardener liked the change. It made him feel responsible.

'I can't understand how that branch came to fall, sir,' he said on the Monday.

'What branch?'

'Why, the branch on the apple tree. The one we were looking at before I left.'

'It was rotten, I suppose. I told you the tree was dead.'

'Nothing rotten about it, sir. Why, look at it. Broke clean off.'

Once again the owner was obliged to follow his man up the

126

slope above the terrace. Willis picked up the branch. The lichen upon it was wet, bedraggled looking, like matted hair.

'You didn't come again to test the branch, over the weekend, and loosen it in some fashion, did you, sir?' asked the gardener.

'I most certainly did not,' replied the owner, irritated. 'As a matter of fact I heard the branch fall, during the night. I was opening the bedroom window at the time.'

'Funny. It was a still night too.'

'These things often happen to old trees. Why you bother about this one I can't imagine. Anyone would think . . .'

He broke off; he did not know how to finish the sentence.

'Anyone would think that the tree was valuable,' he said.

The gardener shook his head. 'It's not the value,' he said. 'I don't reckon for a moment that this tree is worth any money at all. It's just that after all this time, when we thought her dead, she's alive and kicking, as you might say. Freak of nature, I call it. We'll hope no other branches fall before she blossoms.'

Later, when the owner set off for his afternoon walk, he saw the man cutting away the grass below the tree and placing new wire around the base of the trunk. It was quite ridiculous. He did not pay the fellow a fat wage to tinker about with a half-dead tree. He ought to be in the kitchen garden, growing vegetables. It was too much effort, though, to argue with him.

He returned home about half past five. Tea was a discarded meal since Midge had died, and he was looking forward to his armchair by the fire, his pipe, his whisky-and-soda, and silence.

The fire had not long been lit and the chimney was smoking. There was a queer, rather sickly smell about the living-room. He threw open the windows and went upstairs to change his heavy shoes. When he came down again the smoke still clung about the room and the smell was as strong as ever. Impossible to name it. Sweetish, strange. He called to the woman out in the kitchen.

'There's a funny smell in the house,' he said. 'What is it?'

The woman came out into the hall from the back.

'What sort of a smell, sir?' she said, on the defensive.

'It's in the living-room,' he said. 'The room was full of smoke just now. Have you been burning something?'

Her face cleared. 'It must be the logs,' she said. 'Willis cut them up specially, sir, he said you would like them.'

'What logs are those?'

'He said it was apple wood, sir, from a branch he had sawed up. Apple wood burns well, I've always heard. Some people fancy it very much. I don't notice any smell myself, but I've got a slight cold.'

Together they looked at the fire. Willis had cut the logs small. The woman, thinking to please him, had piled several on top of one another, to make a good fire to last. There was no great blaze. The smoke that came from them was thin and poor. Greenish in colour. Was it possible she did not notice that sickly rancid smell?

'The logs are wet,' he said abruptly. 'Willis should have known better. Look at them. Quite useless on my fire.'

The woman's face took on a set, rather sulky expression. 'I'm very sorry,' she said. 'I didn't notice anything wrong with them when I came to light the fire. They seemed to start well. I've always understood apple wood was very good for burning, and Willis said the same. He told me to be sure and see that you had these on the fire this evening, he had made a special job of cutting them for you. I thought you knew about it and had given orders.'

'Oh, all right,' he answered, abruptly. 'I dare say they'll burn in time. It's not your fault.'

He turned his back on her and poked at the fire, trying to separate the logs. While she remained in the house there was nothing he could do. To remove the damp smouldering logs and throw them somewhere round the back, and then light the fire afresh with dry sticks would arouse comment. He would have to go through the kitchen to the back passage where the kindling wood was kept, and she would stare at him, and come forward and say, 'Let me do it, sir. Has the fire gone out then?' No, he must wait until after supper, when she had cleared away and washed up and gone off for the night. Meanwhile, he would endure the smell of the apple wood as best he could.

128

He poured out his drink, lit his pipe and stared at the fire. It gave out no heat at all, and with the central heating off in the house the living-room struck chill. Now and again a thin wisp of the greenish smoke puffed from the logs, and with it seemed to come that sweet sickly smell, unlike any sort of wood smoke that he knew. That interfering fool of a gardener . . . Why saw up the logs? He must have known they were damp. Riddled with damp. He leant forward, staring more closely. Was it damp, though, that oozed there in a thin trickle from the pale logs? No, it was sap, unpleasant, slimy.

He seized the poker, and in a fit of irritation thrust it between the logs, trying to stir them to flame, to change that green smoke into a normal blaze. The effort was useless. The logs would not burn. And all the while the trickle of sap ran on to the grate and the sweet smell filled the room, turning his stomach. He took his glass and his book and went and turned on the electric fire in the study and sat in there instead.

It was idiotic. It reminded him of the old days, how he would make a pretence of writing letters, and go and sit in the study because of Midge in the living-room. She had a habit of yawning in the evenings, when her day's work was done; a habit of which she was quite unconscious. She would settle herself on the sofa with her knitting, the click-click of the needles going fast and furious; and suddenly they would start, those shattering yawns, rising from the depths of her, a prolonged 'Ah . . . Ah . . . Hi-Oh!' followed by the inevitable sigh. Then there would be silence except for the knitting needles, but as he sat behind his book, waiting, he knew that within a few minutes another yawn would come, another sigh.

A hopeless sort of anger used to stir within him, a longing to throw down his book and say, 'Look, if you are so tired, wouldn't it be better if you went to bed?'

Instead, he controlled himself, and after a little while, when he could bear it no longer, he would get up and leave the living-room, and take refuge in the study. Now he was doing the same thing, all over again, because of the apple logs. Because of the damned sickly smell of the smouldering wood.

He went on sitting in his chair by the desk, waiting for supper. It was nearly nine o'clock before the daily woman had cleared up, turned down his bed and gone for the night.

He returned to the living-room, which he had not entered since leaving it earlier in the evening. The fire was out. It had made some effort to burn, because the logs were thinner than they had been before, and had sunk low into the basket grate. The ash was meagre, yet the sickly smell clung to the dying embers. He went out into the kitchen and found an empty scuttle and brought it back into the living-room. Then he lifted the logs into it, and the ashes too. There must have been some damp residue in the scuttle, or the logs were still not dry, because as they settled there they seemed to turn darker than before, with a kind of scum upon them. He carried the scuttle down to the cellar, opened the door of the central heating furnace, and threw the lot inside.

He remembered then, too late, that the central heating had been given up now for two or three weeks, owing to the spring weather, and that unless he relit it now the logs would remain there, untouched, until the following winter. He found paper, matches, and a can of paraffin, and setting the whole alight closed the door of the furnace, and listened to the roar of flames. That would settle it. He waited a moment and then went up the steps, back to the kitchen passage, to lay and relight the fire in the living-room. The business took time, he had to find kindling and coal, but with patience he got the new fire started, and finally settled himself down in his arm-chair before it.

He had been reading perhaps for twenty minutes before he became aware of the banging door. He put down his book and listened. Nothing at first. Then, yes, there it was again. A rattle, a slam of an unfastened door in the kitchen quarters. He got up and went along to shut it. It was the door at the top of the cellar stairs. He could have sworn he had fastened it. The catch must have worked loose in some way. He switched on the light at the head of the stairs, and bent to examine the catch. There seemed nothing wrong with it. He was about to close the door firmly

130

when he noticed the smell again. The sweet sickly smell of smouldering apple wood. It was creeping up from the cellar, finding its way to the passage above.

Suddenly, for no reason, he was seized with a kind of fear, a feeling of panic almost. What if the smell filled the whole house through the night, came up from the kitchen quarters to the floor above, and while he slept found its way into his bedroom, choking him, stifling him, so that he could not breathe? The thought was ridiculous, insane — and yet . . .

Once more he forced himself to descend the steps into the cellar. No sound came from the furnace, no roar of flames. Wisps of smoke, thin and green, oozed their way from the fastened furnace door; it was this that he had noticed from the passage above.

He went to the furnace and threw open the door. The paper had all burnt away, and the few shavings with them. But the logs, the apple logs, had not burnt at all. They lay there as they had done when he threw them in, one charred limb above another, black and huddled, like the bones of someone darkened and dead by fire. Nausea rose in him. He thrust his handkerchief into his mouth, choking. Then, scarcely knowing what he did, he ran up the steps to find the empty scuttle, and with a shovel and tongs tried to pitch the logs back into it, scraping for them through the narrow door of the furnace. He was retching in his belly all the while. At last the scuttle was filled, and he carried it up the steps and through the kitchen to the back door.

He opened the door. Tonight there was no moon and it was raining. Turning up the collar of his coat he peered about him in the darkness, wondering where he should throw the logs. Too wet and dark to stagger all the way to the kitchen garden and chuck them on the rubbish heap, but in the field behind the garage the grass was thick and long and they might lie there hidden. He crunched his way over the gravel drive, and coming to the fence beside the field threw his burden on to the concealing grass. There they could rot and perish, grow sodden with rain, and in the end become part of the mouldy earth; he did not

131

care. The responsibility was his no longer. They were out of his house, and it did not matter what became of them.

He returned to the house, and this time made sure the cellar door was fast. The air was clear again, the smell had gone.

He went back to the living-room to warm himself before the fire, but his hands and feet, wet with the rain, and his stomach, still queasy from the pungent smoke, combined together to chill his whole person, and he sat there, shuddering.

He slept badly when he went to bed that night, and awoke in the morning feeling out of sorts. He had a headache, and an ill-tasting tongue. He stayed indoors. His liver was thoroughly upset. To relieve his feelings he spoke sharply to the daily woman.

'I've caught a bad chill,' he said to her, 'trying to get warm last night. So much for apple wood. The smell of it has affected my inside as well. You can tell Willis, when he comes tomorrow.'

She looked at him in disbelief.

'I'm sure I'm very sorry,' she said. 'I told my sister about the wood last night, when I got home, and that you had not fancied it. She said it was most unusual. Apple wood is considered quite a luxury to burn, and burns well, what's more.'

'This lot didn't, that's all I know,' he said to her, 'and I never want to see any more of it. As for the smell . . . I can taste it still, it's completely turned me up.'

Her mouth tightened. 'I'm sorry,' she said. And then, as she left the dining-room, her eye fell on the empty whisky bottle on the sideboard. She hesitated a moment, then put it on her tray.

'You've finished with this, sir?' she said.

Of course he had finished with it. It was obvious. The bottle was empty. He realized the implication, though. She wanted to suggest that the idea of apple-wood smoke upsetting him was all my eye, he had done himself too well. Damned impertinence.

'Yes,' he said, 'you can bring another in its place.'

That would teach her to mind her own business.

He was quite sick for several days, queasy and giddy, and finally rang up the doctor to come and have a look at him. The story

132

of the apple wood sounded nonsense, when he told it, and the doctor, after examining him, appeared unimpressed.

'Just a chill on the liver,' he said, 'damp feet, and possibly something you've eaten combined. I hardly think wood smoke has much to do with it. You ought to take more exercise, if you're inclined to have a liver. Play golf. I don't know how I should keep fit without my weekend golf.' He laughed, packing up his bag. 'I'll make you up some medicine,' he said, 'and once this rain has cleared off I should get out and into the air. It's mild enough, and all we want now is a bit of sunshine to bring everything on. Your garden is farther ahead than mine. Your fruit trees are ready to blossom.' And then, before leaving the room, he added, 'You mustn't forget, you had a bad shock a few months ago. It takes time to get over these things. You're still missing your wife, you know. Best thing is to get out and about and see people. Well, take care of yourself.'

His patient dressed and went downstairs. The fellow meant well, of course, but his visit had been a waste of time. 'You're still missing your wife, you know.' How little the doctor understood. Poor Midge . . . At least he himself had the honesty to admit that he did not miss her at all, that now she was gone he could breathe, he was free, and that apart from the upset liver he had not felt so well for years.

During the few days he had spent in bed the daily woman had taken the opportunity to spring-clean the living-room. An unnecessary piece of work, but he supposed it was part of the legacy Midge had left behind her. The room looked scrubbed and straight and much too tidy. His own personal litter cleared, books and papers neatly stacked. It was an infernal nuisance, really, having anyone to do for him at all. It would not take much for him to sack her and fend for himself as best he could. Only the bother, the tie of cooking and washing up, prevented him. The ideal life, of course, was that led by a man out East, or in the South Seas, who took a native wife. No problem there. Silence, good service, perfect waiting, excellent cooking, no need for conversation; and then, if you wanted something more than that,

133

there she was, young, warm, a companion for the dark hours. No criticism ever, the obedience of an animal to its master, and the light-hearted laughter of a child. Yes, they had wisdom all right, those fellows who broke away from convention. Good luck to them.

He strolled over to the window and looked out up the sloping lawn. The rain was stopping and tomorrow it would be fine; he would be able to get out, as the doctor had suggested. The man was right, too, about the fruit trees. The little one near the steps was in flower already, and a blackbird had perched himself on one of the branches, which swayed slightly under his weight.

The rain-drops glistened and the opening buds were very curled and pink, but when the sun broke through tomorrow they would turn white and soft against the blue of the sky. He must find his old camera, and put a film in it, and photograph the little tree. The others would be in flower, too, during the week. As for the old one, there on the left, it looked as dead as ever; or else the so-called buds were so brown they did not show up from this distance. Perhaps the shedding of the branch had been its finish. And a good job too.

He turned away from the window and set about rearranging the room to his taste, spreading his things about. He liked pottering, opening drawers, taking things out and putting them back again. There was a red pencil in one of the side tables that must have slipped down behind a pile of books and been found during the turn-out. He sharpened it, gave it a sleek fine point. He found a new film in another drawer, and kept it out to put in his camera in the morning. There were a number of papers and old photographs in the drawer, heaped in a jumble, and snap-shots too, dozens of them. Midge used to look after these things at one time and put them in albums; then during the war she must have lost interest, or had too many other things to do.

All this junk could really be cleared away. It would have made a fine fire the other night, and might have got even the apple logs to burn. There was little sense in keeping any of it. This appalling photo of Midge, for instance, taken heaven knows how many years ago, not long after their marriage, judging from the style of it. Did she really wear her hair that way? That fluffy mop, much too thick and bushy for her face, which was long and narrow even then. The low neck, pointing to a V, and the dangling earrings, and the smile, too eager, making her mouth seem larger than it was. In the left-hand corner she had written 'To my own darling Buzz, from his loving Midge'. He had completely forgotten his old nickname. It had been dropped years back, and he seemed to remember he had never cared for it: he had found it ridiculous and embarrassing and had chided her for using it in front of people.

He tore the photograph in half and threw it on the fire. He watched it curl up upon itself and burn, and the last to go was that vivid smile. My own darling Buzz . . . Suddenly he remembered the evening dress in the photograph. It was green, not her colour ever, turning her sallow; and she had bought it for some special occasion, some big dinner party with friends who were celebrating their wedding anniversary. The idea of the dinner had been to invite all those friends and neighbours who had been married roughly around the same time, which was the reason Midge and he had gone.

There was a lot of champagne, and one or two speeches, and much conviviality, laughter, and joking – some of the joking rather broad – and he remembered that when the evening was over, and they were climbing into the car to drive away, his host, with a gust of laughter, said, 'Try paying your addresses in a top hat, old boy, they say it never fails!' He had been aware of Midge beside him, in that green evening frock, sitting very straight and still, and on her face that same smile which she had worn in the photograph just destroyed, eager yet uncertain, doubtful of the meaning of the words that her host, slightly intoxicated, had let fall upon the evening air, yet wishing to seem advanced, anxious to please, and more than either of these things desperately anxious to attract.

When he had put the car away in the garage and gone into the house he had found her waiting there, in the living-room, for no reason at all. Her coat was thrown off to show the evening dress, and the smile, rather uncertain, was on her face.

He yawned, and settling himself down in a chair picked up a book. She waited a little while, then slowly took up her coat and went upstairs. It must have been shortly afterwards that she had that photograph taken. 'My own darling Buzz, from his loving Midge.' He threw a great handful of dry sticks on to the fire. They crackled and split and turned the photograph to ashes. No damp green logs tonight . . .

It was fine and warm the following day. The sun shone, and the birds sang. He had a sudden impulse to go to London. It was a day for sauntering along Bond Street, watching the passing crowds. A day for calling in at his tailors, for having a hair-cut, for eating a dozen oysters at his favourite bar. The chill had left him. The pleasant hours stretched before him. He might even look in at a matinée.

The day passed without incident, peaceful, untiring, just as he had planned, making a change from day-by-day country routine. He drove home about seven o'clock, looking forward to his drink and to his dinner. It was so warm he did not need his overcoat, not even now, with the sun gone down. He waved a hand to the farmer, who happened to be passing the gate as he turned into the drive.

'Lovely day,' he shouted.

The man nodded, smiled. 'Can do with plenty of these from now on,' he shouted back. Decent fellow. They had always been very matey since those war days, when he had driven the tractor.

He put away the car and had a drink, and while waiting for supper took a stroll around the garden. What a difference those hours of sunshine had made to everything. Several daffodils were out, narcissi too, and the green hedgerows fresh and sprouting. As for the apple trees, the buds had burst, and they were all of them in flower. He went to his little favourite and touched the blossom. It felt soft to his hand and he gently shook a bough. It was firm, well-set, and would not fall. The scent was scarcely perceptible as yet, but in a day or two, with a little more sun, perhaps a shower or two, it would come from the open flower and softly fill the air, never pungent, never strong, a modest scent. A scent which you would have to find for yourself, as the bees did. Once found it stayed with you, it lingered always, alluring, comforting, and sweet. He patted the little tree, and went down the steps into the house.

Next morning, at breakfast, there came a knock on the dining-room window, and the daily woman said that Willis was outside and wanted to have a word with him. He asked Willis to step in.

The gardener looked aggrieved. Was it trouble, then?

'I'm sorry to bother you, sir,' he said, 'but I had a few words with Mr Jackson this morning. He's been complaining.'

Jackson was the farmer, who owned the neighbouring fields.

'What's he complaining about?'

'Says I've been throwing wood over the fence into his field, and the young foal out there, with the mare, tripped over it and went lame. I've never thrown wood over the fence in my life, sir. Quite nasty he was, sir. Spoke of the value of the foal, and it might spoil his chances to sell it.'

'I hope you told him, then, it wasn't true.'

'I did, sir. But the point is someone has been throwing wood over the fence. He showed me the very spot. Just behind the garage. I went with Mr Jackson, and there they were. Logs had been tipped there, sir. I thought it best to come to you about it before I spoke in the kitchen, otherwise you know how it is, there would be unpleasantness.'

He felt the gardener's eye upon him. No way out, of course. And it was Willis's fault in the first place.

'No need to say anything in the kitchen, Willis,' he said. 'I threw the logs there myself. You brought them into the house, without my asking you to do so, with the result that they put out my fire, filled the room with smoke, and ruined an evening. I chucked them over the fence in a devil of a temper, and if they have damaged Jackson's foal you can apologize for me, and tell him I'll pay him compensation. All I ask is that you don't bring any more logs like those into the house again.'

137

'No sir, I understood they had not been a success. I didn't think, though, that you would go so far as to throw them out.'

'Well, I did. And there's an end to it.'

'Yes, sir.' He made as if to go, but before he left the dining-room he paused and said, 'I can't understand about the logs not burning, all the same. I took a small piece back to the wife, and it burnt lovely in our kitchen, bright as anything.'

'It did not burn here.'

'Anyway, the old tree is making up for one spoilt branch, sir. Have you seen her this morning?'

'No.'

'It's yesterday's sun that has done it, sir, and the warm night. Quite a treat she is, with all the blossom. You should go out and take a look at her directly.'

Willis left the room, and he continued his breakfast.

Presently he went out on to the terrace. At first he did not go up on to the lawn; he made a pretence of seeing to other things, of getting the heavy garden seat out, now that the weather was set fair. And then, fetching a pair of clippers, he did a bit of pruning to the few roses, under the windows. Yet, finally, something drew him to the tree.

It was just as Willis said. Whether it was the sun, the warmth, the mild still night, he could not tell; but the small brown buds had unfolded themselves, had ripened into flower, and now spread themselves above his head into a fantastic cloud of white, moist blossom. It grew thickest at the top of the tree, the flowers so clustered together that they looked like wad upon wad of soggy cotton wool, and all of it, from the topmost branches to those nearer to the ground, had this same pallid colour of sickly white.

It did not resemble a tree at all; it might have been a flapping tent, left out in the rain by campers who had gone away, or else a mop, a giant mop, whose streaky surface had been caught somehow by the sun, and so turned bleached. The blossom was too thick, too great a burden for the long thin trunk, and the moisture clinging to it made it heavier still. Already, as if the

138

effort had been too much, the lower flowers, those nearest the ground, were turning brown; yet there had been no rain.

Well, there it was. Willis had been proved right. The tree had blossomed. But instead of blossoming to life, to beauty, it had somehow, deep in nature, gone awry and turned a freak. A freak which did not know its texture or its shape, but thought to please. Almost as though it said, self-conscious, with a smirk, 'Look. All this is for you.'

Suddenly he heard a step behind him. It was Willis.

'Fine sight, sir, isn't it?'

'Sorry, I don't admire it. The blossom is far too thick.'

The gardener stared at him and said nothing. It struck him that Willis must think him very difficult, very hard, and possibly eccentric. He would go and discuss him in the kitchen with the daily woman.

He forced himself to smile at Willis.

'Look here,' he said, 'I don't mean to damp you. But all this blossom doesn't interest me. I prefer it small and light and colourful, like the little tree. But you take some of it back home, to your wife. Cut as much of it as you like, I don't mind at all. I'd like you to have it.'

He waved his arm, generously. He wanted Willis to go now, and fetch a ladder, and carry the stuff away.

The man shook his head. He looked quite shocked.

'No, thank you, sir, I wouldn't dream of it. It would spoil the tree. I want to wait for the fruit. That's what I'm banking on, the fruit.'

There was no more to be said.

'All right, Willis. Don't bother, then.'

He went back to the terrace. But when he sat down there in the sun, looking up the sloping lawn, he could not see the little tree at all, standing modest and demure above the steps, her soft flowers lifting to the sky. She was dwarfed and hidden by the freak, with its great cloud of sagging petals, already wilting, dingy white, on to the grass beneath. And whichever way he turned his chair, this way or that upon the terrace, it seemed to him

139

that he could not escape the tree, that it stood there above him, reproachful, anxious, desirous of the admiration that he could not give.

That summer he took a longer holiday than he had done for many years – a bare ten days with his old mother in Norfolk, instead of the customary month that he had been used to spend with Midge, and the rest of August and the whole of September in Switzerland and Italy.

He took his car, and so was free to motor from place to place as the mood inclined. He cared little for sight-seeing or excursions, and was not much of a climber. What he liked most was to come upon a little town in the cool of the evening, pick out a small but comfortable hotel, and then stay there, if it pleased him, for two or three days at a time, doing nothing, mooching.

He liked sitting about in the sun all morning, at some café or restaurant, with a glass of wine in front of him, watching the people; so many gay young creatures seemed to travel nowadays. He enjoyed the chatter of conversation around him, as long as he did not have to join in; and now and again a smile would come his way, a word or two of greeting from some guest in the same hotel, but nothing to commit him, merely a sense of being in the swim, of being a man of leisure on his own, abroad.

The difficulty in the old days, on holiday anywhere with Midge, would be her habit of striking up acquaintance with people, some other couple who struck her as looking 'nice' or, as she put it, 'our sort'. It would start with conversation over coffee, and then pass on to mutual planning of shared days, car drives in foursomes – he could not bear it, the holiday would be ruined.

Now, thank heaven, there was no need for this. He did what he liked, in his own time. There was no Midge to say, 'Well, shall we be moving?' when he was still sitting contentedly over his wine, no Midge to plan a visit to some old church that did not interest him.

He put on weight during his holiday, and he did not mind.

There was no one to suggest a good long walk to keep fit after the rich food, thus spoiling the pleasant somnolence that comes with coffee and dessert; no one to glance, surprised, at the sudden wearing of a jaunty shirt, a flamboyant tie.

Strolling through the little towns and villages, hatless, smoking a cigar, receiving smiles from the jolly young folk around him, he felt himself a dog. This was the life, no worries, no cares. No 'We have to be back on the fifteenth because of that committee meeting at the hospital'; no 'We can't possibly leave the house shut up for longer than a fortnight, something might happen'. Instead, the bright lights of a little country fair, in a village whose name he did not even bother to find out; the tinkle of music, boys and girls laughing, and he himself, after a bottle of the local wine, bowing to a young thing with a gay handkerchief round her head and sweeping her off to dance under the hot tent. No matter if her steps did not harmonize with his – it was years since he had danced – this was the thing, this was it. He released her when the music stopped, and off she ran, giggling, back to her young friends, laughing at him no doubt. What of it? He had had his fun.

He left Italy when the weather turned, at the end of September, and was back home the first week in October. No problem to it. A telegram to the daily woman, with the probable date of arrival, and that was all. Even a brief holiday with Midge and the return meant complications. Written instructions about groceries, milk, and bread; airing of beds, lighting of fires, reminders about the delivery of the morning papers. The whole business turned into a chore.

He turned into the drive on a mellow October evening and there was smoke coming from the chimneys, the front door open, and his pleasant home awaiting him. No rushing through to the back regions to learn of possible plumbing disasters, breakages, water shortages, food difficulties; the daily woman knew better than to bother him with these. Merely, 'Good evening, sir. I hope you had a good holiday. Supper at the usual time?' And then silence. He could have his drink, light his pipe, and relax; the

141

small pile of letters did not matter. No feverish tearing of them open, and then the start of the telephoning, the hearing of those endless one-sided conversations between women friends. 'Well? How are things? Really? My dear . . . And what did you say to that? . . . She did? . . . I can't possibly on Wednesday . . .'

He stretched himself contentedly, stiff after his drive, and gazed comfortably around the cheerful, empty living-room. He was hungry, after his journey up from Dover, and the chop seemed rather meagre after foreign fare. But there it was, it wouldn't hurt him to return to plainer food. A sardine on toast followed the chop, and then he looked about him for dessert.

There was a plate of apples on the sideboard. He fetched them and put them down in front of him on the dining-room table. Poor-looking things. Small and wizened, dullish brown in colour. He bit into one, but as soon as the taste of it was on his tongue he spat it out. The thing was rotten. He tried another. It was just the same. He looked more closely at the pile of apples. The skins were leathery and rough and hard; you would expect the insides to be sour. On the contrary they were pulpy soft, and the cores were yellow. Filthy-tasting things. A stray piece stuck to his tooth and he pulled it out. Stringy, beastly . . .

He rang the bell, and the woman came through from the kitchen.

'Have we any other dessert?' he said.

'I am afraid not, sir. I remembered how fond you were of apples, and Willis brought in these from the garden. He said they were especially good, and just ripe for eating.'

'Well, he's quite wrong. They're uneatable.'

'I'm very sorry, sir. I wouldn't have put them through had I known. There's a lot more outside, too. Willis brought in a great basketful.'

'All the same sort?'

'Yes, sir. The small brown ones. No other kind, at all.'

'Never mind, it can't be helped. I'll look for myself in the morning.'

He got up from the table and went through to the living-room.

142

He had a glass of port to take away the taste of the apples, but it seemed to make no difference, not even a biscuit with it. The pulpy rotten tang clung to his tongue and the roof of his mouth, and in the end he was obliged to go up to the bathroom and clean his teeth. The maddening thing was that he could have done with a good clean apple, after that rather indifferent supper: something with a smooth clear skin, the inside not too sweet, a little sharp in flavour. He knew the kind. Good biting texture. You had to pick them, of course, at just the right moment.

He dreamt that night he was back again in Italy, dancing under the tent in the little cobbled square. He woke with the tinkling music in his ear, but he could not recall the face of the peasant girl or remember the feel of her, tripping against his feet. He tried to recapture the memory, lying awake, over his morning tea, but it eluded him.

He got up out of bed and went over to the window, to glance at the weather. Fine enough, with a slight nip in the air.

Then he saw the tree. The sight of it came as a shock, it was so unexpected. Now he realized at once where the apples had come from the night before. The tree was laden, bowed down, under her burden of fruit. They clustered, small and brown, on every branch, diminishing in size as they reached the top, so that those on the high boughs, not grown yet to full size, looked like nuts. They weighed heavy on the tree, and because of this it seemed bent and twisted out of shape, the lower branches nearly sweeping the ground; and on the grass, at the foot of the tree, were more and yet more apples, windfalls, the first-grown, pushed off by their clamouring brothers and sisters. The ground was covered with them, many split open and rotting where the wasps had been. Never in his life had he seen a tree so laden with fruit. It was a miracle that it had not fallen under the weight.

He went out before breakfast – curiosity was too great – and stood beside the tree, staring at it. There was no mistake about it, these were the same apples that had been put in the dining-room last night. Hardly bigger than tangerines, and many of them smaller than that, they grew so close together on the branches that to pick one you would be forced to pick a dozen.

There was something monstrous in the sight, something distasteful; yet it was pitiful too that the months had brought this agony upon the tree, for agony it was, there could be no other word for it. The tree was tortured by fruit, groaning under the weight of it, and the frightful part about it was that not one of the fruit was eatable. Every apple was rotten through and through. He trod them underfoot, the windfalls on the grass, there was no escaping them; and in a moment they were mush and slime, clinging about his heels – he had to clean the mess off with wisps of grass.

It would have been far better if the tree had died, stark and bare, before this ever happened. What use was it to him or anyone, this load of rotting fruit, littering up the place, fouling the ground? And the tree itself humped, as it were, in pain, and yet he could almost swear triumphant, gloating.

Just as in spring, when the mass of fluffy blossom, colourless and sodden, dragged the reluctant eye away from the other trees, so it did now. Impossible to avoid seeing the tree, with its burden of fruit. Every window in the front part of the house looked out upon it. And he knew how it would be. The fruit would cling there until it was picked, staying upon the branches through October and November, and it never would be picked, because nobody could eat it. He could see himself being bothered with the tree throughout the autumn. Whenever he came out on to the terrace there it would be, sagging and loathsome.

It was extraordinary the dislike he had taken to the tree. It was a perpetual reminder of the fact that he . . . well, he was blessed if he knew what . . . a perpetual reminder of all the things he most detested, and always had, he could not put a name to them. He decided then and there that Willis should pick the fruit and take it away, sell it, get rid of it, anything, as long as he did not have to eat it, and as long as he was not forced to watch the tree drooping there, day after day, throughout the autumn.

He turned his back upon it and was relieved to see that none

144

of the other trees had so degraded themselves to excess. They carried a fair crop, nothing out of the way, and as he might have known the young tree, to the right of the old one, made a brave little show on its own, with a light load of medium-sized, rosy-looking apples, not too dark in colour, but freshly reddened where the sun had ripened them. He would pick one now, and take it in, to eat with breakfast. He made his choice, and the apple fell at the first touch into his hand. It looked so good that he bit into it with appetite. That was it, juicy, sweet-smelling, sharp, the dew upon it still. He did not look back at the old tree. He went indoors, hungry, to breakfast.

It took the gardener nearly a week to strip the tree, and it was plain he did it under protest.

'I don't care what you do with them,' said his employer. 'You can sell them and keep the money, or you can take them home and feed them to your pigs. I can't stand the sight of them, and that's all there is to it. Find a long ladder, and start on the job right away.'

It seemed to him that Willis, from sheer obstinacy, spun out the time. He would watch the man from the windows act as though in slow motion. First the placing of the ladder. Then the laborious climb, and the descent to steady it again. After that the performance of plucking off the fruit, dropping them, one by one, into the basket. Day after day it was the same. Willis was always there on the sloping lawn with his ladder, under the tree, the branches creaking and groaning, and beneath him on the grass baskets, pails, basins, any receptacle that would hold the apples.

At last the job was finished. The ladder was removed, the baskets and pails also, and the tree was stripped bare. He looked out at it, the evening of that day, in satisfaction. No more rotting fruit to offend his eye. Every single apple gone.

Yet the tree, instead of seeming lighter from the loss of its burden, looked, if it were possible, more dejected than ever. The branches still sagged, and the leaves, withering now to the cold autumnal evening, folded upon themselves and shivered. 'Is this my reward?' it seemed to say. 'After all I've done for you?'

As the light faded, the shadow of the tree cast a blight upon the dank night. Winter would soon come. And the short, dull days.

He had never cared much for the fall of the year. In the old days, when he went up to London every day to the office, it had meant that early start by train, on a nippy morning. And then, before three o'clock in the afternoon, the clerks were turning on the lights, and as often as not there would be fog in the air, murky and dismal, and a slow chugging journey home, daily bread-ers like himself sitting five abreast in a carriage, some of them with colds in their heads. Then the long evening followed, with Midge opposite him before the living-room fire, and he listening, or feigning to listen, to the account of her days and the things that had gone wrong.

If she had not shouldered any actual household disaster, she would pick upon some current event to cast a gloom. 'I see fares are going up again, what about your season ticket?', or 'This business in South Africa looks nasty, quite a long bit about it on the six o'clock news', or yet again 'Three more cases of polio over at the isolation hospital. I don't know, I'm sure, what the medical world thinks it's doing . . .'

Now, at least, he was spared the role of listener, but the memory of those long evenings was with him still, and when the lights were lit and the curtains were drawn he would be reminded of the click-click of the needles, the aimless chatter, and the 'Heigh-ho' of the yawns. He began to drop in, sometimes before supper, sometimes afterwards, at the Green Man, the old public house a quarter of a mile away on the main road. Nobody bothered him there. He would sit in a corner, having said good evening to genial Mrs Hill, the proprietress, and then, with a cigarette and a whisky-and-soda, watch the local inhabitants stroll in to have a pint, to throw a dart, to gossip.

In a sense it made a continuation of his summer holiday. It bore resemblance, admittedly slight, to the care-free atmosphere of the cafés and the restaurants; and there was a kind of warmth

146

about the bright smoke-filled bar, crowded with working men who did not bother him, which he found pleasant, comforting. These visits cut into the length of the dark winter evenings, making them more tolerable.

A cold in the head, caught in mid-December, put a stop to this for more than a week. He was obliged to keep to the house. And it was odd, he thought to himself, how much he missed the Green Man, and how sick to death he became of sitting about in the living-room or in the study, with nothing to do but read or listen to the wireless. The cold and the boredom made him morose and irritable, and the enforced inactivity turned his liver sluggish. He needed exercise. Whatever the weather, he decided towards the end of yet another cold grim day, he would go out tomorrow. The sky had been heavy from mid-afternoon and threatened snow, but no matter, he could not stand the house for a further twenty-four hours without a break.

The final edge to his irritation came with the fruit tart at supper. He was in that final stage of a bad cold when the taste is not yet fully returned, appetite is poor, but there is a certain emptiness within that needs ministration of a particular kind. A bird might have done it. Half a partridge, roasted to perfection, followed by a cheese soufflé. As well ask for the moon. The daily woman, not gifted with imagination, produced plaice, of all fish the most tasteless, the most dry. When she had borne the remains of this away – he had left most of it upon his plate – she returned with a tart, and because hunger was far from being satisfied he helped himself to it liberally.

One taste was enough. Choking, spluttering, he spat out the contents of his spoon upon the plate. He got up and rang the bell.

The woman appeared, a query on her face, at the unexpected summons.

'What the devil is this stuff?'

'Jam tart, sir.'

'What sort of jam?'

'Apple jam, sir. Made from my own bottling.'

He threw down his napkin on the table.

'I guessed as much. You've been using some of those apples that I complained to you about months ago. I told you and Willis quite distinctly that I would not have any of those apples in the house.'

The woman's face became tight and drawn.

'You said, sir, not to cook the apples, or to bring them in for dessert. You said nothing about not making jam. I thought they would taste all right as jam. And I made some myself, to try. It was perfectly all right. So I made several bottles of jam from the apples Willis gave me. We always made jam here, madam and myself.'

'Well, I'm sorry for your trouble, but I can't eat it. Those apples disagreed with me in the autumn, and whether they are made into jam or whatever you like they will do so again. Take the tart away, and don't let me see it, or the jam, again. I'll have some coffee in the living-room.'

He went out of the room, trembling. It was fantastic that such a small incident should make him feel so angry. God! What fools people were. She knew, Willis knew, that he disliked the apples, loathed the taste and smell of them, but in their cheese-paring way they decided that it would save money if he was given home-made jam, jam made from the apples he particularly detested.

He swallowed down a stiff whisky and lit a cigarette.

In a moment or two she appeared with the coffee. She did not retire immediately on putting down the tray.

'Could I have a word with you, sir?'

'What is it?'

'I think it would be for the best if I gave in my notice.'

Now this, on top of the other. What a day, what an evening.

'What reason? Because I can't eat apple-tart?'

'It's not just that, sir. Somehow I feel things are very different from what they were. I have meant to speak several times.'

'I don't give much trouble, do I?'

'No, sir. Only in the old days, when madam was alive, I felt my work was appreciated. Now it's as though it didn't matter one way or the other. Nothing's ever said, and although I try to do my best I can't be sure. I think I'd be happier if I went where there was a lady again who took notice of what I did.'

'You are the best judge of that, of course. I'm sorry if you haven't liked it here lately.'

'You were away so much too, sir, this summer. When madam was alive it was never for more than a fortnight. Everything seems so changed. I don't know where I am, or Willis either.'

'So Willis is fed up too?'

'That's not for me to say, of course. I know he was upset about the apples, but that's some time ago. Perhaps he'll be speaking to you himself.'

'Perhaps he will. I had no idea I was causing so much concern to you both. All right, that's quite enough. Goodnight.'

She went out of the room. He stared moodily about him. Good riddance to them both, if that was how they felt. Things aren't the same. Everything so changed. Damned nonsense. As for Willis being upset about the apples, what infernal impudence. Hadn't he a right to do what he liked with his own tree? To hell with his cold and with the weather. He couldn't bear sitting about in front of the fire thinking about Willis and the cook. He would go down to the Green Man and forget the whole thing.

He put on his overcoat and muffler and his old cap and walked briskly down the road, and in twenty minutes he was sitting in his usual corner in the Green Man, with Mrs Hill pouring out his whisky and expressing her delight to see him back. One or two of the habitués smiled at him, asked after his health.

'Had a cold, sir? Same everywhere. Everyone's got one.'

'That's right.'

'Well, it's the time of year, isn't it?'

'Got to expect it. It's when it's on the chest it's nasty.'

'No worse than being stuffed up, like, in the head.'

'That's right. One's as bad as the other. Nothing to it.'

Likeable fellows. Friendly. Not harping at one, not bothering.

'Another whisky, please.'

'There you are, sir. Do you good. Keep out the cold.'

Mrs Hill beamed behind the bar. Large, comfortable old soul. Through a haze of smoke he heard the chatter, the deep laughter, the click of the darts, the jocular roar at a bull's eye.

'. . . and if it comes on to snow, I don't know how we shall manage,' Mrs Hill was saying, 'them being so late delivering the coal. If we had a load of logs it would help us out, but what do you think they're asking? Two pounds a load. I mean to say . . .'

He leant forward and his voice sounded far away, even to himself.

'I'll let you have some logs,' he said.

Mrs Hill turned round. She had not been talking to him.

'Excuse me?' she said.

'I'll let you have some logs,' he repeated. 'Got an old tree, up at home, needed sawing down for months. Do it for you tomorrow.'

He nodded, smiling.

'Oh no, sir. I couldn't think of putting you to the trouble. The coal will turn up, never fear.'

'No trouble at all. A pleasure. Like to do it for you, the exercise, you know, do me good. Putting on weight. You count on me.'

He got down from his seat and reached, rather carefully, for his coat.

'It's apple wood,' he said. 'Do you mind apple wood?'

'Why no,' she answered, 'any wood will do. But can you spare it, sir?'

He nodded, mysteriously. It was a bargain, it was a secret.

'I'll bring it down to you in my trailer tomorrow night,' he said.

'Careful, sir,' she said, 'mind the step . . .'

He walked home, through the cold crisp night, smiling to himself. He did not remember undressing or getting into bed, but when he woke the next morning the first thought that came to his mind was the promise he had made about the tree.

It was not one of Willis's days, he realized with satisfaction. There would be no interfering with his plan. The sky was heavy and snow had fallen in the night. More to come. But as yet nothing to worry about, nothing to hamper him.

He went through to the kitchen garden, after breakfast, to the tool shed. He took down the saw, the wedges, and the axe. He might need all of them. He ran his thumb along the edges. They would do. As he shouldered his tools and walked back to the front garden he laughed to himself, thinking that he must resemble an executioner of old days, setting forth to behead some wretched victim in the Tower.

He laid his tools down beneath the apple tree. It would be an act of mercy, really. Never had he seen anything so wretched, so utterly woebegone, as the apple tree. There couldn't be any life left in it. Not a leaf remained. Twisted, ugly, bent, it ruined the appearance of the lawn. Once it was out of the way the whole setting of the garden would change.

A snow-flake fell on to his hand, then another. He glanced down past the terrace to the dining-room window. He could see the woman laying his lunch. He went down the steps and into the house. 'Look,' he said, 'if you like to leave my lunch ready in the oven, I think I'll fend for myself today. I may be busy, and I don't want to be pinned down for time. Also it's going to snow. You had better go off early today and get home, in case it becomes really bad. I can manage perfectly well. And I prefer it.'

Perhaps she thought his decision came through offence at her giving notice the night before. Whatever she thought, he did not mind. He wanted to be alone. He wanted no face peering from the window.

She went off at about twelve-thirty, and as soon as she had gone he went to the oven and got his lunch. He meant to get it over, so that he could give up the whole short afternoon to the felling of the tree.

No more snow had fallen, apart from a few flakes that did not lie. He took off his coat, rolled up his sleeves, and seized the saw. With his left hand he ripped away the wire at the base of the tree. Then he placed the saw about a foot from the bottom and began to work it, backwards, forwards.

151

For the first dozen strokes all went smoothly. The saw bit into the wood, the teeth took hold. Then after a few moments the saw began to bind. He had been afraid of that.

He tried to work it free, but the opening that he had made was not yet large enough, and the tree gripped upon the saw and held it fast. He drove in the first wedge, with no result. He drove in the second, and the opening gaped a little wider, but still not wide enough to release the saw.

He pulled and tugged at the saw, to no avail. He began to lose his temper. He took up his axe and started hacking at the tree, pieces of the trunk flying outwards, scattering on the grass.

That was more like it. That was the answer.

Up and down went the heavy axe, splitting and tearing at the tree. Off came the peeling bark, the great white strips of underwood, raw and stringy. Hack at it, blast at it, gouge at the tough tissue, throw the axe away, claw at the rubbery flesh with the bare hands. Not far enough yet, go on, go on.

There goes the saw, the wedge, released. Now up with the axe again. Down there, heavy, where the stringy threads cling so steadfast. Now she's groaning, now she's splitting, now she's rocking and swaying, hanging there upon one bleeding strip. Boot her, then. That's it, kick her, kick her again, one final blow, she's over, she's falling . . . she's down . . . damn her, blast her . . . she's down, splitting the air with sound, and all her branches spread about her on the ground.

He stood back, wiping the sweat from his forehead, from his chin. The wreckage surrounded him on either side, and below him, at his feet, gaped the torn, white, jagged stump of the axed tree.

It began snowing.

His first task, after felling the apple tree, was to hack off the branches and the smaller boughs, and so to grade the wood in stacks, which made it easier to drag away.

The small stuff, bundled and roped, would do for kindling; Mrs Hill would no doubt be glad of that as well. He brought

152

the car, with the trailer attached, to the garden gate, hard by the terrace. This chopping up of the branches was simple work; much of it could be done with a hook. The fatigue came with bending and tying the bundles, and then heaving them down past the terrace and through the gate up on to the trailer. The thicker branches he disposed of with the axe, then split them into three or four lengths, which he could also rope and drag, one by one, to the trailer.

He was fighting all the while against time. The light, what there was of it, would be gone by half past four, and the snow went on falling. The ground was already covered, and when he paused for a moment in his work, and wiped the sweat away from his face, the thin frozen flakes fell upon his lips and made their way, insidious and soft, down his collar to his neck and body. If he lifted his eyes to the sky he was blinded at once. The flakes came thicker, faster, swirling about his head, and it was as though the heaven had turned itself into a canopy of snow, ever descending, coming nearer, closer, stifling the earth. The snow fell upon the torn boughs and the hacked branches, hampering his work. If he rested but an instant to draw breath and renew his strength, it seemed to throw a protective cover, soft and white, over the pile of wood.

He could not wear gloves. If he did so he had no grip upon his hook or his axe, nor could he tie the rope and drag the branches. His fingers were numb with cold, soon they would be too stiff to bend. He had a pain now, under the heart, from the strain of dragging the stuff on to the trailer; and the work never seemed to lessen. Whenever he returned to the fallen tree the pile of wood would appear as high as ever, long boughs, short boughs, a heap of kindling there, nearly covered with the snow, which he had forgotten: all must be roped and fastened and carried or pulled away.

It was after half past four, and almost dark, when he had disposed of all the branches, and nothing now remained but to drag the trunk, already hacked into three lengths, over the terrace to the waiting trailer.

He was very nearly at the point of exhaustion. Only his will to be rid of the tree kept him to the task. His breath came slowly, painfully, and all the while the snow fell into his mouth and into his eyes and he could barely see.

He took his rope and slid it under the cold slippery trunk, knotting it fiercely. How hard and unyielding was the naked wood, and the bark was rough, hurting his numb hands.

'That's the end of you,' he muttered, 'that's your finish.'

Staggering to his feet he bore the weight of the heavy trunk over his shoulder, and began to drag it slowly down over the slope to the terrace and to the garden gate. It followed him, bump . . . bump . . . down the steps of the terrace. Heavy and lifeless, the last bare limbs of the apple tree dragged in his wake through the wet snow.

It was over. His task was done. He stood panting, one hand upon the trailer. Now nothing more remained but to take the stuff down to the Green Man before the snow made the drive impossible. He had chains for the car, he had thought of that already.

He went into the house to change the clothes that were clinging to him and to have a drink. Never mind about his fire, never mind about drawing curtains, seeing what there might be for supper, all the chores the daily woman usually did – that would come later. He must have his drink and get the wood away.

His mind was numb and weary, like his hands and his whole body. For a moment he thought of leaving the job until the following day, flopping down into the armchair, and closing his eyes. No, it would not do. Tomorrow there would be more snow, tomorrow the drive would be two or three feet deep. He knew the signs. And there would be the trailer, stuck outside the garden gate, with the pile of wood inside it, frozen white. He must make the effort and do the job tonight.

He finished his drink, changed, and went out to start the car. It was still snowing, but now that darkness had fallen a colder, cleaner feeling had come into the air, and it was freezing. The dizzy, swirling flakes came more slowly now, with precision.

The engine started and he began to drive downhill, the trailer in tow. He drove slowly, and very carefully, because of the heavy load. And it was an added strain, after the hard work of the afternoon, peering through the falling snow, wiping the windscreen. Never had the lights of the Green Man shone more cheerfully as he pulled up into the little yard.

He blinked as he stood within the doorway, smiling to himself. 'Well, I've brought your wood,' he said.

Mrs Hill stared at him from behind the bar, one or two fellows turned and looked at him, and a hush fell upon the dart-players.

'You never . . .' began Mrs Hill, but he jerked his head at the door and laughed at her.

'Go and see,' he said, 'but don't ask me to unload it tonight.'

He moved to his favourite corner, chuckling to himself, and there they all were, exclaiming and talking and laughing by the door, and he was quite a hero, the fellows crowding round with questions, and Mrs Hill pouring out his whisky and thanking him and laughing and shaking her head. 'You'll drink on the house tonight,' she said.

'Not a bit of it,' he said, 'this is my party. Rounds one and two to me. Come on, you chaps.'

It was festive, warm, jolly, and good luck to them all, he kept saying, good luck to Mrs Hill, and to himself, and to the whole world. When was Christmas? Next week, the week after? Well, here's to it, and a merry Christmas. Never mind the snow, never mind the weather. For the first time he was one of them, not isolated in his corner. For the first time he drank with them, he laughed with them, he even threw a dart with them, and there they all were in that warm stuffy smoke-filled bar, and he felt they liked him, he belonged, he was no longer 'the gentleman' from the house up the road.

The hours passed, and some of them went home, and others took their place, and he was still sitting there, hazy, comfortable, the warmth and the smoke blending together. Nothing of what he heard or saw made very much sense but somehow it did not

155

seem to matter, for there was jolly, fat, easy-going Mrs Hill to minister to his needs, her face glowing at him over the bar.

Another face swung into his view, that of one of the labourers from the farm, with whom, in the old war days, he had shared the driving of the tractor. He leant forward, touching the fellow on the shoulder.

'What happened to the little girl?' he said.

The man lowered his tankard. 'Beg pardon, sir?' he said.

'You remember. The little land-girl. She used to milk the cows, feed the pigs, up at the farm. Pretty girl, dark curly hair, always smiling.'

Mrs Hill turned round from serving another customer.

'Does the gentleman mean May, I wonder?' she asked.

'Yes, that's it, that was the name, young May,' he said.

'Why, didn't you ever hear about it, sir?' said Mrs Hill, filling up his glass. 'We were all very much shocked at the time, everyone was talking of it, weren't they, Fred?'

'That's right, Mrs Hill.'

The man wiped his mouth with the back of his hand.

'Killed,' he said, 'thrown from the back of some chap's motor-bike. Going to be married very shortly. About four years ago, now. Dreadful thing, eh? Nice kid too.'

'We all sent a wreath, from just around,' said Mrs Hill. 'Her mother wrote back, very touched, and sent a cutting from the local paper, didn't she, Fred? Quite a big funeral they had, ever so many floral tributes. Poor May. We were all fond of May.'

'That's right,' said Fred.

'And fancy you never hearing about it, sir!' said Mrs Hill.

'No,' he said, 'no, nobody ever told me. I'm sorry about it. Very sorry.'

He stared in front of him at his half-filled glass.

The conversation went on around him but he was no longer part of the company. He was on his own again, silent, in his corner. Dead. That poor, pretty girl was dead. Thrown off a motor-bike. Been dead for three or four years. Some careless, bloody fellow, taking a corner too fast, the girl behind him, clinging on to his belt, laughing probably in his ear, and then crash . . . finish. No more curling hair, blowing about her face, no more laughter.

May, that was the name; he remembered clearly now. He could see her smiling over her shoulder, when they called to her. 'Coming,' she sang out, and put a clattering pail down in the yard and went off, whistling, with big clumping boots. He had put his arm about her and kissed her for one brief, fleeting moment. May, the land-girl, with the laughing eyes.

'Going, sir?' said Mrs Hill.

'Yes. Yes, I think I'll be going now.'

He stumbled to the entrance and opened the door. It had frozen hard during the past hour and it was no longer snowing. The heavy pall had gone from the sky and the stars shone.

'Want a hand with the car, sir?' said someone.

'No, thank you,' he said, 'I can manage.'

He unhitched the trailer and let it fall. Some of the wood lurched forward heavily. That would do tomorrow. Tomorrow, if he felt like it, he would come down again and help to unload the wood. Not tonight. He had done enough. Now he was really tired; now he was spent.

It took him some time to start the car, and before he was halfway up the side-road leading to his house he realized that he had made a mistake to bring it at all. The snow was heavy all about him, and the track he had made earlier in the evening was now covered. The car lurched and slithered, and suddenly the right wheel dipped and the whole body plunged sideways. He had got into a drift.

He climbed out and looked about him. The car was deep in the drift, impossible to move without two or three men to help him, and even then, if he went for assistance, what hope was there of trying to continue further, with the snow just as thick ahead? Better leave it. Try again in the morning, when he was fresh. No sense in hanging about now, spending half the night pushing and shoving at the car, all to no purpose. No harm would come to it, here on the side-road; nobody else would be coming this way tonight.

157

He started walking up the road towards his own drive. It was bad luck that he had got the car into the drift. In the centre of the road the going was not bad and the snow did not come above his ankles. He thrust his hands deep in the pockets of his overcoat and ploughed on, up the hill, the countryside a great white waste on either side of him.

He remembered that he had sent the daily woman home at midday and that the house would strike cheerless and cold on his return. The fire would have gone out, and in all probability the furnace too. The windows, uncurtained, would stare bleakly down at him, letting in the night. Supper to get into the bargain. Well, it was his own fault. No one to blame but himself. This was the moment when there should be someone waiting, someone to come running through from the living-room to the hall, opening the front-door, flooding the hall with light. 'Are you all right, darling? I was getting anxious.'

He paused for breath at the top of the hill and saw his home, shrouded by trees, at the end of the short drive. It looked dark and forbidding, without a light in any window. There was more friendliness in the open, under the bright stars, standing on the crisp white snow, than in the sombre house.

He had left the side-gate open, and he went through that way to the terrace, shutting the gate behind him. What a hush had fallen upon the garden – there was no sound at all. It was as though some spirit had come and put a spell upon the place, leaving it white and still.

He walked softly over the snow towards the apple trees.

Now the young one stood alone, above the steps, dwarfed no longer; and with her branches spread, glistening white, she belonged to the spirit world, a world of fantasy and ghosts. He wanted to stand beside the little tree and touch the branches, to make certain she was still alive, that the snow had not harmed her, so that in the spring she would blossom once again.

She was almost within his reach when he stumbled and fell, his foot twisted underneath him, caught in some obstacle hidden by the snow. He tried to move his foot but it was jammed, and he knew suddenly, by the sharpness of the pain biting his ankle, that what had trapped him was the jagged split stump of the old apple tree he had felled that afternoon.

He leant forward on his elbows, in an attempt to drag himself along the ground, but such was his position, in falling, that his leg was bent backwards, away from his foot, and every effort that he made only succeeded in imprisoning the foot still more firmly in the grip of the trunk. He felt for the ground, under the snow, but where he felt his hands touched the small broken twigs from the apple tree that had scattered there, when the tree fell, and then were covered by the falling snow. He shouted for help, knowing in his heart no one could hear.

'Let me go,' he shouted, 'let me go,' as though the thing that held him there in its mercy had the power to release him, and as he shouted tears of frustration and of fear ran down his face. He would have to lie there all night, held fast in the clutch of the old apple tree. There was no hope, no escape, until they came to find him in the morning, and supposing it was then too late, that when they came he was dead, lying stiffly in the frozen snow?

Once more he struggled to release his foot, swearing and sobbing as he did so. It was no use. He could not move. Exhausted, he laid his head upon his arms, and wept. He sank deeper, ever deeper into the snow, and when a stray piece of brushwood, cold and wet, touched his lips, it was like a hand, hesitant and timid feeling its way towards him in the darkness.

The Little Photographer

T he Marquise lay on her chaise-longue on the balcony of the hotel. She wore only a wrapper, and her sleek gold hair, newly set in pins, was bound close to her head in a turquoise bandeau that matched her eyes. Beside her chair stood a little table, and on it were three bottles of nail varnish all of a different shade.

She had dabbed a touch of colour on to three separate finger-nails, and now she held her hand in front of her to see the effect. No, the varnish on the thumb was too red, too vivid, giving a heated look to her slim olive hand, almost as if a spot of blood had fallen there from a fresh-cut wound.

In contrast, her fore-finger was a striking pink, and this too seemed to her false, not true to her present mood. It was the elegant rich pink of drawing-rooms, of ball-gowns, of herself standing at some reception, slowly moving to and fro her ostrich feather fan, and in the distance the sound of violins.

The middle finger was touched with a sheen of silk neither crimson nor vermilion, but somehow softer, subtler; the sheen of a peony in bud, not yet opened to the heat of the day but with the dew of the morning upon it still. A peony, cool and close, looking down upon lush grass from some terraced border, and later, at high noon, the petals unfolding to the sun.

Yes, that was the colour. She reached for cotton-wool and wiped away the offending varnish from her other finger-nails, and then slowly, carefully, she dipped the little brush into the chosen varnish and, like an artist, worked with swift, deft strokes.

When she had finished she leant back in her chaise-longue, exhausted, waving her hands before her in the air to let the varnish harden – a strange gesture, like that of a priestess. She

160

looked down at her toes, appearing from her sandals, and decided that presently, in a few moments, she would paint them too; olive hands, olive feet, subdued and quiet, surprised into sudden life.

Not yet, though. She must rest, relax. It was too hot to move from the supporting back of the chaise-longue and lean forward, crouching, eastern fashion, for the adorning of her feet. There was plenty of time. Time, in fact, stretched before her in an unwinding pattern through the whole long, languorous day.

She closed her eyes.

The distant sound of hotel life came to her as in a dream, and the sounds were hazy, pleasant, because she was part of that life yet free as well, bound no longer to the tyranny of home. Someone on a balcony above scraped back a chair. Below, on the terrace, the waiters set up the gay striped umbrellas over the little luncheon tables; she could hear the *maître d'hôtel* call directions from the dining-room. The *femme de chambre* was doing the rooms in the adjoining suite. Furniture was moved, a bed creaked, the *valet de chambre* came out on to the next balcony and swept the boards with a straw brush. Their voices murmured, grumbled. Then they went away. Silence again. Nothing but the lazy splash of the sea, as effortlessly it licked the burning sand; and somewhere, far away, too distant to make an irritation, the laughter of children playing, her own amongst them.

A guest ordered coffee on the terrace below. The smoke of his cigar came floating upwards to the balcony. The Marquise sighed, and her lovely hands dropped down like lilies on either side of the chaise-longue. This was peace, this was contentment. If she could hold the moment thus for one more hour . . . But something warned her, when the hour was past, the old demon of dissatisfaction, of tedium, would return, even here where she was free at last, on holiday.

A bumble-bee flew on to the balcony, hovered over the bottle of nail varnish and entered the open flower, picked by one of the children, lying beside it. His humming ceased when he was inside the flower. The Marquise opened her eyes and saw the bee crawl forth, intoxicated. Then dizzily once more he took the air and hummed his way. The spell was broken. The Marquise picked up the letter from Édouard, her husband, that had fallen on to the floor of the balcony: '. . . And so, my dearest, I find it impossible to get to you and the children after all. There is so much business to attend to, here at home, and you know I can rely on no one but myself. I shall, of course, make every effort to come and fetch you at the end of the month. Meanwhile, enjoy yourself, bathing and resting. I know the sea air will do you good. I went to see Maman yesterday, and Madeleine, and it seems the old curé . . .'

The Marquise let the letter fall back again on to the balcony floor. The little droop at the corner of her mouth, the one tell-tale sign that spoilt the smooth lovely face, intensified. It had happened again. Always his work. The estate, the farms, the forests, the business men that he must see, the sudden journeys that he must take, so that in spite of his devotion for her he had no time to spare, Édouard, her husband.

They had told her, before her marriage, how it would be. *'C'est un homme très sérieux, Monsieur le Marquis, vous comprenez.'* How little she had minded, how gladly she had agreed, for what could be better in life than a Marquis who was also *un homme sérieux*? What more lovely than that château and those vast estates? What more imposing than the house in Paris, the retinue of servants, humble, bowing, calling her Madame la Marquise? A fairy-tale world to someone like herself, brought up in Lyon, the daughter of a hard-working surgeon, an ailing mother. But for the sudden arrival of Monsieur le Marquis she might have found herself married to her father's young assistant, and that same day-by-day in Lyon continuing forever.

A romantic match, surely. Frowned on at first by his rela-tives, most certainly. But Monsieur le Marquis, *homme sérieux*, was past forty. He knew his own mind. And she was beautiful. There was no further argument. They married. They had two little girls. They were happy. Yet sometimes . . . The Marquise rose from the chaise-longue and, going into the bedroom, sat down before the dressing-table and removed the pins from her hair. Even this effort exhausted her. She threw off her wrapper and sat naked before her mirror. Sometimes she found herself regretting that day-by-day in Lyon. She remembered the laughter, the joking with other girls, the stifled giggles when a passing man looked at them in the street, the confidences, the exchange of letters, the whispering in bedrooms when her friends came to tea.

Now, as Madame la Marquise, she had no one with whom to share confidences, laughter. Everyone about her was middle-aged, dull, rooted to a life long-lived that never changed. Those interminable visits of Édouard's relatives to the château. His mother, his sisters, his brothers, his sisters-in-law. In the winter, in Paris, it was just the same. Never a new face, never the arrival of a stranger. The only excitement was the appearance, perhaps, to luncheon of one of Édouard's business friends, who, surprised at her beauty when she entered the salon, flickered a daring glance of admiration, then bowed, and kissed her hand.

Watching such a one, during luncheon, she would make a fantasy to herself of how they would meet in secret, how a taxi would take her to his apartment, and entering a small, dark *ascenseur* she would ring a bell and vanish into a strange unknown room. But, the long luncheon over, the business friend would bow and go his way. And afterwards, she would think to herself, he was not even passably good-looking; even his teeth were false. But the glance of admiration, swiftly suppressed – she wanted that.

Now she combed her hair before the mirror, and parting it on one side tried a new effect; a ribbon, the colour of her fingernails, threaded through the gold. Yes, yes . . . And the white frock, later, and that chiffon scarf, thrown carelessly over the shoulders, so that when she went out on to the terrace, followed by the children and the English governess, and the *maître d'hôtel*, bowing, led the way to the little table at the corner, under the striped umbrella, people would stare, would whisper, and the eyes would follow her, as deliberately she would stoop to one of the children, pat its curls in a fond maternal gesture, a thing of grace, of beauty.

But now, before the mirror, only the naked body and the sad

163

sulky mouth. Other women would have lovers. Whispers or scandal came to her ears, even during those long heavy dinners, with Édouard at the far end of the table. Not only in the smart riff-raff society to which she never penetrated, but even amongst the old *noblesse* to which she now belonged. '*On dit, vous savez . . .*' and the suggestion, the murmur, passed from one to the other, with a lifted eye-brow, a shrug of the shoulder.

Sometimes, after a tea-party, a guest would leave early, before six o'clock, giving as an excuse that she was expected elsewhere, and the Marquise, echoing regrets, bidding the guest *au revoir*, would wonder – is she going to a rendezvous? Could it be that in twenty minutes, less perhaps, that dark, rather ordinary little comtesse would be shivering, smiling secretly, as she let her clothes slip to the floor?

Even Élise, her friend of *lycée* days in Lyons, married now six years, had a lover. She never wrote of him by name. She always called him '*mon ami*'. Yet they managed to meet twice a week, on Mondays and Thursdays. He had a car and drove her into the country, even in winter. And Élise would write to the Marquise and say, 'But how plebeian my little affair must seem to you, in high society. How many admirers you must have, and what adventures! Tell me of Paris, and the parties, and who is the man of your choice this winter.' The Marquise would reply, hinting, suggesting, laughing off the question, and launch into a description of her frock, worn at some reception. But she did not say that the reception ended at midnight, that it was formal, dull and that all she, the Marquise, knew of Paris was the drives she took in the car with the children, and the drives to the *couturier* to be fitted for yet another frock, and the drives to the *coiffeur* to have her hair re-arranged and set to perhaps a different style. As to life at the château, she would describe the rooms, yes, the many guests, the solemn long avenue of trees, the acres of woodland; but not the rain in spring, day after day, nor the parching heat of early summer, when silence fell upon the place like a great white pall.

'*Ah! Pardon, je croyais que madame était sortie . . .*' He had come in without knocking, the *valet de chambre*, his straw brush in his hand, and now he backed out of the room again, discreetly, but not before he had seen her there, naked before the mirror. And surely he must have known she had not gone out, when only a few moments before she had been lying on the balcony? Was it compassion she saw in his eyes as well as admiration, before he left the room? As though to say, 'So beautiful, and all alone? We are not used to that in this hotel, where people come for pleasure . . .'

Heavens, it was hot. No breeze even from the sea. Trickles of perspiration ran down from her arms to her body.

She dressed languidly, putting on the cool white dress, and then, strolling out on to the balcony once more, pulled up the sun-blind, let the full heat of the day fall upon her. Dark glasses hid her eyes. The only touch of colour lay on her mouth, her feet, her hands, and in the scarf, thrown about her shoulders. The dark lenses gave a deep tone to the day. The sea, by natural eye a periwinkle blue, had turned to purple, and the white sands to olive brown. The gaudy flowers in their tubs upon the terrace had a tropical texture. As the Marquise leant upon the balcony the heat of the wooden rail burnt her hands. Once again the smell of a cigar floated upwards from some source unknown. There was a tinkle of glasses as a waiter brought apéritifs to a table on the terrace. Somewhere a woman spoke, and a man's voice joined with the woman's, laughing.

An Alsatian dog, his tongue dripping moisture, padded along the terrace towards the wall, searching for a cold stone slab on which to lie. A group of young people, bare and bronzed, the salt from the warm sea scarce dried upon their bodies, came running up from the sands, calling for Martinis. Americans, of course. They flung their towels upon the chairs. One of them whistled to the Alsatian, who did not move. The marquise looked down upon them with disdain, yet merged with her disdain was a kind of envy. They were free to come and go, to climb into a car, to move onward to some other place. They lived in a state of blank, ferocious gaiety. Always in groups. Six or eight of them.

They paired off, of course, they pawed each other, forming into couples. But – and here she gave full play to her contempt – their gaiety held no mystery. In their open lives there could be no moment of suspense. No one waited, in secret, behind a half-closed door.

The savour of a love affair should be quite otherwise, thought the Marquise, and breaking off a rose that climbed the trellis of the balcony, she placed it in the opening of her dress, below her neck. A love affair should be a thing of silence, soft, unspoken. No raucous voice, no burst of sudden laughter, but the kind of stealthy curiosity that comes with fear, and when the fear has gone, a brazen confidence. Never the give-and-take between good friends, but passion between strangers. . .

One by one they came back from the sands, the visitors to the hotel. The tables began to fill up. The terrace, hot and deserted all the morning, became alive once more. And guests, arriving by car for luncheon only, mingled with the more familiar figures belonging to the hotel. A party of six in the right-hand corner. A party of three below. And now more bustle, more chatter, more tinkling of glasses and clatter of plates, so that the splash of the sea, which had been the foremost sound since early morning, now seemed secondary, remote. The tide was going out, the water rippling away across the sands.

Here came the children with their governess, Miss Clay. They prinked their way like little dolls across the terrace, followed by Miss Clay in her striped cotton dress, her crimped hair strag-gling from her bathe, and suddenly they looked up to the balcony, they waved their hands, '*Maman . . . maman . .* .' She leant down, smiling at them; and then, as usual, the little clamour brought distraction. Somebody glanced up with the children, smiling, some man, at a left-hand table, laughed and pointed to his companion, and it began, the first wave of admiration that would come again in full measure when she descended, the Marquise, the beautiful Marquise and her cherubic children, whispers wafting towards her in the air like the smoke from the cigarettes, like the conversation the guests at the other tables shared with

166

one another. This, then, was all that *déjeuner* on the terrace would bring to her, day after day, the ripple of admiration, respect, and then oblivion. Each and all went his way, to swim, to golf, to tennis, to drive, and she was left, beautiful, unruffled, with the children and Miss Clay.

'Look, *maman*, I found a little star-fish on the beach, I am going to take him home with me when we go.'

'No, no, that isn't fair, it's mine. I saw it first.'

The little girls, with flushed faces, fell out with one another.

'Hush, Céleste and Hélène: you make my head ache.'

'Madame is tired? You must rest after lunch. It will do you good, in such heat.' Miss Clay, tactful, bent down to scold the children. 'Everyone is tired. It will do us all good to rest,' she said.

Rest . . . But, thought the Marquise, I never do anything else. My life is one long rest. *Il faut reposer. Repose-toi, ma chérie, tu as mauvaise mine.* Winter and summer, those were the words she heard. From her husband, from the governess, from sisters-in-law, from all those aged, tedious friends. Life was one long sequence of resting, of getting up, and of resting again. Because with her pallor, with her reserve, they thought her delicate.

Heavens above, the hours of her married life she had spent resting, the bed turned down, the shutters closed. In the house in Paris, in the château in the country. Two to four, resting, always resting.

'I'm not in the least tired,' she said to Miss Clay, and for once her voice, usually melodious and soft, was sharp, high-pitched. 'I shall go walking after lunch. I shall go into the town.'

The children stared at her, round-eyed, and Miss Clay, her goat-face startled to surprise, opened her mouth in protest.

'You'll kill yourself, in the heat. Besides, the few shops always close between one and three. Why not wait until after tea? Surely it would be wiser to wait until after tea? The children could go with you and I could do some ironing.'

The Marquise did not answer. She rose from the table, and now, because the children had lingered over *déjeuner* – Céleste was always slow with her food – the terrace was almost deserted.

No one of any importance would watch the progress back to the hotel.

The Marquise went upstairs and once again touched her face with powder, circled her mouth, dipped her fore-finger in scent. Next door she could hear the droning of the children as Miss Clay settled them to rest and closed the shutters. The Marquise took her handbag, made of plaited straw, put in her purse a roll of film, a few odds and ends, and tip-toeing past the children's room went downstairs again, and out of the hotel grounds into the dusty road.

The gravel forced its way at once into her open sandals and the glare of the sun beat down upon her head, and at once what had seemed to her, on the spur of the moment, an unusual thing to do struck her now, in the doing of it, as foolish, pointless. The road was deserted, the sands were deserted, the visitors who had played and walked all morning, while she had lain idle on her balcony, were now taking their ease in their rooms, like Miss Clay and the children. Only the Marquise trod the sun-baked road into the little town.

And here it was even as Miss Clay had warned her. The shops were closed, the sun-blinds were all down, the hour of siesta, inviolate, unbroken, held sway over the shops and their inhabitants.

The Marquise strolled along the street, her straw handbag swinging from her hand, the one walker in a sleeping, yawning world. Even the café at the corner was deserted, and a sand-coloured dog, his face between his paws, snapped with closed eyes at the flies that bothered him. Flies were everywhere. They buzzed at the window of the *pharmacie*, where dark bottles, filled with mysterious medicine, rubbed glass shoulders with skin tonic, sponges, and cosmetics. Flies danced behind the panes of the shop filled with sun-shades, spades, pink dolls, and rope-soled shoes. They crawled upon the empty blood-stained slab of the butcher's shop, behind the iron shutter. From above the shop came the jarring sound of the radio, suddenly switched off, and the heavy sigh of someone who would sleep and would

168

not be disturbed. Even the *bureau de poste* was shut. The Marquise, who had thought to buy stamps, rattled the door to no purpose.

Now she could feel the sweat trickling under her dress, and her feet, in the thin sandals, ached from the short distance she had walked. The sun was too strong, too fierce, and as she looked up and down the empty street, and at the houses, with the shops between, every one of them closed from her, withdrawn into the blessed peace of their siesta, she felt a sudden longing for any place that might be cool, that might be dark – a cellar, perhaps, where there was dripping water from a tap. The sound of water, falling to a stone floor, would soothe her nerves, now jagged from the sun.

Frustrated, almost crying, she turned into an alley-way between two shops. She came to steps, leading down to a little court where there was no sun, and paused there a moment, her hand against the wall, so cold and firm. Beside her there was a window, shuttered, against which she leant her head, and suddenly, to her confusion, the shutter was withdrawn and a face looked out upon her from some dark room within.

'*Je regrette . . .*' she began, swept to absurdity that she should be discovered here, intruding, like one peering into the privacy and squalor of life below a shop. And then her voice dwindled and died away, foolishly, for the face that looked out upon her from the open window was so unusual, so gentle, that it might have come straight from a stained-glass saint in a cathedral. His face was framed in a cloud of dark curled hair, his nose was small and straight, his mouth a sculptured mouth, and his eyes, so solemn, brown and tender, were like the eyes of a gazelle.

'*Vous désirez, Madame la Marquise,*' he said, in answer to her unfinished words.

He knows me, she thought in wonder, he has seen me before, but even this was not so unexpected as the quality of his voice, not rough, not harsh, not the voice of someone in a cellar under a shop, but cultivated, liquid, a voice that matched the eyes of the gazelle.

'It was so hot up in the street,' she said. 'The shops were closed and I felt faint. I came down the steps. I am very sorry, it is private, of course.'

The face disappeared from the window. He opened a door somewhere that she had not seen, and suddenly she found a chair beneath her and she was sitting down, inside the doorway, and it was dark and cool inside the room, even like the cellar she had imagined, and he was giving her water from an earthenware cup.

'Thank you,' she said, 'thank you very much.' Looking up, she saw that he was watching her, with humility, with reverence, the pitcher of water in his hand; and he said to her in his soft, gentle voice, 'Is there anything else I can get for you, Madame la Marquise?'

She shook her head, but within her stirred the feeling she knew so well, the sense of secret pleasure that came with admiration, and, conscious of herself for the first time since he had opened the window, she drew her scarf closer about her shoulders, the gesture deliberate, and she saw the gazelle eyes fall to the rose, tucked in the bodice of her dress.

She said, 'How do you know who I am?'

He answered, 'You came into my shop three days ago. You had your children with you. You bought a film for your camera.'

She stared at him, puzzled. She remembered buying the film from the little shop that advertised Kodaks in the window, and she remembered too the ugly, shuffling crippled woman who had served her behind the counter. The woman had walked with a limp, and afraid that the children would notice and laugh, and that she herself, from nervousness, would be betrayed to equally heartless laughter, she had ordered some things to be sent to the hotel, and then departed.

'My sister served you,' he said, in explanation. 'I saw you from the inner room. I do not often go behind the counter. I take photographs of people, of the countryside, and then they are sold to the visitors who come here in the summer.'

'Yes,' she said, 'I see, I understand.'

And she drank again from the earthenware cup, and drank too the adoration in his eyes.

'I have brought a film to be developed,' she said. 'I have it here in my bag. Would you do that for me?'

'Of course, Madame la Marquise,' he said. 'I will do anything for you, whatever you ask. Since that day you came into my shop I . . .' Then he stopped, a flush came over his face, and he looked away from her, deeply embarrassed.

The Marquise repressed a desire to laugh. It was quite absurd, his admiration. Yet, funny . . . it gave her a sense of power.

'Since I came into your shop, what?' she asked.

He looked at her again. 'I have thought of nothing else, but nothing,' he said to her, and with such intensity that it almost frightened her.

She smiled, she handed back the cup of water. 'I am quite an ordinary woman,' she said. 'If you knew me better, I should disappoint you.' How odd it is, she thought to herself, that I am so much mistress of this situation, I am not at all outraged or shocked. Here I am, in the cellar of a shop, talking to a photographer who has just expressed his admiration for me. It is really most amusing, and yet he, poor man, is in earnest, he really means what he says.

'Well,' she said, 'are you going to take my film?'

It was as though he could not drag his eyes away from her, and boldly she stared him out of face, so that his eyes fell and he flushed again.

'If you will go back the way you came,' he said, 'I will open up the shop for you.' And now it was she who let her eyes linger upon him; the open vest, no shirt, the bare arms, the throat, the head of curling hair, and she said, 'Why cannot I give you the film here?'

'It would not be correct, Madame la Marquise,' he said to her.

She turned, laughing, and went back up the steps to the hot street. She stood on the pavement, she heard the rattle of the key in the door behind, she heard the door open. And then presently, in her own time, having deliberately stood outside to keep him waiting, she went into the shop which was stuffy now, and close, unlike the cool quiet cellar.

171

He was behind the counter and she saw, with disappointment, that he had put on his coat, a grey cheap coat worn by any man serving in a shop, and his shirt was much too stiff, and much too blue. He was ordinary, a shopkeeper, reaching across the counter for the film.

'When will you have them ready?' she said.

'Tomorrow,' he answered, and once again he looked at her with his dumb brown eyes. And she forgot the common coat and the blue stiff shirt, and saw the vest under the coat, and the bare arms.

'If you are a photographer,' she said, 'why don't you come to the hotel and take some photographs of me and my children?'

'You would like me to do that?' he asked.

'Why not?' she answered.

A secret look came into his eyes and went again, and he bent below the counter, pretending to search for string. But she thought, smiling to herself, this is exciting to him, his hands are trembling; and for the same reason her heart beat faster than before.

'Very well, Madame la Marquise,' he said, 'I will come to the hotel at whatever time is convenient to you.'

'The morning, perhaps, is best,' she said, 'at eleven o'clock.'

Casually she strolled away. She did not even say goodbye.

She walked across the street, and looking for nothing in the window of a shop opposite she saw, through the glass, that he had come to the door of his own shop and was watching her. He had taken off his jacket and his shirt. The shop would be closed again, the siesta was not yet over. Then she noticed, for the first time, that he too was crippled, like his sister. His right foot was encased in a high-fitted boot. Yet, curiously, the sight of this did not repel her nor bring her to nervous laughter, as it had done before when she had seen the sister. His high boot had a fascination, strange, unknown.

The Marquise walked back to the hotel along the dusty road.

At eleven o'clock the next morning the concierge of the hotel sent up word that Monsieur Paul, the photographer, was below in the hall, and awaited the instructions of Madame la Marquise.

The instructions were sent back that Madame la Marquise would be pleased if Monsieur Paul would go upstairs to the suite. Presently she heard the knock on the door, hesitant, timid.

'*Entrez*,' she called, and standing, as she did, on the balcony, her arms around the two children, she made a tableau, ready set, for him to gaze upon.

Today she was dressed in silk shantung the colour of chartreuse, and her hair was not the little-girl hair of yesterday, with the ribbon, but parted in the centre and drawn back to show her ears, with the gold clips upon them.

He stood in the entrance of the doorway, he did not move. The children, shy, gazed with wonder at the high boot, but they said nothing. Their mother had warned them not to mention it.

'These are my babies,' said the Marquise. 'And now you must tell us how to pose, and where you want us placed.'

The children did not make their usual curtsey, as they did to guests. Their mother had told them it would not be necessary. Monsieur Paul was a photographer, from the shop in the little town.

'If it would be possible, Madame la Marquise,' he said, 'to have one pose just as you are standing now. It is quite beautiful. So very natural, so full of grace.'

'Why, yes, if you like. Stand still, Hélène.'

'Pardon. It will take a few moments to fix the camera.'

His nervousness had gone. He was busy with the mechanical tricks of his trade. And as she watched him set up the tripod, fix the velvet cloth, make the adjustments to his camera, she noticed his hands, deft and efficient, and they were not the hands of an artisan, of a shopkeeper, but the hands of an artist.

Her eyes fell to the boot. His limp was not so pronounced as the sister's, he did not walk with that lurching, jerky step that produced stifled hysteria in the watcher. His step was slow, more dragging, and the Marquise felt a kind of compassion for his deformity, for surely the misshapen foot beneath the boot must pain him constantly, and the high boot, especially in hot weather, crush and sear his flesh.

'Now, Madame la Marquise,' he said, and guiltily she raised

173

her eyes from the boot and struck her pose, smiling gracefully, her arms embracing the children.

'Yes,' he said, 'just so. It is very lovely.'

The dumb brown eyes held hers. His voice was low, gentle. The sense of pleasure came upon her just as it had done in the shop the day before. He pressed the bulb. There was a little clicking sound.

'Once more,' he said.

She went on posing, the smile on her lips; and she knew that the reason he paused this time before pressing the bulb was not from professional necessity, because she or the children had moved, but because it delighted him to gaze upon her.

'There,' she said, and breaking the pose, and the spell, she moved towards the balcony, humming a little song.

After half an hour the children became tired, restless.

The Marquise apologized. 'It's so very hot,' she said, 'you must excuse them. Céleste, Hélène, get your toys and play on the other corner of the balcony.'

They ran chattering to their own room. The Marquise turned her back upon the photographer. He was putting fresh plates into his camera.

'You know what it is with children,' she said. 'For a few minutes it is a novelty, then they are sick of it, they want something else. You have been very patient, Monsieur Paul.'

She broke off a rose from the balcony, and cupping it in her hands bent her lips to it.

'Please,' he said with urgency, 'if you would permit me, I scarcely like to ask you . . .'

'What?' she said.

'Would it be possible for me to take one or two photographs of you alone, without the children?'

She laughed. She tossed the rose over the balcony to the terrace below.

'But of course,' she said, 'I am at your disposal. I have nothing else to do.'

She sat down on the edge of the chaise-longue, and leaning back against the cushion rested her head against her arm.

'Like this?' she said.

He disappeared behind the velvet cloth, and then, after an adjustment to the camera, came limping forward.

'If you will permit me,' he said, 'the hand should be raised a little, so . . . And the head, just slightly on one side.'

He took her hand and placed it to his liking; and then gently, with hesitation, put his hand under her chin, lifting it. She closed her eyes. He did not take his hand away. Almost imperceptibly his thumb moved, lingering, over the long line of her neck, and his fingers followed the movement of the thumb. The sensation was feather-weight, like the brushing of a bird's wing against her skin.

'Just so,' he said, 'that is perfection.'

She opened her eyes. He limped back to his camera.

The Marquise did not tire as the children had done. She permitted Monsieur Paul to take one photograph, then another, then another. The children returned, as she had bidden them, and played together at the far end of the balcony, and their chatter made a background to the business of the photography, so that, both smiling at the prattle of the children, a kind of adult intimacy developed between the Marquise and the photographer, and the atmosphere was not so tense as it had been.

He became bolder, more confident of himself. He suggested poses and she acquiesced, and once or twice she placed herself badly and he told her of it.

'No, Madame la Marquise. Not like that. Like this.'

Then he would come over to the chair, kneel beside her, move her foot perhaps, or turn her shoulder, and each time he did so his touch became more certain, became stronger. Yet when she forced him to meet her eyes he looked away, humble and diffident, as though he was ashamed of what he did, and his gentle eyes, mirroring his nature, would deny the impulse of his hands. She sensed a struggle within him, and it gave her pleasure.

At last, after he had rearranged her dress the second time, she

175

noticed that he had gone quite white and there was perspiration on his forehead.

'It is very hot,' she said, 'perhaps we have done enough for today.'

'If you please, Madame la Marquise,' he answered, 'it is indeed very warm. I think it is best that we should stop now.'

She rose from the chair, cool and at her ease. She was not tired, nor was she troubled. Rather was she invigorated, full of a new energy. When he had gone she would walk down to the sea and swim. It was very different for the photographer. She saw him wipe his face with his handkerchief, and as he packed up his camera and his tripod, and put them in the case, he looked exhausted and dragged his high boot more heavily than before.

She made a pretence of glancing through the snap-shots he had developed for her from her own film.

'These are very poor,' she said lightly. 'I don't think I handle my camera correctly. I should take lessons from you.'

'It is just a little practice that you need, Madame la Marquise,' he said. 'When I first started I had a camera much the same as yours. Even now, when I take exteriors, I wander out on the cliffs above the sea, with a small camera, and the effects are just as good as with the larger one.'

She put the snap-shots down on the table. He was ready to go. He carried the case in his hand.

'You must be very busy in the season,' she said. 'How do you get time to take exteriors?'

'I make time, Madame la Marquise,' he said. 'I prefer it, actually, to taking studio portraits. It is only occasionally that I find true satisfaction in photographing people. Like, for instance, today.'

She looked at him and she saw again the devotion, the humility, in his eyes. She stared at him until he dropped his eyes, abashed.

'The scenery is very beautiful along the coast,' he said. 'You must have noticed it, when walking. Most afternoons I take my

176

small camera and go out on to the cliffs, above the big rock that stands there so prominent, to the right of the bathing beach.'

He pointed from the balcony and she followed the direction of his hand. The green headland shimmered hazily in the intense heat.

'It was only by chance that you found me at home yesterday,' he said. 'I was in the cellar, developing prints that had been promised for visitors who were to leave today. But usually I go walking on the cliff at that time.'

'It must be very hot,' she said.

'Perhaps,' he answered. 'But above the sea there is a little breeze. And best of all, between one and four there are so few people. They are all taking their siesta in the afternoon. I have all that beautiful scenery to myself.'

'Yes,' said the Marquise, 'I understand.'

For a moment they both stood silent. It was as though something unspoken passed between them. The Marquise played with her chiffon handkerchief, then tied it loosely round her wrist, a casual, lazy gesture.

'Some time I must try it for myself,' she said at last, 'walking in the heat of the day.'

Miss Clay came on to the balcony, calling the children to come and be washed before *déjeuner*. The photographer stepped to one side, deferential, apologizing. And the Marquise, glancing at her watch, saw that it was already *midi*, and that the tables below on the terrace were filled with people and the usual bustle and chatter was going on, the tinkle of glasses, the rattle of plates, and she had noticed none of it.

She turned her shoulder to the photographer, dismissing him, deliberately cool and indifferent now that the session was over and Miss Clay had come to fetch the children.

'Thank you,' she said. 'I shall call in at the shop to see the proofs in a few days' time. Good morning.'

He bowed, he went away, an employee who had fulfilled his orders.

177

'I hope he has taken some good photographs,' said Miss Clay. 'The Marquis will be very pleased to see the results.'

The Marquise did not answer. She was taking off the gold clips from her ears that now, for some reason, no longer matched her mood. She would go down to *déjeuner* without jewellery, without rings; she felt, for today, her own beauty would suffice.

Three days passed, and the Marquise did not once descend into the little town. The first day she swam, she watched the tennis in the afternoon. The second day she spent with the children, giving Miss Clay leave of absence to take a tour by charabanc to visit the old walled cities, further inland, along the coast. The third day, she sent Miss Clay and the children into the town to inquire for the proofs, and they returned with them wrapped in a neat package. The Marquise examined them. They were very good indeed, and the studies of herself the best she had ever had taken.

Miss Clay was in raptures. She begged for copies to send home to England. 'Who would believe it,' she exclaimed, 'that a little photographer, by the sea like this, could take such splendid pictures? And then you go and pay heaven knows what to real professionals in Paris.'

'They are not bad,' said the Marquise, yawning. 'He certainly took a lot of trouble. They are better of me than they are of the children.' She folded the package and put it away in a drawer. 'Did Monsieur Paul seem pleased with them himself?' she asked the governess.

'He did not say,' replied Miss Clay. 'He seemed disappointed that you had not gone down for them yourself; he said they had been ready since yesterday. He asked if you were well, and the children told him *maman* had been swimming. They were quite friendly with him.'

'It's much too hot and dusty, down in the town,' said the Marquise.

The next afternoon, when Miss Clay and the children were resting and the hotel itself seemed asleep under the glare of the

178

sun, the Marquise changed into a short sleeveless frock, very simple and plain, and softly, so as not to disturb the children, went downstairs, her small box camera slung over her arm, and walking through the hotel grounds on to the sands she followed a narrow path that led upwards, to the greensward above. The sun was merciless. Yet she did not mind. Here on the springing grass there was no dust, and presently, by the cliff's edge, the bracken, growing thicker, brushed her bare legs.

The little path wound in and out amongst the bracken, at times coming so close to the cliff's edge that a false step, bringing a stumble, would spell danger. But the Marquise, walking slowly, with the lazy swing of the hips peculiar to her, felt neither frightened nor exhausted. She was merely intent on reaching a spot that overlooked the great rock, standing out from the coast in the middle of the bay. She was quite alone on the headland. No one was in sight. Away behind her, far below, the white walls of the hotel, and the rows of bathing cabins on the beach, looked like bricks, played with by children. The sea was very smooth and still. Even where it washed upon the rock in the bay it left no ripple.

Suddenly the Marquise saw something flash in the bracken ahead of her. It was the lens of a camera. She took no notice. Turning her back, she pretended to examine her own camera, and took up a position as though to photograph the view. She took one, took another, and then she heard the swish of someone walking towards her through the bracken.

She turned, surprised. 'Why, good afternoon, Monsieur Paul,' she said.

He had discarded the cheap stiff jacket and the bright blue shirt. He was not on business. It was the hour of the siesta, when he walked, as it were, incognito. He wore only the vest and a pair of dark blue trousers, and the grey squash hat, which she had noticed with dismay the morning he had come to the hotel, was also absent. His thick dark hair made a frame to his gentle face. His eyes had such a rapturous expression at the sight of her that she was forced to turn away to hide her smile.

'You see,' she said lightly, 'I have taken your advice, and strolled up here to look at the view. But I am sure I don't hold my camera correctly. Show me how.'

He stood beside her and, taking her camera, steadied her hands, moving them to the correct position.

'Yes, of course,' she said, and then moved away from him, laughing a little, for it had seemed to her that when he stood beside her and guided her hands she had heard his heart beating and the sound brought excitement, which she wished to conceal from him.

'Have you your own camera?' she said.

'Yes, Madame la Marquise,' he answered, 'I left it over in the bracken there, with my coat. It is a favourite spot of mine, close to the edge of the cliff. In spring I come here to watch the birds and take photographs of them.'

'Show me,' she said.

He led the way, murmuring 'Pardon,' and the path he had made for himself took them to a little clearing, like a nest, hidden on all sides by bracken that was now waist-high. Only the front of the clearing was open, and this was wide to the cliff face, and the sea.

'But how lovely,' she said, and passing through the bracken into the hiding-place she looked about her, smiling, and sitting down, gracefully, naturally, like a child at a picnic, she picked up the book that was lying on top of his coat beside his camera.

'You read much?' she said.

'Yes, Madame la Marquise,' he answered. 'I am very fond of reading.' She glanced at the cover, and read the title. It was a cheap romance, the sort of book she and her friends had smuggled into their satchels at the *lycée*, in old days. She had not read that sort of stuff for years. Once again she had to hide her smile. She put the book back on the coat.

'Is it a good story?' she asked him.

He looked down at her solemnly, with his great eyes like a gazelle's.

'It is very tender, Madame la Marquise,' he said.

Tender . . . What an odd expression. She began to talk about the proofs of the photographs, and how she preferred one to another, and all the while she was conscious of an inner triumph that she was in such command of the situation. She knew exactly what to do, what to say, when to smile, when to look serious. It reminded her strangely of childhood days, when she and her young friends would dress up in their mothers' hats and say, 'Let's pretend to be ladies.' She was pretending now; not to be a lady, as then, but to be – what? She was not sure. But something other than the self who now, for so long, was in truth a real lady, sipping tea in the salon at the château, surrounded by so many ancient things and people that each one of them had the mustiness of death.

The photographer did not talk much. He listened to the Marquise. He agreed, nodded his head, or simply remained silent, and she heard her own voice trilling on in a sort of wonder. He was merely a witness she could ignore, a lay-figure, while she listened to the brilliant, charming woman that had suddenly become herself.

At last there came a pause in the one-sided conversation, and he said to her, shyly, 'May I dare to ask you something?'

'Of course,' she said.

'Could I photograph you here, alone, with this background?'

Was that all? How timid he was, and how reluctant. She laughed.

'Take as many as you want,' she said, 'it is very pleasant sitting here. I may even go to sleep.'

'*La belle au bois dormant*,' he said quickly, and then, as if ashamed of his familiarity, he murmured, 'Pardon' once more and reached for the camera behind her.

This time he did not ask her to pose, to change position. He photographed her as she sat, lazily nibbling at a stem of grass, and it was he who moved, now here, now there, so that he had shots of her from every angle, full-face, profile, three-quarter.

She began to feel sleepy. The sun beat down upon her un-covered head, and the dragon-flies, gaudy and green and gold, swung and hovered before her eyes. She yawned and leant back against the bracken.

'Would you care for my coat as a pillow for your head, Madame la Marquise?' he asked her.

Before she could reply he had taken his coat, folded it neatly, and placed it in a little roll against the bracken. She leant back against it, and the despised grey coat made a softness to her head, easy and comfortable.

He knelt beside her, intent upon his camera, doing something to the film, and she watched him, yawning, between half-closed eyes, and noticed that as he knelt he kept his weight upon one knee only, thrusting the deformed foot in the high boot to one side. Idly, she wondered if it hurt to lean upon it. The boot was highly polished, much brighter than the leather shoe upon the left foot, and she had a sudden vision of him taking great pains with the boot every morning when he dressed, polishing it, rubbing it, perhaps, with a wash-leather cloth.

A dragon-fly settled on her hand. It crouched, waiting, a sheen upon its wings. What was it waiting for? She blew upon it and it flew away. Then it came back again, hovering, insistent.

Monsieur Paul had put aside his camera but he was still kneeling in the bracken beside her. She was aware of him, watching her, and she thought to herself, 'If I move he will get up, and it will all be over.'

She went on staring at the glittering, shivering dragon-fly, but she knew that in a moment or two she must look somewhere else, or the dragon-fly would go, or the present silence would become so tense and so strained that she would break it with a laugh and so spoil everything. Reluctantly, against her will, she turned to the photographer, and his large eyes, humble and devoted, were fixed upon her with all the deep abasement of a slave.

'Why don't you kiss me?' she said, and her own words startled her, shocked her into sudden apprehension.

He said nothing. He did not move. He went on gazing at her. She closed her eyes, and the dragon-fly went from her hand.

Presently, when the photographer bent to touch her, it was not what she expected. There was no sudden crude embrace. It was just as though the dragon-fly had returned, and now with silken wings brushed and stroked the smooth surface of her skin.

When he went away it was with tact and delicacy. He left her to herself so that there should be no aftermath of awkwardness, of embarrassment, no sudden strain of conversation.

The Marquise lay back in the bracken, her hands over her eyes, thinking about what had happened to her, and she had no sense of shame. She was clear-headed and quite calm. She began to plan how she would walk back to the hotel in a little while, giving him good time to gain the sands before her, so that if by chance people from the hotel should see him they would not connect him with her, who would follow after, say in half an hour.

She got up, rearranged her dress, took out her powder-compact from her pocket, with her lipstick, and, having no mirror, judged carefully how much powder to put upon her face. The sun had lost its power, and a cool breeze blew inland from the sea.

'If the weather holds,' thought the Marquise as she combed her hair, 'I can come out here every day, at the same time. No one will ever know. Miss Clay and the children always rest in the afternoon. If we walk separately and go back separately, as we have done today, and come to this same place, hidden by the bracken, we cannot possibly be discovered. There are over three weeks still to the holiday. The great thing is to pray for this hot weather to continue. If it should rain . . .'

As she walked back to the hotel she wondered how they would manage, should the weather break. She could not very well set out to walk the cliffs in a mackintosh, and then lie down while the rain and the wind beat the bracken. There was of course the cellar, beneath the shop. But she might be seen in the village. That would be dangerous. No, unless it rained in torrents the cliff was safest.

That evening she sat down and wrote a letter to her friend

Élise. '. . . This is a wonderful place,' she wrote, 'and I am amusing myself as usual, and without my husband, *bien entendu!*' But she gave no details of her conquest, though she mentioned the bracken and the hot afternoon. She felt that if she left it vague Élise would picture to herself some rich American, travelling for pleasure, alone, without his wife.

The next morning, dressing herself with great care – she stood for a long while before her wardrobe, finally choosing a frock rather more elaborate than was usual for the sea-side, but this was deliberate on her part – she went down into the little town, accompanied by Miss Clay and the children. It was market-day, and the cobbled streets and the square were full of people. Many came from the countryside around, but there were quantities of visitors, English and American, who strolled to see the sights, to buy souvenirs and picture-postcards, or to sit down at the café at the corner and look about them.

The Marquise made a striking figure, walking in her indolent way in her lovely dress, hatless, carrying a sunshade, with the two little girls prancing beside her. Many people turned to look at her, or even stepped aside to let her pass, in unconscious homage to her beauty. She dawdled in the market-place and made a few purchases, which Miss Clay put into the shopping-bag she carried, and then still casual, still answering with gay, lazy humour the questions of the children, she turned into the shop which displayed Kodaks and photographs in the window.

It was full of visitors waiting their turn to be served, and the Marquise, who was in no hurry, pretended to examine a book of local views, while at the same time she could see what was happening in the shop. They were both there, Monsieur Paul and his sister, he in his stiff shirt, an ugly pink this time, worse even than the blue, and the cheap grey coat, while the sister, like all women who served behind a counter, was in drab black, a shawl over her shoulders.

He must have seen her come into the shop, because almost at once he came forward from the counter, leaving the queue of visitors to the care of his sister, and was by her side, humble, polite, anxious to know in what manner he could serve her. There was no trace of familiarity, no look of knowledge in his eyes, and she took care to assure herself of this by staring directly at him. Then deliberately, bringing the children and Miss Clay into the conversation, asking Miss Clay to make her choice of the proofs which were to be sent to England, she kept him there by her side, treating him with condescension, with a sort of *hauteur*, even finding fault with certain of the proofs, which, so she told him, did not do the children justice, and which she could not possibly send to her husband, the Marquis. The photographer apologized. Most certainly the proofs mentioned did not do the children justice. He would be willing to come again to the hotel and try again, at no extra charge, of course. Perhaps on the terrace or in the gardens the effect would be better.

One or two people turned to look at the Marquise as she stood there. She could feel their eyes upon her, absorbing her beauty, and still in a tone of condescension, coldly, almost curtly, she told the photographer to show her various articles in his shop, which he hastened to do in his anxiety to please.

The other visitors were becoming restive, they shuffled their feet waiting for the sister to serve them, and she, hemmed about with customers, limped wretchedly from one end of the counter to the other, now and again raising her head, peering to see if her brother, who had so suddenly deserted her, would come to the rescue.

At last the Marquise relented. She had had her fill. The delicious furtive sense of excitement that had risen in her since her entrance to the shop died down and was appeased.

'One of these mornings I will let you know,' she said to Monsieur Paul, 'and then you can come out and photograph the children again. Meanwhile, let me pay what I owe. Miss Clay, attend to it, will you?'

And she strolled from the shop, not bidding him good morning, putting out her hands to the two children.

She did not change for *déjeuner*. She wore the same enchanting frock, and the hotel terrace, more crowded than ever because of the many visitors who had come on an excursion, seemed to her to buzz and hum with a murmur of conversation, directed at her and her beauty, and at the effect she made, sitting there at the table in the corner. The *maître d'hôtel*, the waiters, even the manager himself, were drawn towards her, obsequious, smiling, and she could hear her name pass from one to the other.

All things combined to her triumph; the proximity of people, the smell of food and wine and cigarettes, the scent of the gaudy flowers in their tubs, the feel of the hot sun beating down, the close sound of the splashing sea. When she rose at last with the children and went upstairs, she had a sense of happiness that she felt must only come to a prima donna after the clamour of long applause.

The children, with Miss Clay, went to their rooms to rest; and swiftly, hurriedly, the Marquise changed her frock and her shoes and tip-toed down the stairs and out of the hotel, across the burning sands to the path and the bracken headland.

He was waiting for her, as she expected, and neither of them made any reference to her visit in the morning, or to what brought her there on the cliff this afternoon. They made at once for the little clearing by the cliff's edge and sat down of one accord, and the Marquise, in a tone of banter, described the crowd at lunch, and the fearful bustle and fatigue of the terrace with so many people, and how delicious it was to get away from them all to the fresh clean air of the headland, above the sea.

He agreed with her humbly, watching her as she spoke of such mundane matters as though the wit of the world flowed in her speech, and then, exactly as on the previous day, he begged to take a few photographs of her, and she consented, and presently she lay back in the bracken and closed her eyes.

There was no sense of time to the long, languorous afternoon. Just as before the dragon-flies winged about her in the bracken, and the sun beat down upon her body, and with her sense of deep enjoyment of all that happened went the curiously satisfying knowledge that what she did was without emotion of any sort. Her mind and her affections were quite untouched. She

186

might almost have been relaxing in a beauty parlour, back in Paris, having the first tell-tale lines smoothed from her face and her hair shampooed, although these things brought only a lazy contentment and no pleasure.

Once again he departed, leaving her without a word, tactful and discreet, so that she could arrange herself in privacy. And once again, when she judged him out of sight, she rose to her feet and began the long walk back to the hotel.

Her good luck held and the weather did not break. Every afternoon, as soon as *déjeuner* was over and the children had gone to rest, the Marquise went for her promenade, returning about half past four, in time for tea. Miss Clay, at first exclaiming at her energy, came to accept the walk as a matter of routine. If the Marquise chose to walk in the heat of the day, it was her own affair; certainly it seemed to do her good. She was more human towards her, Miss Clay, and less nagging to the children. The constant headaches and attacks of migraine were forgotten, and it seemed that the Marquise was really enjoying this simple sea-side holiday alone with Miss Clay and the two little girls.

When a fortnight had passed, the Marquise discovered that the first delight and bliss of her experience were slowly fading. It was not that Monsieur Paul failed her in any way, but that she herself was becoming used to the daily ritual. Like an inoculation that 'took' at the first with very great success, on constant repetition the effect lessened, dulled, and the Marquise found that to recapture her enjoyment she was obliged to treat the photographer no longer as a lay-figure, or as she would a *coiffeur* who had set her hair, but as a person whose feelings she could wound. She would find fault with his appearance, complain that he wore his hair too long, that his clothes were cheap, ill-cut, or even that he ran his little shop in the town with inefficiency, that the material and paper he used for his prints were shoddy.

She would watch his face when she told him this, and she would see anxiety and pain come into his large eyes, pallor to his skin, a look of dejection fall upon his whole person as he realized how unworthy he was of her, how inferior in every way,

187

and only when she saw him thus did the original excitement kindle in her again.

Deliberately she began to cut down the hours of the afternoon. She would arrive late at the rendezvous in the bracken and find him waiting for her with that same look of anxiety on his face, and if her mood was not sufficiently ripe for what should happen she would get through the business quickly, with an ill grace, and then dispatch him hastily on his return journey, picturing him limping back, tired and unhappy, to the shop in the little town.

She permitted him to take photographs of her still. This was all part of the experience, and she knew that it troubled him to do this, to see her to perfection, so she delighted in taking advantage of it, and would sometimes tell him to come to the hotel during the morning, and then she would pose in the grounds, exquisitely dressed, the children beside her, Miss Clay an admiring witness, the visitors watching from their rooms or from the terrace.

The contrast of these mornings, when as an employee he limped back and forth at her bidding, moving the tripod first here, first there, while she gave him orders, with the sudden intimacy of the afternoons in the bracken under the hot sun, proved, during the third week, to be her only stimulation.

Finally, a day breaking when quite a cold breeze blew in from the sea, and she did not go to the rendezvous as usual but rested on her balcony reading a novel, the change in the routine came as a real relief.

The following day was fine and she decided to go to the headland, and for the first time since they had encountered one another in the cool dark cellar below the shop he upbraided her, his voice sharp with anxiety.

'I waited for you all yesterday afternoon,' he said. 'What happened?'

She stared at him in astonishment.

'It was an unpleasant day,' she replied. 'I preferred to read on my balcony in the hotel.'

'I was afraid you might have been taken ill,' he went on. 'I very nearly called at the hotel to inquire for you. I hardly slept last night, I was so upset.'

He followed her to the hiding-place in the bracken, his eyes still anxious, lines of worry on his brow, and though in a sense it was a stimulation to the Marquise to witness his distress, at the same time it irritated her that he should so forget himself as to find fault in her conduct. It was a though her *coiffeur* in Paris, or her masseur, expressed anger when she broke an appointment fixed for a certain day.

'If you think I feel myself bound to come here every afternoon you are very much mistaken,' she said. 'I have plenty of other things to do.'

At once he apologized, he was abject. He begged her to forgive him.

'You cannot understand what this means to me,' he said. 'Since I have known you, everything in my life is changed. I live only for these afternoons.'

His subjection pleased her, whipping her to a renewal of interest, and pity came to her too, as he lay by her side, pity that this creature should be so utterly devoted, depending on her like a child. She touched his hair, feeling for a moment quite compassionate, almost maternal. Poor fellow, limping all this way because of her, and then sitting in the biting wind of yesterday, alone and wretched. She imagined the letter she would write to her friend Élise.

'I am very much afraid I have broken Paul's heart. He has taken this little *affaire de vacance au sérieux*. But what am I to do? After all, these things must have an end. I cannot possibly alter my life because of him. *Enfin*, he is a man, he will get over it.' Élise would picture the beautiful blond American play-boy climbing wearily into his Packard, setting off in despair to the unknown.

The photographer did not leave her today, when the afternoon session had ended. He sat up in the bracken and stared out towards the great rock jutting out into the sea.

'I have made up my mind about the future,' he said quietly.

189

The Marquise sensed the drama in the air. Did he mean he was going to kill himself? How very terrible. He would wait, of course, until she had left the hotel and had returned home. She need never know.

'Tell me,' she said gently.

'My sister will look after the shop,' he said. 'I will make it all over to her. She is very capable. For myself, I shall follow you, wherever you go, whether it is to Paris, or to the country. I shall be close at hand; whenever you want me, I shall be there.'

The Marquise swallowed. Her heart went still.

'You can't possibly do that,' she said. 'How would you live?'

'I am not proud,' he said. 'I know, in the goodness of your heart, you would allow me something. My needs would be very small. But I know that it is impossible to live without you, therefore the only thing to do is to follow you, always. I will find a room close to your house in Paris, and in the country too. We will find ways and means of being together. When love is as strong as this there are no difficulties.'

He spoke with his usual humility, but there was a force behind his words that was unexpected, and she knew that for him this was no false drama, ill-timed to the day, but true sincerity. He meant every word. He would in truth give up the shop, follow her to Paris, follow her also to the château in the country.

'You are mad,' she said violently, sitting up, careless of her appearance and her dishevelled hair. 'Once I have left here I am no longer free. I cannot possibly meet you anywhere, the danger of discovery would be too great. You realize my position? What it would mean to me?'

He nodded his head. His face was sad, but quite determined. 'I have thought of everything,' he answered, 'but as you know, I am very discreet. You need never be apprehensive on that score. It has occurred to me that it might be possible to obtain a place in your service as footman. It would not matter to me, the loss of personal dignity. I am not proud. But in such a capacity our life together could continue much as it does now. Your husband, the Marquis, must be a very busy man, often out during the day, and your children and the English miss no doubt go walking in the country in the afternoon. You see, everything would be very simple if we had the courage.'

The Marquise was so shocked that she could not answer. She could not imagine anything more terrible, more disastrous, than that the photographer should take a place in the house as footman. Quite apart from his disability – she shuddered to think of him limping round the table in the great *salle à manger* – what misery she would suffer knowing that he was there, in the house, that he was waiting for her to go up to her room in the afternoon, and then, timidly, the knock upon the door, the hushed whisper. The degradation of this – this creature, there was really no other word for him – in the house, always waiting, always hoping.

'I am afraid,' she said firmly, 'that what you are suggesting is utterly impossible. Not only the idea of coming to my house as a servant, but of our ever being able to meet again once I return home. Your own common sense must tell you so. These afternoons have been – have been pleasant, but my holiday is very nearly over. In a few days' time my husband will be coming to fetch me and the children, and that finishes everything.'

To show finality she got up, brushed her crumpled frock, combed her hair, powdered her nose, and reaching for her bag fumbled inside it for her note-case.

She drew out several ten-thousand-franc notes.

'This is for the shop,' she said, 'any little fittings it may require. And buy something for your sister. And remember, I shall always think of you with great tenderness.'

To her consternation his face went dead white, then his mouth began to work violently and he rose to his feet.

'No, no,' he said, 'I will never take them. You are cruel, wicked to suggest it.' And suddenly he began to sob, burying his face in his hands, his shoulders heaving with emotion.

The Marquise watched him helplessly, uncertain whether to go or to stay. His sobs were so violent that she was afraid of hysteria, and she did not know what might happen. She was sorry for him, deeply sorry, but even more sorry for herself, because now, on parting, he cut such a ridiculous figure in her eyes. A man who gave way to emotion was pitiable. And it seemed to her that the clearing in the bracken took on a sordid, shameful appearance, which once had seemed so secret and so warm. His shirt, lying on a stem of bracken, looked like old linen spread by washerwomen in the sun to dry. Beside it lay his tie and the cheap trilby hat. It needed only orange peel and silver paper from a chocolate carton to complete the picture.

'Stop that noise,' she said, in sudden fury. 'For God's sake pull yourself together.'

The crying ceased. He took his hands away from his ravaged face. He stared at her, trembling, his brown eyes blind with pain. 'I have been mistaken in you,' he said. 'I know you now for what you are. You are a wicked woman and you go about ruining the lives of innocent men like myself. I shall tell your husband everything.'

The Marquise said nothing. He was unbalanced, mad . . .

'Yes,' said the photographer, still catching at his breath, 'that is what I shall do. As soon as your husband comes to fetch you I will tell him everything. I will show him the photographs I have taken, here on the headland. I will prove to him without a doubt that you are false to him, that you are bad. And he will believe me. He cannot help but believe me. What he does to me does not matter. I cannot suffer more than I suffer now. But your life, that will be finished, I promise you. He will know, the English miss will know, the manager of the hotel will know, I will tell everybody how you have been spending your afternoons.'

He reached for his coat, he reached for his hat, he slung his camera around his shoulder, and panic seized the Marquise, rose from her heart to her throat. He would do all that he threatened to do, he would wait there, in the hall of the hotel by the reception desk, he would wait for Edouard to come.

'Listen to me,' she began, 'we will think of something, we can perhaps come to some arrangement . . .'

But he ignored her. His face was set and pale. He stooped,

by the opening at the cliff's edge, to pick up his stick, and as he did so the terrible impulse was born in her, and flooded her whole being, and would not be denied. Leaning forward, her hands outstretched, she pushed his stooping body. He did not utter a single cry. He fell, and was gone.

The Marquise sank back on her knees. She did not move. She waited. She felt the sweat trickle down her face, to her throat, to her body. Her hands were also wet. She waited there in the clearing, upon her knees, and presently, when she was cooler, she took her handkerchief and wiped away the sweat from her forehead, and her face, and her hands.

It seemed suddenly cold. She shivered. She stood up and her legs were firm; they did not give way, as she feared. She looked about her, over the bracken, and no one was in sight. As always, she was alone upon the headland. Five minutes passed, and then she forced herself to the brink of the cliff and looked down. The tide was in. The sea was washing the base of the cliff below. It surged, and swept the rocks, and sank, and surged again. There was no sign of his body on the cliff face, nor could there be, because the cliff was sheer. No sign of his body in the water and had he fallen and floated it would have shown there, on the surface of the still blue sea. When he fell he must have sunk immediately.

The Marquise turned back from the opening. She gathered her things together. She tried to pull the flattened bracken to its original height, and so smooth out the signs of habitation, but the hiding-place had been made so long that this was impossible. Perhaps it did not matter. Perhaps it would be taken for granted that people came out upon the cliff and took their ease.

Suddenly her knees began to tremble and she sat down. She waited a few moments, then glanced at her watch. She knew that it might be important to remember the time. A few minutes after half past three. If she was asked, she could say, 'Yes, I was out on the headland at about half past three, but I heard nothing.' That would be the truth. She would not be lying. It would be the truth.

She remembered with relief that today she had brought her mirror in her bag. She glanced at it, fearfully. Her face was chalk white, blotched and strange. She powdered, carefully, gently; it seemed to make no difference. Miss Clay would notice something was wrong. She dabbed dry rouge on to her cheeks, but this stood out, like the painted spots on a clown's face.

'There is only one thing to do,' she thought, 'and that is to go straight to the bathing-cabin on the beach, and undress, and put on my swimming-suit, and bathe. Then if I return to the hotel with my hair wet, and my face wet too, it will seem natural, and I shall have been swimming, and that also will be true.'

She began to walk back along the cliff, but her legs were weak, as though she had been lying ill in bed for many days, and when she came to the beach at last she was trembling so much she thought she would fall. More than anything she longed to lie down on her bed, in the hotel bedroom, and close the shutters, even the windows, and hide there by herself in the darkness. Yet she must force herself to play the part she had decided.

She went to the bathing-cabin and undressed. Already there were several people lying on the sands, reading or sleeping, the hour of siesta drawing to its close. She walked down to the water's edge, kicked off her rope-soled shoes, drew on her cap, and as she swam to and fro in the still, tepid water, and dipped her face, she wondered how many of the people on the beach noticed her, watched her, and afterwards might say, 'But don't you remember, we saw a woman come down from the headland in the middle of the afternoon?'

She began to feel very cold, but she continued swimming, backwards and forwards, with stiff, mechanical strokes, until suddenly, seeing a little boy who was playing with a dog point out to sea, and the dog run in barking towards some dark object that might have been a piece of timber, nausea and terror combined to turn her faint, and she stumbled from the sea back to the bathing-cabin and lay on the wooden floor, her face in her hands. It might be, she thought, that had she gone on swimming she would have touched him with her feet, as his body came floating in towards her on the water.

In five days' time the Marquis was due to arrive by car and pick up his wife, the governess, and the children, and drive them home. The Marquise put a call through to him at the château, and asked if it would be possible for him to come sooner. Yes, the weather was still good, she said, but somehow she had become tired of the place. It was now getting too full of people, it was noisy, and the food had gone off. In fact she had turned against it. She longed to be back at home, she told her husband, amongst her own things, and the gardens would be looking lovely.

The Marquis regretted very much that she was bored, but surely she could stick it out for just the three days, he said. He had made all his arrangements, and he could not come sooner. He had to pass through Paris anyway for an important business meeting. He would promise to reach her by the morning of the Thursday, and then they could leave immediately after lunch.

'I had hoped,' he said, 'that you would want to stay on for the weekend, so that I too could get some bathing. The rooms are held surely until the Monday?'

But no, she had told the manager, she said, that they would not require the rooms after Thursday, and he had already let them to someone else. The place was crowded. The charm of it had gone, she assured him. Édouard would not care for it at all, and at the weekend it became quite insupportable. So would he make every effort to arrive in good time on the Thursday, and then they could leave after an early lunch?

The Marquise put down the receiver and went out to the balcony to the chaise-longue. She took up a book and pretended to read, but in reality she was listening, waiting for the sound of footsteps, voices, at the entrance to the hotel, and presently for her telephone to ring, and it would be the manager asking her, with many apologies, if she would mind descending to his office. The fact was, the matter was delicate . . . but the police were with him. They had some idea that she could help them. The telephone did not ring. There were no voices. No footsteps. Life continued as before. The long hours dragged through the interminable day. Lunch on the terrace, the waiters bustling, obsequious, the tables filled with the usual faces or with new visitors to take the place of old, the children chattering, Miss Clay reminding them of their manners. And all the while the Marquise listened, waited . . . She forced herself to eat, but the food she put in her mouth tasted of sawdust. Lunch over, she mounted to her room, and while the children rested she lay on the chaise-longue on the balcony. They descended to the terrace again for tea, but when the children went to the beach for their second bathe of the day she did not go with them. She had a little chill, she told Miss Clay; she did not fancy the water. So she went on sitting there, on her balcony.

When she closed her eyes at night and tried to sleep, she felt his stooping shoulders against her hands once more, and the sensation that it had given her when she pushed them hard. The ease with which he fell and vanished, one moment there, and the next, nothing. No stumble, no cry.

In the daytime she used to strain her eyes towards the headland in search of figures walking there, amongst the bracken – would they be called 'a cordon of police'? But the headland shimmered under the pitiless sun, and no one walked there in the bracken.

Twice Miss Clay suggested going down into the town in the mornings to make purchases, and each time the Marquise made an excuse.

'It's always so crowded,' she said, 'and so hot. I don't think it's good for the children. The gardens are more pleasant, the lawn at the back of the hotel is shady and quiet.'

She herself did not leave the hotel. The thought of the beach brought back the pain in her belly, and the nausea. Nor did she walk.

'I shall be quite all right,' she told Miss Clay, 'when I have thrown off this tiresome chill.'

She lay there on the balcony, turning over the pages of the magazines she had read a dozen times.

On the morning of the third day, just before *déjeuner*, the children came running on to the balcony, waving little windmill flags.

'Look, *maman*,' said Hélène, 'mine is red, and Céleste's is blue. We are going to put them on our sand-castles after tea.'

'Where did you get them?' asked the Marquise.

'In the market-place,' said the child. 'Miss Clay took us to the town this morning instead of playing in the garden. She wanted to pick up her snap-shots that were to be ready today.'

A feeling of shock went through the Marquise. She sat very still.

'Run along,' she said, 'and get ready for *déjeuner*.'

She could hear the children chattering to Miss Clay in the bathroom. In a moment or two Miss Clay came in. She closed the door behind her. The Marquise forced herself to look up at the governess. Miss Clay's long, rather stupid face was grave and concerned.

'Such a dreadful thing has happened,' she said, her voice low. 'I don't want to speak of it in front of the children. I am sure you will be very distressed. It's poor Monsieur Paul.'

'Monsieur Paul?' said the Marquise. Her voice was perfectly calm. But her tone had the right quality of interest.

'I went down to the shop to fetch my snap-shots,' said Miss Clay, 'and I found it shut. The door was locked and the shutters were up. I thought it rather odd, and I went into the *pharmacie* next door and asked if they knew whether the shop was likely to be open after tea. They said no, Mademoiselle Paul was too upset, she was being looked after by relatives. I asked what had happened, and they told me there had been an accident, that poor Monsieur Paul's body had been found by some fishermen three miles up the coast, drowned.'

Miss Clay had quite lost colour as she told her tale. She was obviously deeply shocked. The Marquise, at sight of her, gained courage.

'How perfectly terrible,' she said. 'Does anybody know when it happened?'

197

'I couldn't go into details at the *pharmacie* because of the children,' said Miss Clay, 'but I think they found the body yesterday. Terribly injured, they said. He must have hit some rocks before falling into the sea. It's so dreadful I can't bear to think of it. And his poor sister, whatever will she do without him?'

The Marquise put up her hand for silence and made a warning face. The children were coming into the room.

They went down to the terrace for *déjeuner* and the Marquise ate better than she had done for three days. For some reason her appetite had returned. Why this should be so she could not tell. She wondered if it could possibly be that part of the burden of her secret was now lifted. He was dead. He had been found. These things were known. After *déjeuner* she told Miss Clay to ask the manager if he knew anything of the sad accident. Miss Clay was to say that the Marquise was most concerned and grieved. While Miss Clay went about this business the Marquise took the children upstairs.

Presently the telephone rang. The sound that she had dreaded. Her heart missed a beat. She took off the receiver and listened.

It was the manager. He said Miss Clay had just been to him. He said it was most gracious of Madame la Marquise to show concern at the unfortunate accident that had befallen Monsieur Paul. He would have spoken of it when the accident was discovered yesterday, but he did not wish to distress the clientèle. A drowning disaster was never very pleasant at a sea-side resort, it made people feel uncomfortable. Yes, of course, the police had been called in directly the body was found. It was assumed that he had fallen from the cliffs somewhere along the coast. It seemed he was very fond of photographing the sea views. And of course, with his disability, he could easily slip. His sister had often warned him to be careful. It was very sad. He was such a good fellow. Everyone liked him. He had no enemies. And such an artist, too, in his way. Madame la Marquise had been pleased with the studies Monsieur Paul had done of herself and the children? The manager was so glad. He would make a point of letting Mademoiselle Paul know this, and also of the concern shown by Madame la Marquise. Yes, indeed, she would be deeply grateful for flowers, and for a note of sympathy. The poor woman was quite broken-hearted. No, the day of the funeral had not yet been decided . . .

When he had finished speaking, the Marquise called to Miss Clay, and told her she must order a taxi and drive to the town seven miles inland, where the shops were larger, and where she seemed to remember there was an excellent florist. Miss Clay was to order flowers, lilies for choice, and to spare no expense, and the Marquise would write a note to go with them; and then if Miss Clay gave them to the manager when she returned he would see that they reached Mademoiselle Paul.

The Marquise wrote the note for Miss Clay to take with her to pin on the flowers. 'In deepest sympathy at your great loss.' She gave Miss Clay some money, and the governess went off to find a taxi.

Later the Marquise took the children to the beach.

'Is your chill better, *maman*?' asked Céleste.

'Yes, chérie, now *maman* can bathe again.'

And she entered the warm yielding water with the children, and splashed with them.

Tomorrow Édouard would arrive, tomorrow Édouard would come in his car and drive them away, and the white dusty roads would lengthen the distance between her and the hotel. She would not see it any more, nor the headland, nor the town, and the holiday would be blotted out like something that had never been.

'When I die,' thought the Marquise, as she stared out across the sea, 'I shall be punished. I don't fool myself. I am guilty of taking life. When I die, God will accuse me. Until then, I will be a good wife to Édouard, and a good mother to Céleste and Hélène. I will try to be a good woman from now. I will try and atone for what I have done by being kinder to everyone, to relations, friends, servants.'

She slept well for the first time for four days.

Her husband arrived the next morning while she was still having her breakfast. She was so glad to see him that she sprang

199

from her bed and flung her arms round his neck. The Marquis was touched at this reception.

'I believe my girl has missed me after all,' he said.

'Missed you? But of course I've missed you. That's why I rang up. I wanted you to come so much.'

'And you are quite determined to leave today after lunch?'

'Oh, yes, yes . . . I couldn't bear to stay. Our packing is done, there are only the last things to put in the suitcases.'

He sat on the balcony drinking coffee, laughing with the children, while she dressed and stripped the room of her personal possessions. The room that had been hers for a whole month became bare once more, and quite impersonal. In a fever of hurry she cleared the dressing-table, mantelpiece, the table by her bed. It was finished with. The *femme de chambre* would come in presently with clean sheets and make all fresh for the next visitor. And she, the Marquise, would have gone.

'Listen, Édouard,' she said, 'why must we stay for *déjeuner*? Wouldn't it be more fun to lunch somewhere on the way? There is always something a little dreary in lunching at a hotel when one has already paid the bill. Tipping, everything, has been done. I cannot bear a sense of anti-climax.'

'Just as you like,' he said. She had given him such a welcome that he was prepared to gratify every whim. Poor little girl. She had been really lonely without him. He must make up to her for it.

The Marquise was making up her mouth in front of the mirror in the bathroom when the telephone rang.

'Answer it, will you?' she called to her husband. 'It is probably the *concierge* about the luggage.'

The Marquis did so, and in a few moments he shouted through to his wife.

'It's for you, dear. It's a Mademoiselle Paul who has called to see you, and asks if she may thank you for her flowers before you go.'

The Marquise did not answer at once, and when his wife came into the bedroom it seemed to him that the lipstick had not enhanced her appearance. It made her look almost haggard, older. How very strange. She must have changed the colour. It was not becoming.

'Well,' he asked, 'what shall I say? You probably don't want to be bothered with her now, whoever she is. Would you like me to go down and get rid of her?'

The Marquise seemed uncertain, troubled. 'No,' she said, 'no, I think I had better see her. The fact is, it's a very tragic thing. She and her brother kept a little shop in the town – I had some photographs done of myself and the children – and then a dreadful thing happened, the brother was drowned. I thought it only right to send flowers.'

'How thoughtful of you,' said her husband, 'a very kind gesture. But do you need to bother now? Why, we are ready to go.'

'Tell her that,' said his wife, 'tell her that we are leaving almost immediately.'

The Marquis turned to the telephone again, and after a word or two put his hand over the receiver and whispered to his wife.

'She is very insistent,' he said. 'She says she has some prints belonging to you that she wants to give to you personally.'

A feeling of panic came over the Marquise. Prints? What prints?

'But everything is paid for,' she whispered back. 'I don't know what she can mean.'

The Marquis shrugged his shoulders.

'Well, what am I to say? She sounds as if she is crying.'

The Marquise went back into the bathroom, dabbed more powder on her nose.

'Tell her to come up,' she said, 'but repeat that we are leaving in five minutes. Meanwhile, you go down, take the children to the car. Take Miss Clay with you. I will see the woman alone.'

When he had gone she looked about the room. Nothing remained but her gloves, her handbag. One last effort, and then the closing door, the *ascenseur*, the farewell bow to the manager, and freedom.

There was a knock at the door. The Marquise waited by the entrance to the balcony, her hands clasped in front of her.

'*Entrez,*' she said.

Mademoiselle Paul opened the door. Her face was blotched and ravaged from weeping, her old-fashioned mourning dress was long, nearly touching the ground. She hesitated, then lurched forward, her limp grotesque, as though each movement must be agony.

'Madame la Marquise . . .' she began, then her mouth worked, she began to cry.

'Please don't,' said the Marquise gently. 'I am so dreadfully sorry for what has happened.'

Mademoiselle Paul took her handkerchief and blew her nose.

'He was all I had in the world,' she said. 'He was so good to me. What am I to do now? How am I to live?'

'You have relatives?'

'They are poor folk, Madame la Marquise. I cannot expect them to support me. Nor can I keep the shop alone, without my brother. I haven't the strength. My health has always been my trouble.'

The Marquise was fumbling in her bag. She took out a twenty-thousand-franc note.

'I know this is not much,' she said, 'but perhaps it will help just a little. I am afraid my husband has not many contacts in this part of the country, but I will ask him, perhaps he will be able to make some suggestions.'

Mademoiselle Paul took the note. It was strange. She did not thank the Marquise. 'This will keep me until the end of the month,' she said. 'It will help to pay the funeral expenses.'

She opened her bag. She took out three prints.

'I have more, similar to these, back in the shop,' she said. 'It seemed to me that perhaps, going away suddenly as you are doing, you had forgotten all about them. I found them amongst my poor brother's other prints and negatives in the cellar, where he used to develop them.'

She handed the prints to the Marquise. The Marquise went cold when she saw them. Yes, she had forgotten. Or rather, she had not been aware of their existence. They were three views of her taken in the bracken. Careless, abandoned, half-sleeping, with

202

her head against his coat for a pillow, she had heard the click-click of the camera, and it had added a sort of zest to the afternoon. Some he had shown her. But not these.

She took the photographs and put them in her bag.

'You say you have others?' she asked, her voice without expression.

'Yes, Madame la Marquise.'

She forced herself to meet the woman's eyes. They were swollen still with weeping, but the glint was unmistakable.

'What do you want me to do?' asked the Marquise.

Mademoiselle Paul looked about her in the hotel bedroom. Tissue paper strewn on the floor, odds and ends thrown into the waste-paper basket, the tumbled, unmade bed.

'I have lost my brother,' she said, 'my supporter, my reason for being alive. Madame la Marquise has had an enjoyable holiday and now returns home. I take it that Madame la Marquise would not desire her husband or her family to see these prints?'

'You are right,' said the Marquise, 'I do not even wish to see them myself.'

'In which case,' said Mademoiselle Paul, 'twenty thousand francs is really very little return for a holiday that Madame la Marquise so much enjoyed.'

The Marquise looked in her bag again. She had two mille notes and a few hundred francs.

'This is all I have,' she said, 'you are welcome to these as well.'

Mademoiselle Paul blew her nose once more.

'I think it would be more satisfactory for both of us if we came to a more permanent arrangement,' she said. 'Now my poor brother has gone the future is very uncertain. I might not even wish to live in a neighbourhood that holds such sad memories. I cannot but ask myself how my brother met his death. The afternoon before he disappeared he went out to the headland and came back very distressed. I knew something had upset him, but I did not ask him what. Perhaps he had hoped to meet a friend, and the friend had not appeared. The next day he went again,

203

and that night he did not return. The police were informed, and then three days later his body was found. I have said nothing of possible suicide to the police, but have accepted it, as they have done, as accidental. But my brother was a very sensitive soul, Madame la Marquise. Unhappy, he would have been capable of anything. If I make myself wretched thinking over these things, I might go to the police, I might suggest he did away with himself after an unhappy love affair. I might even give them leave to search through his effects for photographs.'

In agony the Marquise heard her husband's footsteps outside the door.

'Are you coming, dearest?' he called, bursting it open and entering the room. 'The luggage is all in, the children are clamouring to be off.'

He said good morning to Mademoiselle Paul. She curtseyed.

'I will give you my address,' said the Marquise, 'both in Paris, and in the country.' She sought in her bag feverishly for cards. 'I shall expect to hear from you in a few weeks' time.'

'Possibly before that, Madame la Marquise,' said Mademoiselle Paul. 'If I leave here, and find myself in your neighbourhood, I would come and pay my humble respects to you and Miss, and the little children. I have friends not so very far away. I have friends in Paris too. I have always wanted to see Paris.'

The Marquise turned with a terrible bright smile to her husband.

'I have told Mademoiselle Paul,' she said, 'that if there is anything I can do for her at any time she has only to let me know.'

'Of course,' said her husband. 'I am so sorry to hear of your tragedy. The manager here has been telling me all about it.'

Mademoiselle Paul curtseyed again, looking from him back to the Marquise.

'He was all I had in the world, Monsieur le Marquis,' she said. 'Madame la Marquise knows what he meant to me. It is good to know that I may write to her, and that she will write to me, and when that happens I shall not feel alone and isolated. Life can be very hard for someone who is alone in the world. May

I wish you a pleasant journey, Madame la Marquise, and happy memories of your holidays, and above all no regrets?'

Once more Mademoiselle Paul curtseyed, then turned and limped from the room.

'Poor woman,' said the Marquis, 'and what an appearance. I understand from the manager that the brother was crippled too?'

'Yes . . .' She fastened her handbag. Took her gloves. Reached for her dark glasses.

'Curious thing, but it often runs in families,' said the Marquis, as they walked along the corridor. He paused and rang the bell for the *ascenseur*. 'You have never met Richard du Boulay, have you, an old friend of mine? He was crippled, much as this unfortunate little photographer seems to have been, but for all that a charming, perfectly normal girl fell in love with him, and they got married. A son was born, and he turned out to be a hopeless club-foot like his father. You can't fight that sort of thing. It's a taint in the blood that passes on.'

They stepped into the *ascenseur* and the doors closed upon them.

'Sure you won't change your mind and stay for lunch? You look pale. We've got a long drive before us, you know.'

'I'd rather go.'

They were waiting in the hall to see her off. The manager, the receptionist, the *concierge*, the *maître d'hôtel*.

'Come again, Madame la Marquise. There will always be a welcome for you here. It has been such a pleasure looking after you. The hotel will not be the same once you have gone.'

'Goodbye . . . Goodbye . . .'

The Marquise climbed into the car beside her husband. They turned out of the hotel grounds into the road. Behind her lay the headland, the hot sands, and the sea. Before her lay the long straight road to home and safety. Safety . . .?

Kiss Me Again, Stranger

I looked around for a bit, after leaving the army and before settling down, and then I found myself a job up Hampstead way, in a garage it was, at the bottom of Haverstock Hill near Chalk Farm, and it suited me fine. I'd always been one for tinkering with engines, and in REME that was my work and I was trained to it – it had always come easy to me, anything mechanical.

My idea of having a good time was to lie on my back in my greasy overalls under a car's belly, or a lorry's, with a spanner in my hand, working on some old bolt or screw, with the smell of oil about me, and someone starting up an engine, and the other chaps around clattering their tools and whistling. I never minded the smell or the dirt. As my old Mum used to say when I'd be that way as a kid, mucking about with a grease can, 'It won't hurt him, it's clean dirt,' and so it is, with engines.

The boss at the garage was a good fellow, easy-going, cheerful, and he saw I was keen on my work. He wasn't much of a mechanic himself, so he gave me the repair jobs, which was what I liked.

I didn't live with my old Mum – she was too far off, over Shepperton way, and I saw no point in spending half the day getting to and from my work. I like to be handy, have it on the spot, as it were. So I had a bedroom with a couple called Thompson, only about ten minutes' walk away from the garage. Nice people, they were. He was in the shoe business, cobbler I suppose he'd be called, and Mrs Thompson cooked the meals and kept the house for him over the shop. I used to eat with them, breakfast and supper – we always had a cooked supper – and being the only lodger I was treated as family.

I'm one for routine. I like to get on with my job, and then when the day's work's over settle down to a paper and a smoke and a bit of music on the wireless, variety or something of the sort, and then turn in early. I never had much use for girls, not even when I was doing my time in the army. I was out in the Middle East, too, Port Said and that.

No, I was happy enough living with the Thompsons, carrying on much the same day after day, until that one night, when it happened. Nothing's been the same since. Nor ever will be. I don't know . . .

The Thompsons had gone to see their married daughter up at Highgate. They asked me if I'd like to go along, but somehow I didn't fancy barging in, so instead of staying home alone after leaving the garage I went down to the picture palace, and taking a look at the poster saw it was cowboy and Indian stuff – there was a picture of a cowboy sticking a knife into the Indian's guts. I like that – proper baby I am for westerns – so I paid my one and twopence and went inside. I handed my slip of paper to the usherette and said, 'Back row, please,' because I like sitting far back and leaning my head against the board.

Well, then I saw her. They dress the girls up no end in some of these places, velvet tams and all, making them proper guys. They hadn't made a guy out of this one, though. She had copper hair, page-boy style I think they call it, and blue eyes, the kind that look short-sighted but see further than you think, and go dark by night, nearly black, and her mouth was sulky-looking, as if she was fed up, and it would take someone giving her the world to make her smile. She hadn't freckles, nor a milky skin, but warmer than that, more like a peach, and natural too. She was small and slim, and her velvet coat – blue it was – fitted her close, and the cap on the back of her head showed up her copper hair.

I bought a programme – not that I wanted one, but to delay going in through the curtain – and I said to her, 'What's the picture like?'

She didn't look at me. She just went on staring into nothing, at the opposite wall. 'The knifing's amateur,' she said, 'but you can always sleep.'

I couldn't help laughing. I could see she was serious though. She wasn't trying to have me on or anything.

'That's no advertisement,' I said. 'What if the manager heard you?'

Then she looked at me. She turned those blue eyes in my direction, still fed-up they were, not interested, but there was something in them I'd not seen before, and I've never seen it since, a kind of laziness like someone waking from a long dream and glad to find you there. Cat's eyes have that gleam sometimes, when you stroke them, and they purr and curl themselves into a ball and let you do anything you want. She looked at me this way a moment, and there was a smile lurking somewhere behind her mouth if you gave it a chance, and tearing my slip of paper in half she said, 'I'm not paid to advertise. I'm paid to look like this and lure you inside.'

She drew aside the curtains and flashed her torch in the darkness. I couldn't see a thing. It was pitch black, like it always is at first until you get used to it and begin to make out the shapes of the other people sitting there, but there were two great heads on the screen and some chap saying to the other, 'If you don't come clean I'll put a bullet through you,' and somebody broke a pane of glass and a woman screamed.

'Looks all right to me,' I said, and began groping for somewhere to sit.

She said, 'This isn't the picture, it's the trailer for next week,' and she flicked on her torch and showed me a seat in the back row, one away from the gangway.

I sat through the advertisements and the news reel, and then some chap came and played the organ, and the colours of the curtains over the screen went purple and gold and green – funny, I suppose they think they have to give you your money's worth – and looking around I saw the house was half empty – and I guessed the girl had been right, the big picture wasn't going to be much, and that's why nobody much was there.

Just before the hall went dark again she came sauntering down the aisle. She had a tray of ice-creams, but she didn't even bother to call them out and try and sell them. She could have been walking in her sleep, so when she went up the other aisle I beckoned to her.

'Got a sixpenny one?' I said.

She looked across at me. I might have been something dead under her feet, and then she must have recognized me, because that half-smile came back again, and the lazy look in the eye, and she walked round the back of the seats to me.

'Wafer or cornet?' she said.

I didn't want either, to tell the truth. I just wanted to buy something from her and keep her talking.

'Which do you recommend?' I asked.

She shrugged her shoulders. 'Cornets last longer,' she said, and put one in my hand before I had time to give her my choice.

'How about one for you too?' I said.

'No thanks,' she said, 'I saw them made.'

And she walked off, and the place went dark, and there I was sitting with a great sixpenny cornet in my hand looking a fool. The damn thing slopped all over the edge of the holder, spilling on to my shirt, and I had to ram the frozen stuff into my mouth as quick as I could for fear it would all go on my knees, and I turned sideways, because someone came and sat in the empty seat beside the gangway.

I finished it at last, and cleaned myself up with my pocket handkerchief, and then concentrated on the story flashing across the screen. It was a western all right, carts lumbering over prairies, and a train full of bullion being held to ransom, and the heroine in breeches one moment and full evening dress the next. That's the way pictures should be, not a bit like real life at all; but as I watched the story I began to notice the whiff of scent in the air, and I didn't know what it was or where it came from, but it was there just the same. There was a man to the right of me, and on my left were two empty seats, and it certainly wasn't the people in front, and I couldn't keep turning round and sniffing.

I'm not a great one for liking scent. It's too often cheap and nasty, but this was different. There was nothing stale about it, or stuffy, or strong; it was like the flowers they sell up in the West End in the big flower shops before you get them on the barrows – three bob a bloom sort of touch, rich chaps buy them for actresses and such – and it was so darn good, the smell of it there, in that murky old picture palace full of cigarette smoke, that it nearly drove me mad.

At last I turned right round in my seat, and I spotted where it came from. It came from the girl, the usherette; she was leaning on the back board behind me, her arms folded across it.

'Don't fidget,' she said. 'You're wasting one and twopence. Watch the screen.'

But not out loud, so that anyone could hear. In a whisper, for me alone. I couldn't help laughing to myself. The cheek of it! I knew where the scent came from now, and somehow it made me enjoy the picture more. It was as though she was beside me in one of the empty seats and we were looking at the story together.

When it was over, and the lights went on, I saw I'd sat through the last showing and it was nearly ten. Everyone was clearing off for the night. So I waited a bit, and then she came down with her torch and started squinting under the seats to see if anybody had dropped a glove or a purse, the way they do and only remember about afterwards when they get home, and she took no more notice of me than if I'd been a rag which no one would bother to pick up.

I stood up in the back row, alone – the house was clear now – and when she came to me she said, 'Move over, you're blocking the gangway,' and flashed about with her torch, but there was nothing there, only an empty packet of Player's which the cleaners would throw away in the morning. Then she straightened herself and looked me up and down, and taking off the ridiculous cap from the back of her head that suited her so well she fanned herself with it and said, 'Sleeping here tonight?' and then went off, whistling under her breath, and disappeared through the curtains.

210

It was proper maddening. I'd never been taken so much with a girl in my life. I went into the vestibule after her, but she had gone through a door to the back, behind the box-office place, and the commissionaire chap was already getting the doors to and fixing them for the night. I went out and stood in the street and waited. I felt a bit of a fool, because the odds were that she would come out with a bunch of others, the way girls do. There was the one who had sold me my ticket, and I dare say there were other usherettes up in the balcony, and perhaps a cloak-room attendant too, and they'd all be giggling together, and I wouldn't have the nerve to go up to her.

In a few minutes, though, she came swinging out of the place alone. She had a mac on, belted, and her hands in her pockets, and she had no hat. She walked straight up the street, and she didn't look to right or left of her. I followed, scared that she would turn round and see me off, but she went on walking, fast and direct, staring straight in front of her, and as she moved her copper page-boy hair swung with her shoulders.

Presently she hesitated, then crossed over and stood waiting for a bus. There was a queue of four or five people, so she didn't see me join the queue, and when the bus came she climbed on to it, ahead of the others, and I climbed too, without the slightest notion where it was going, and I couldn't have cared less. Up the stairs she went with me after her, and settled herself in the back seat, yawning, and closed her eyes.

I sat myself down beside her, nervous as a kitten, the point being that I never did that sort of thing as a rule and expected a rocket, and when the conductor stumped up and asked for fares I said, 'Two sixpennies, please,' because I reckoned she would never be going the whole distance and this would be bound to cover her fare and mine too.

He raised his eyebrows – they like to think themselves smart, some of these fellows – and he said, 'Look out for the bumps when the driver changes gear. He's only just passed his test.' And he went down the stairs chuckling, telling himself he was no end of a wag, no doubt.

The sound of his voice woke the girl, and she looked at me out of her sleepy eyes, and looked too at the tickets in my hand – she must have seen by the colour they were sixpennies – and she smiled, the first real smile I had got out of her that evening, and said without any sort of surprise, 'Hullo, stranger.'

I took out a cigarette, to put myself at ease, and offered her one, but she wouldn't take it. She just closed her eyes again, to settle herself to sleep. Then, seeing there was no one else to notice up on the top deck, only an Air Force chap in the front slopped over a newspaper, I put out my hand and pulled her head down on my shoulder, and got my arm round her, snug and comfortable, thinking of course she'd throw it off and blast me to hell. She didn't though. She gave a sort of laugh to herself, and settled down like as if she might have been in an armchair, and she said, 'It's not every night I get a free ride and a free pillow. Wake me at the bottom of the hill, before we get to the cemetery.'

I didn't know what hill she meant, or what cemetery, but I wasn't going to wake her, not me. I had paid for two sixpennies, and I was darn well going to get value for my money.

So we sat there together, jogging along in the bus, very close and very pleasant, and I thought to myself that it was a lot more fun than sitting at home in the bed-sit reading the football news, or spending an evening up Highgate at Mr and Mrs Thompson's daughter's place.

Presently I got more daring, and let my head lean against hers, and tightened up my arm a bit, not too obvious-like, but nicely. Anyone coming up the stairs to the top deck would have taken us for a courting couple.

Then, after we had had about fourpenny-worth, I got anxious. The old bus wouldn't be turning round and going back again, when we reached the sixpenny limit; it would pack up for the night, we'd have come to the terminus. And there we'd be, the girl and I, stuck out somewhere at the back of beyond, with no return bus, and I'd got about six bob in my pocket and no more. Six bob would never pay for a taxi, not with a tip and all. Besides, there probably wouldn't be any taxis going.

What a fool I'd been not to come out with more money. It was silly, perhaps, to let it worry me, but I'd acted on impulse right from the start, and if only I'd known how the evening was going to turn out I'd have had my wallet filled. It wasn't often I went out with a girl, and I hate a fellow who can't do the thing in style. Proper slap-up do at a Corner House – they're good these days with that help-yourself service – and if she had a fancy for something stronger than coffee or orangeade, well, of course as late as this it wasn't much use, but nearer home I knew where to go. There was a pub where my boss went, and you paid for your gin and kept it there, and could go in and have a drink from your bottle when you felt like it. They have the same sort of racket at the posh night clubs up West, I'm told, but they make you pay through the nose for it.

Anyway, here I was riding a bus to the Lord knows where, with my girl beside me – I called her 'my girl' just as if she really was and we were courting – and bless me if I had the money to take her home. I began to fidget about, from sheer nerves, and I fumbled in one pocket after another, in case by a piece of luck I should come across a half-crown, or even a ten-bob note I had forgotten all about, and I suppose I disturbed her with all this, because she suddenly pulled my ear and said, 'Stop rocking the boat.'

Well, I mean to say . . . It just got me. I can't explain why. She held my ear a moment before she pulled it, like as though she were feeling the skin and liked it, and then she just gave it a lazy tug. It's the kind of thing anyone would do to a child, and the way she said it, as if she had known me for years and we were out picnicking together, 'Stop rocking the boat.' Chummy, matey, yet better than either.

'Look here,' I said, 'I'm awfully sorry, I've been and done a darn silly thing. I took tickets to the terminus because I wanted to sit beside you, and when we get there we'll be turned out of the bus, and it will be miles from anywhere, and I've only got six bob in my pocket.'

'You've got legs, haven't you?' she said.

'What d'you mean, I've got legs?'

213

'They're meant to walk on. Mine were,' she answered.

Then I knew it didn't matter, and she wasn't angry either, and the evening was going to be all right. I cheered up in a second, and gave her a squeeze, just to show I appreciated her being such a sport – most girls would have torn me to shreds – and I said, 'We haven't passed a cemetery, as far as I know. Does it matter very much?'

'Oh, there'll be others,' she said. 'I'm not particular.'

I didn't know what to make of that. I thought she wanted to get out at the cemetery stopping point because it was her nearest stop for home, like the way you say, 'Put me down at Woolworth's' if you live handy. I puzzled over it for a bit, and then I said, 'How do you mean, there'll be others? It's not a thing you see often along a bus route.'

'I was speaking in general terms,' she answered. 'Don't bother to talk, I like you silent best.'

It wasn't a slap on the face, the way she said it. Fact was, I knew what she meant. Talking's all very pleasant with people like Mr and Mrs Thompson, over supper, and you say how the day has gone, and one of you reads a bit out of the paper, and the other says, 'Fancy, there now,' and so it goes on, in bits and pieces until one of you yawns, and somebody says, 'Who's for bed?' Or it's nice enough with a chap like the boss, having a cuppa mid-morning, or about three when there's nothing doing, 'I'll tell you what I think, those blokes in the government are making a mess of things, no better than the last lot,' and then we'll be inter-rupted with someone coming to fill up with petrol. And I like talking to my old Mum when I go and see her, which I don't do often enough, and she tells me how she spanked my bottom when I was a kid, and I sit on the kitchen table like I did then, and she bakes rock cakes and gives me peel, saying, 'You always were one for peel.' That's talk, that's conversation.

But I didn't want to talk to my girl. I just wanted to keep my arm round her the way I was doing, and rest my chin against her head, and that's what she meant when she said she liked me silent. I liked it too.

One last thing bothered me a bit, and that was whether I could kiss her before the bus stopped and we were turned out at the terminus. I mean, putting an arm round a girl is one thing, and kissing her is another. It takes a little time as a rule to warm up. You start off with a long evening ahead of you, and by the time you've been to a picture or a concert, and then had something to eat and to drink, well, you've got yourselves acquainted, and it's the usual thing to end up with a bit of kissing and a cuddle, the girls expect it. Truth to tell, I was never much of a one for kissing. There was a girl I walked out with back home, before I went into the army, and she was quite a good sort, I liked her. But her teeth were a bit prominent, and even if you shut your eyes and tried to forget who it was you were kissing, well, you knew it was her, and there was nothing to it. Good old Doris from next door. But the opposite kind are even worse, the ones that grab you and nearly eat you. You come across plenty of them, when you're in uniform. They're much too eager, and they muss you about, and you get the feeling they can't wait for a chap to get busy about them. I don't mind saying it used to make me sick. Put me dead off, and that's a fact. I suppose I was born fussy. I don't know.

But now, this evening in the bus, it was all quite different. I don't know what it was about the girl – the sleepy eyes, and the copper hair, and somehow not seeming to care if I was there yet liking me at the same time; I hadn't found anything like this before. So I said to myself, 'Now, shall I risk it, or shall I wait?', and I knew, from the way the driver was going and the conductor was whistling below and saying 'goodnight' to the people getting off, that the final stop couldn't be far away; and my heart began to thump under my coat, and my neck grew hot below the collar – darn silly, only a kiss you know, she couldn't kill me – and then . . . It was like diving off a spring-board. I thought, 'Here goes,' and I bent down, and turned her face to me, and lifted her chin with my hand, and kissed her good and proper.

Well, if I was poetical, I'd say what happened then was a revelation. But I'm not poetical, and I can only say that she kissed

215

me back, and it lasted a long time, and it wasn't a bit like Doris.

Then the bus stopped with a jerk, and the conductor called out in a sing-song voice, 'All out, please.' Frankly, I could have wrung his neck.

She gave me a kick on the ankle. 'Come on, move,' she said, and I stumbled from my seat and racketed down the stairs, she following behind, and there we were, standing in a street. It was beginning to rain too, not badly but just enough to make you notice and want to turn up the collar of your coat, and we were right at the end of a great wide street, with deserted unlighted shops on either side, the end of the world it looked to me, and sure enough there was a hill over to the left, and at the bottom of the hill a cemetery. I could see the railings and the white tombstones behind, and it stretched a long way, nearly half-way up the hill. There were acres of it.

'God darn it,' I said, 'is this the place you meant?'

'Could be,' she said, looking over her shoulder vaguely, and then she took my arm. 'What about a cup of coffee first?' she said.

First . . .? I wondered if she meant before the long trudge home, or was this home? It didn't really matter. It wasn't much after eleven. And I could do with a cup of coffee, and a sandwich too. There was a stall across the road, and they hadn't shut up shop.

We walked over to it, and the driver was there too, and the conductor, and the Air Force fellow who had been up in front on the top deck. They were ordering cups of tea and sandwiches, and we had the same, only coffee. They cut them tasty at the stalls, the sandwiches, I've noticed it before, nothing stingy about it, good slices of ham between thick white bread, and the coffee is piping hot, full cups too, good value, and I thought to myself 'Six bob will see this lot all right.'

I noticed my girl looking at the Air Force chap, sort of thoughtful-like, as though she might have seen him before, and he looked at her too. I couldn't blame him for that. I didn't mind either; when you're out with a girl it gives you a kind of pride

216

if other chaps notice her. And you couldn't miss this one. Not my girl.

Then she turned her back on him, deliberate, and leant with her elbows on the stall, sipping her hot coffee, and I stood beside her doing the same. We weren't stuck up or anything, we were pleasant and polite enough, saying good evening all round, but anyone could tell that we were together, the girl and I, we were on our own. I liked that. Funny, it did something to me inside, gave me a protective feeling. For all they knew we might have been a married couple on our way home.

They were chaffing a bit, the other three and the chap serving the sandwiches and tea, but we didn't join in.

'You want to watch out, in that uniform,' said the conductor to the Air Force fellow, 'or you'll end up like those others. It's late too, to be out on your own.'

They all started laughing. I didn't quite see the point, but I supposed it was a joke.

'I've been awake a long time,' said the Air Force fellow. 'I know a bad lot when I see one.'

'That's what the others said, I shouldn't wonder,' remarked the driver, 'and we know what happened to them. Makes you shudder. But why pick on the Air Force, that's what I want to know?'

'It's the colour of our uniform,' said the fellow. 'You can spot it in the dark.'

They went on laughing in that way. I lighted up a cigarette, but my girl wouldn't have one.

'I blame the war for all that's gone wrong with the women,' said the coffee-stall bloke, wiping a cup and hanging it up behind. 'Turned a lot of them barmy, in my opinion. They don't know the difference between right or wrong.'

''Tisn't that, it's sport that's the trouble,' said the conductor. 'Develops their muscles and that, what weren't never meant to be developed. Take my two youngsters, f'r instance. The girl can knock the boy down any time, she's a proper little bully. Makes you think.'

217

'That's right,' agreed the driver, 'equality of the sexes, they call it, don't they? It's the vote that did it. We ought never to have given them the vote.'

'Garn,' said the Air Force chap, 'giving them the vote didn't turn the women barmy. They've always been the same, under the skin. The people out East know how to treat 'em. They keep 'em shut up, out there. That's the answer. Then you don't get any trouble.'

'I don't know what my old woman would say if I tried to shut her up,' said the driver. And they all started laughing again.

My girl plucked at my sleeve and I saw she had finished her coffee. She motioned with her head towards the street.

'Want to go home?' I said.

Silly. I somehow wanted the others to believe we were going home. She didn't answer. She just went striding off, her hands in the pockets of her mac. I said goodnight, and followed her, but not before I noticed the Air Force fellow staring after her over his cup of tea.

She walked off along the street, and it was still raining, dreary somehow, made you want to be sitting over a fire somewhere snug, and when she had crossed the street, and had come to the railings outside the cemetery she stopped, and looked up at me, and smiled.

'What now?' I said.

'Tombstones are flat,' she said, 'sometimes.'

'What if they are?' I asked, bewildered-like.

'You can lie down on them,' she said.

She turned and strolled along, looking at the railings, and then she came to one that was bent wide, and the next beside it broken, and she glanced up at me and smiled again.

'It's always the same,' she said. 'You're bound to find a gap if you look long enough.'

She was through that gap in the railings as quick as a knife through butter. You could have knocked me flat.

'Here, hold on,' I said, 'I'm not as small as you.'

But she was off and away, wandering among the graves. I got

through the gap, puffing and blowing a bit, and then I looked around, and bless me if she wasn't lying on a long flat gravestone, with her arms under her head and her eyes closed.

Well, I wasn't expecting anything. I mean, it had been in my mind to see her home and that. Date her up for the next evening. Of course, seeing as it was late, we could have stopped a bit when we came to the doorway of her place. She needn't have gone in right away. But lying there on the gravestone wasn't hardly natural.

I sat down, and took her hand.

'You'll get wet lying there,' I said. Feeble, but I didn't know what else to say.

'I'm used to that,' she said.

She opened her eyes and looked at me. There was a street light not far away, outside the railings, so it wasn't all that dark, and anyway in spite of the rain the night wasn't pitch black, more murky somehow. I wish I knew how to tell about her eyes, but I'm not one for fancy talk. You know how a luminous watch shines in the dark. I've got one myself. When you wake up in the night, there it is on your wrist, like a friend. Somehow my girl's eyes shone like that, but they were lovely too. And they weren't lazy cat's eyes any more. They were loving and gentle, and they were sad, too, all at the same time.

'Used to lying in the rain?' I said.

'Brought up to it,' she answered. 'They gave us a name in the shelters. The dead-end kids, they used to call us, in the war days.'

'Weren't you never evacuated?' I asked.

'Not me,' she said. 'I never could stop any place. I always came back.'

'Parents living?'

'No. Both of them killed by the bomb that smashed my home.' She didn't speak tragic-like. Just ordinary.

'Bad luck,' I said.

She didn't answer that one. And I sat there, holding her hand, wanting to take her home.

'You been on your job some time, at the picture-house?' I asked.

219

'About three weeks,' she said. 'I don't stop anywhere long. I'll be moving on again soon.'

'Why's that?'

'Restless,' she said.

She put up her hands suddenly and took my face and held it. It was gentle the way she did it, not as you'd think.

'You've got a good kind face. I like it,' she said to me.

It was queer. The way she said it made me feel daft and soft, not sort of excited like I had been in the bus, and I thought to myself, well, maybe this is it, I've found a girl at last I really want. But not for an evening, casual. For going steady.

'Got a bloke?' I asked.

'No,' she said.

'I mean, regular.'

'No, never.'

It was a funny line of talk to be having in a cemetery, and she lying there like some figure carved on the old tombstone.

'I haven't got a girl either,' I said. 'Never think about it, the way other chaps do. Faddy, I guess. And then I'm keen on my job. Work in a garage, mechanic you know, repairs, anything that's going. Good pay. I've saved a bit, besides what I send my old Mum. I live in digs. Nice people, Mr and Mrs Thompson, and my boss at the garage is a nice chap too. I've never been lonely, and I'm not lonely now. But since I've seen you, it's made me think. You know, it's not going to be the same any more.'

She never interrupted once, and somehow it was like speaking my thoughts aloud.

'Going home to the Thompsons is all very pleasant and nice,' I said, 'and you couldn't wish for kinder people. Good grub too, and we chat a bit after supper, and listen to the wireless. But d'you know, what I want now is different. I want to come along and fetch you from the cinema, when the programme's over, and you'd be standing there by the curtains, seeing the people out, and you'd give me a bit of a wink to show me you'd be going through to change your clothes and I could wait for you. And then you'd come out into the street, like you did tonight, but

220

you wouldn't go off on your own, you'd take my arm, and if you didn't want to wear your coat I'd carry it for you, or a parcel maybe, or whatever you had. Then we'd go off to the Corner House or some place for supper, handy. We'd have a table reserved – they'd know us, the waitresses and them; they'd keep back something special, just for us.'

I could picture it too, clear as anything. The table with the ticket on 'Reserved'. The waitress nodding at us, 'Got curried eggs tonight.' And we going through to get our trays, and my girl acting like she didn't know me, and me laughing to myself.

'D'you see what I mean?' I said to her. 'It's not just being friends, it's more than that.'

I don't know if she heard. She lay there looking up at me, touching my ear and my chin in that funny, gentle way. You'd say she was sorry for me.

'I'd like to buy you things,' I said, 'flowers sometimes. It's nice to see a girl with a flower tucked in her dress, it looks clean and fresh. And for special occasions, birthdays, Christmas, and that, something you'd seen in a shop window, and wanted, but hadn't liked to go in and ask the price. A brooch perhaps, or a bracelet, something pretty. And I'd go in and get it when you weren't with me, and it'd cost much more than my week's pay, but I wouldn't mind.'

I could see the expression on her face, opening the parcel. And she'd put it on, what I'd bought, and we'd go out together, and she'd be dressed up a bit for the purpose, nothing glaring I don't mean, but something that took the eye. You know, saucy.

'It's not fair to talk about getting married,' I said, 'not in these days, when everything's uncertain. A fellow doesn't mind the uncertainty, but it's hard on a girl. Cooped up in a couple of rooms maybe, and queueing and rations and all. They like their freedom, and being in a job, and not being tied down, the same as us. But it's nonsense the way they were talking back in the coffee stall just now. About girls not being the same as in old days, and the war to blame. As for the way they treat them out East – I've seen some of it. I suppose that fellow meant to be

221

funny, they're all smart Alicks in the Air Force, but it was a silly line of talk, I thought.'

She dropped her hands to her side and closed her eyes. It was getting quite wet there on the tombstone. I was worried for her, though she had her mac of course, but her legs and feet were damp in her thin stockings and shoes.

'You weren't ever in the Air Force, were you?' she said.

Queer. Her voice had gone quite hard. Sharp, and different. Like as if she was anxious about something, scared even.

'Not me,' I said, 'I served my time with REME. Proper lot they were. No swank, no nonsense. You know where you are with them.'

'I'm glad,' she said. 'You're good and kind. I'm glad.'

I wondered if she'd known some fellow in the RAF who had let her down. They're a wild crowd, the ones I've come across. And I remembered the way she'd looked at the boy drinking his tea at the stall. Reflective, somehow. As if she was thinking back. I couldn't expect her not to have been around a bit, with her looks, and then brought up to play about the shelters, without parents, like she said. But I didn't want to think of her being hurt by anyone.

'Why, what's wrong with them?' I said. 'What's the RAF done to you?'

'They smashed my home,' she said.

'That was the Germans, not our fellows.'

'It's all the same, they're killers, aren't they?' she said.

I looked down at her, lying on the tombstone, and her voice wasn't hard any more, like when she'd asked me if I'd been in the Air Force, but it was tired, and sad, and oddly lonely, and it did something queer to my stomach, right in the pit of it, so that I wanted to do the darndest silliest thing and take her home with me, back to where I lived with Mr and Mrs Thompson, and say to Mrs Thompson – she was a kind old soul, she wouldn't mind – 'Look, this is my girl. Look after her.' Then I'd know she'd be safe, she'd be all right, nobody could do anything to hurt her. That was the thing I was afraid of suddenly, that someone would come along and hurt my girl.

I bent down and put my arms round her and lifted her up close.

'Listen,' I said, 'it's raining hard. I'm going to take you home. You'll catch your death, lying here on the wet stone.'

'No,' she said, her hands on my shoulders, 'nobody ever sees me home. You're going back where you belong, alone.'

'I won't leave you here,' I said.

'Yes, that's what I want you to do. If you refuse I shall be angry. You wouldn't want that, would you?'

I stared at her, puzzled. And her face was queer in the murky old light there, whiter than before, but it was beautiful, Jesus Christ, it was beautiful. That's blasphemy. But I can't say it no other way.

'What do you want me to do?' I asked.

'I want you to go and leave me here, and not look back,' she said, 'like someone dreaming, sleep-walking, they call it. Go back walking through the rain. It will take you hours. It doesn't matter, you're young and strong and you've got long legs. Go back to your room, wherever it is, and get into bed, and go to sleep, and wake and have your breakfast in the morning, and go off to work, the same as you always do.'

'What about you?'

'Never mind about me. Just go.'

'Can I call for you at the cinema tomorrow night? Can it be like what I was telling you, you know . . . going steady?'

She didn't answer. She only smiled. She sat quite still, looking in my face, and then she closed her eyes and threw back her head and said, 'Kiss me again, stranger.'

I left her, like she said. I didn't look back. I climbed through the railings of the cemetery, out on to the road. No one seemed to be about, and the coffee stall by the bus stop had closed down, the boards were up.

I started walking the way the bus had brought us. The road was straight, going on for ever. A High Street it must have been. There were shops on either side, and it was right away north-east of

London, nowhere I'd ever been before. I was proper lost, but it didn't seem to matter. I felt like a sleep-walker, just as she said.

I kept thinking of her all the time. There was nothing else, only her face in front of me as I walked. They had a word for it in the army, when a girl gets a fellow that way, so he can't see straight or hear right or know what he's doing; and I thought it a lot of cock, or it only happened to drunks, and now I knew it was true and it had happened to me. I wasn't going to worry any more about how she'd get home; she'd told me not to, and she must have lived handy, she'd never have ridden out so far else, though it was funny living such a way from her work. But maybe in time she'd tell me more, bit by bit. I wouldn't drag it from her. I had one thing fixed in my mind, and that was to pick her up the next evening from the picture palace. It was firm and set, and nothing would budge me from that. The hours in between would just be a blank for me until ten p.m. came round.

I went on walking in the rain, and presently a lorry came along and I thumbed a lift, and the driver took me a good part of the way before he had to turn left in the other direction, and so I got down and walked again, and it must have been close on three when I got home.

I would have felt bad, in an ordinary way, knocking up Mr Thompson to let me in, and it had never happened before either, but I was all lit up inside from loving my girl, and I didn't seem to mind. He came down at last and opened the door. I had to ring several times before he heard, and there he was, grey with sleep, poor old chap, his pyjamas all crumpled from the bed.

'Whatever happened to you?' he said. 'We've been worried, the wife and me. We thought you'd been knocked down, run over. We came back here and found the house empty and your supper not touched.'

'I went to the pictures,' I said.

'The pictures?' He stared up at me, in the passage-way. 'The pictures stop at ten o'clock.'

'I know,' I said, 'I went walking after that. Sorry. Goodnight.'

And I climbed up the stairs to my room, leaving the old chap muttering to himself and bolting the door, and I heard Mrs Thompson calling from her bedroom, 'What is it? Is it him? Is he come home?'

I'd put them to trouble and to worry, and I ought to have gone in there and then and apologized, but I couldn't somehow, it wouldn't have come right; so I shut my door and threw off my clothes and got into bed, and it was like as if she was with me still, my girl, in the darkness.

They were a bit quiet at breakfast the next morning, Mr and Mrs Thompson. They didn't look at me. Mrs Thompson gave me my kipper without a word, and he went on looking at his newspaper.

I ate my breakfast, and then I said, 'I hope you had a nice evening up at Highgate?' and Mrs Thompson, with her mouth a bit tight, she said, 'Very pleasant, thank you, we were home by ten,' and she gave a little sniff and poured Mr Thompson out another cup of tea.

We went on being quiet, no one saying a word, and then Mrs Thompson said, 'Will you be in to supper this evening?' and I said, 'No, I don't think so. I'm meeting a friend,' and then I saw the old chap look at me over his spectacles.

'If you're going to be late,' he said, 'we'd best take the key for you.'

Then he went on reading his paper. You could tell they were proper hurt that I didn't tell them anything, or say where I was going.

I went off to work, and we were busy at the garage that day, one job after the other came along, and any other time I wouldn't have minded. I liked a full day and often worked overtime, but today I wanted to get away before the shops closed; I hadn't thought about anything else since the idea came into my head.

It was getting on for half past four, and the boss came to me and said, 'I promised the doctor he'd have his Austin this evening, I said you'd be through with it by seven-thirty. That's OK, isn't it?'

My heart sank. I'd counted on getting off early, because of

what I wanted to do. Then I thought quickly that if the boss let me off now, and I went out to the shop before it closed, and came back again to do the job on the Austin, it would be all right, so I said, 'I don't mind working a bit of overtime, but I'd like to slip out now, for half an hour, if you're going to be here. There's something I want to buy before the shops shut.'

He told me that suited him, so I took off my overalls and washed and got my coat and I went off to the line of shops down at the bottom of Haverstock Hill. I knew the one I wanted. It was a jeweller's, where Mr Thompson used to take his clock to be repaired, and it wasn't a place where they sold trash at all, but good stuff, solid silver frames and that, and cutlery.

There were rings, of course, and a few fancy bangles, but I didn't like the look of them. All the girls in the NAAFI used to wear bangles with charms on them, quite common it was, and I went on staring in at the window and then I spotted it, right at the back.

It was a brooch. Quite small, not much bigger than your thumbnail, but with a nice blue stone on it and a pin at the back, and it was shaped like a heart. That was what got me, the shape. I stared at it a bit, and there wasn't a ticket to it, which meant it would cost a bit, but I went in and asked to have a look at it. The jeweller got it out of the window for me, and he gave it a bit of a polish and turned it this way and that, and I saw it pinned on my girl, showing up nice on her frock or her jumper, and I knew this was it.

'I'll take it,' I said, and then asked him the price.

I swallowed a bit when he told me, but I took out my wallet and counted the notes, and he put the heart in a box wrapped up careful with cotton wool, and made a neat package of it, tied with fancy string. I knew I'd have to get an advance from the boss before I went off work that evening, but he was a good chap and I was certain he'd give it to me.

I stood outside the jeweller's, with the packet for my girl safe in my breast pocket, and I heard the church clock strike a quarter to five. There was time to slip down to the cinema and make sure she understood about the date for the evening, and then I'd beat it fast up the road and get back to the garage, and I'd have the Austin done by the time the doctor wanted it.

When I got to the cinema my heart was beating like a sledge-hammer and I could hardly swallow. I kept picturing to myself how she'd look, standing there by the curtains going in, with the velvet jacket and the cap on the back of her head.

There was a bit of a queue outside, and I saw they'd changed the programme. The poster of the western had gone, with the cowboy throwing a knife in the Indian's guts, and they had instead a lot of girls dancing, and some chap prancing in front of them with a walking-stick. It was a musical.

I went in, and didn't go near the box office but looked straight to the curtains, where she'd be. There was an usherette there all right, but it wasn't her. This was a great tall girl, who looked silly in the clothes, and she was trying to do two things at once – tear off the slips of tickets as the people went past, and hang on to her torch at the same time.

I waited a moment. Perhaps they'd switched over positions and my girl had gone up to the circle. When the last lot had got in through the curtains and there was a pause and she was free, I went up to her and I said, 'Excuse me, do you know where I could have a word with the other young lady?'

She looked at me. 'What other young lady?'

'The one who was here last night, with copper hair,' I said.

She looked at me closer then, suspicious-like.

'She hasn't shown up today,' she said. 'I'm taking her place.'

'Not shown up?'

'No. And it's funny you should ask. You're not the only one. The police was here not long ago. They had a word with the manager, and the commissionaire too, and no one's said anything to me yet, but I think there's been trouble.'

My heart beat different then. Not excited, bad. Like when someone's ill, took to hospital, sudden.

'The police?' I said. 'What were they here for?'

227

'I told you, I don't know,' she answered, 'but it was something to do with her, and the manager went with them to the police station, and he hasn't come back yet. This way, please, circle on the left, stalls to the right.'

I just stood there, not knowing what to do. It was like as if the floor had been knocked away from under me.

The tall girl tore another slip off a ticket and then she said to me, over her shoulder, 'Was she a friend of yours?'

'Sort of,' I said. I didn't know what to say.

'Well, if you ask me, she was queer in the head, and it wouldn't surprise me if she'd done away with herself and they'd found her dead. No, ice-creams served in the interval, after the news reel.'

I went out and stood in the street. The queue was growing for the cheaper seats, and there were children too, talking, excited. I brushed past them and started walking up the street, and I felt sick inside, queer. Something had happened to my girl. I knew it now. That was why she had wanted to get rid of me last night, and for me not to see her home. She was going to do herself in, there in the cemetery. That's why she talked funny and looked so white, and now they'd found her, lying there on the grave-stone by the railings.

If I hadn't gone away and left her she'd have been all right. If I'd stayed with her just five minutes longer, coaxing her, I'd have got her round to my way of thinking and seen her home, standing no nonsense, and she'd be at the picture palace now, showing the people to their seats.

It might be it wasn't as bad as what I feared. It might be she was found wandering, lost her memory and got picked up by the police and taken off, and then they found out where she worked and that, and now the police wanted to check up with the manager at the cinema to see if it was so. If I went down to the police station and asked them there, maybe they'd tell me what had happened, and I could say she was my girl, we were walking out, and it wouldn't matter if she didn't recognize me even, I'd stick to the story. I couldn't let down my boss, I had

228

to get that job done on the Austin, but afterwards, when I'd finished, I could go down to the police station.

All the heart had gone out of me, and I went back to the garage hardly knowing what I was doing, and for the first time ever the smell of the place turned my stomach, the oil and the grease, and there was a chap roaring up his engine, before backing out his car, and a great cloud of smoke coming from his exhaust, filling the workshop with stink.

I went and got my overalls, and put them on, and fetched the tools, and started on the Austin, and all the time I was wondering what it was that had happened to my girl, if she was down at the police station, lost and lonely, or if she was lying somewhere . . . dead. I kept seeing her face all the time like it was last night.

It took me an hour and a half, not more, to get the Austin ready for the road, filled up with petrol and all, and I had her facing outwards to the street for the owner to drive out, but I was all in by then, dead tired, and the sweat pouring down my face. I had a bit of a wash and put on my coat, and I felt the package in the breast pocket. I took it out and looked at it, done so neat with the fancy ribbon, and I put it back again, and I hadn't noticed the boss come in – I was standing with my back to the door.

'Did you get what you wanted?' he said, cheerful-like and smiling.

He was a good chap, never out of temper, and we got along well.

'Yes,' I said.

But I didn't want to talk about it. I told him the job was done and the Austin was ready to drive away. I went to the office with him so that he could note down the work done, and the overtime, and he offered me a fag from the packet lying on his desk beside the evening paper.

'I see Lady Luck won the three-thirty,' he said. 'I'm a couple of quid up this week.'

He was entering my work in his ledger, to keep the pay-roll right.

229

'Good for you,' I said.

'Only backed it for a place, like a clot,' he said. 'She was twenty-five to one. Still, it's all in the game.'

I didn't answer. I'm not one for drinking, but I needed one bad, just then. I mopped my forehead with my handkerchief. I wished he'd get on with the figures, and say goodnight, and let me go.

'Another poor devil's had it,' he said. 'That's the third now in three weeks, ripped right up the guts, same as the others. He died in hospital this morning. Looks like there's a hoodoo on the RAF.'

'What was it, flying jets?' I asked.

'Jets?' he said. 'No, damn it, murder. Sliced up the belly, poor sod. Don't you ever read the papers? It's the third one in three weeks, done identical, all Air Force fellows, and each time they've found 'em near a graveyard or a cemetery. I was saying just now, to that chap who came in for petrol, it's not only men who go off their rockers and turn sex maniacs, but women too. They'll get this one all right though, you see. It says in the paper they've a line on her, and expect an arrest shortly. About time too, before another poor blighter cops it.'

He shut up his ledger and stuck his pencil behind his ear.

'Like a drink?' he said. 'I've got a bottle of gin in the cupboard.'

'No,' I said, 'no, thanks very much. I've . . . I've got a date.'

'That's right,' he said, smiling, 'enjoy yourself.'

I walked down the street and bought an evening paper. It was like what he said about the murder. They had it on the front page. They said it must have happened about two a.m. Young fellow in the Air Force, in north-east London. He had managed to stagger to a call-box and get through to the police, and they found him there on the floor of the box when they arrived.

He made a statement in the ambulance before he died. He said a girl called to him, and he followed her, and he thought it was just a bit of love-making – he'd seen her with another fellow drinking coffee at a stall a little while before – and he thought she'd thrown this other fellow over and had taken a fancy to him, and then she got him, he said, right in the guts.

230

It said in the paper that he had given the police a full description of her, and it said also that the police would be glad if the man who had been seen with the girl earlier in the evening would come forward to help in identification.

I didn't want the paper any more. I threw it away. I walked about the streets till I was tired, and when I guessed Mr and Mrs Thompson had gone to bed I went home, and groped for the key they'd left on a piece of string hanging inside the letterbox, and I let myself in and went upstairs to my room.

Mrs Thompson had turned down the bed and put a thermos of tea for me, thoughtful-like, and the evening paper, the late edition.

They'd got her. About three o'clock in the afternoon. I didn't read the writing, nor the name nor anything. I sat down on my bed, and took up the paper, and there was my girl staring up at me from the front page.

Then I took the package from my coat and undid it, and threw away the wrapper and the fancy string, and sat there looking down at the little heart I held in my hand.

The Old Man

D id I hear you asking about the Old Man? I thought so. You're a newcomer to the district, here on holiday. We get plenty these days, during the summer months. Somehow they always find their way eventually over the cliffs down to this beach, and then they pause and look from the sea back to the lake. Just as you did.

It's a lovely spot, isn't it? Quiet and remote. You can't wonder at the old man choosing to live here.

I don't remember when he first came. Nobody can. Many years ago, it must have been. He was here when I arrived, long before the war. Perhaps he came to escape from civilization, much as I did myself. Or maybe, where he lived before, the folks around made things too hot for him. It's hard to say. I had the feeling, from the very first, that he had done something, or something had been done to him, that gave him a grudge against the world. I remember the first time I set eyes on him I said to myself, 'I bet that old fellow is one hell of a character.'

Yes, he was living here beside the lake, along of his missus. Funny sort of lash-up they had, exposed to all the weather, but they didn't seem to mind.

I had been warned about him by one of the fellows from the farm, who advised me, with a grin, to give the old man who lived down by the lake a wide berth – he didn't care for strangers. So I went warily, and I didn't stay to pass the time of day. Nor would it have been any use if I had, not knowing a word of his lingo. The first time I saw him he was standing by the edge of the lake, looking out to sea, and from tact I avoided the piece of planking over the stream, which meant passing close to him, and crossed to the other side of the lake by the beach instead.

Then, with an awkward feeling that I was trespassing and had no business to be there, I bobbed down behind a clump of gorse, took out my spy-glass, and had a peep at him.

He was a big fellow, broad and strong – he's aged, of course, lately; I'm speaking of several years back – but even now you can see what he must have been once. Such power and drive behind him, and that fine head, which he carried like a king. There's an idea in that, too. No, I'm not joking. Who knows what royal blood he carries inside him, harking back to some remote ancestor? And now and again, surging in him – not through his own fault – it gets the better of him and drives him fighting mad. I didn't think about that at the time. I just looked at him, and ducked behind the gorse when I saw him turn, and I wondered to myself what went on in his mind, whether he knew I was there, watching him.

If he should decide to come up the lake after me I should look pretty foolish. He must have thought better of it, though, or perhaps he did not care. He went on staring out to sea, watching the gulls and the incoming tide, and presently he ambled off his side of the lake, heading for the missus and home and maybe supper.

I didn't catch a glimpse of her that first day. She just wasn't around. Living as they do, close in by the left bank of the lake, with no proper track to the place, I hardly had the nerve to venture close and come upon her face to face. When I did see her, though, I was disappointed. She wasn't much to look at after all. What I mean is, she hadn't got anything like his character. A placid, mild-tempered creature, I judged her.

They had both come back from fishing when I saw them, and were making their way up from the beach to the lake. He was in front, of course. She tagged along behind. Neither of them took the slightest notice of me, and I was glad, because the old man might have paused, and waited, and told her to get on back home, and then come down towards the rocks where I was sitting. You ask what I would have said, had he done so? I'm damned if I know. Maybe I would have got up, whistling and seeming

233

unconcerned, and then, with a nod and a smile – useless, really, but instinctive, if you know what I mean – said good day and pottered off. I don't think he would have done anything. He'd just have stared after me, with those strange narrow eyes of his, and let me go.

After that, winter and summer, I was always down on the beach or the rocks, and they went on living their curious, remote existence, sometimes fishing in the lake, sometimes at sea. Occasionally I'd come across them in the harbour on the estuary, taking a look at the yachts anchored there, and the shipping. I used to wonder which of them made the suggestion. Perhaps suddenly he would be lured by the thought of the bustle and life of the harbour, and all the things he had either wantonly given up or never known, and he would say to her, 'Today we are going into town.' And she, happy to do whatever pleased him best, followed along.

You see, one thing that stood out – and you couldn't help noticing it – was that the pair of them were devoted to one another. I've seen her greet him when he came back from a day's fishing and had left her back home, and towards evening she'd come down the lake and on to the beach and down to the sea to wait for him. She'd see him coming from a long way off, and I would see him too, rounding the corner of the bay. He'd come straight in to the beach, and she would go to meet him, and they would embrace each other, not caring a damn who saw them. It was touching, if you know what I mean. You felt there was something lovable about the old man, if that's how things were between them. He might be a devil to outsiders, but he was all the world to her. It gave me a warm feeling for him, when I saw them together like that.

You asked if they had any family? I was coming to that. It's about the family I really wanted to tell you. Because there was a tragedy, you see. And nobody knows anything about it except me. I suppose I could have told someone, but if I had, I don't know . . . They might have taken the old man away, and she'd have broken her heart without him, and anyway, when all's said and done, it wasn't my business. I know the evidence against the old man was strong, but I hadn't positive proof, it might have been some sort of accident, and anyway, nobody made any inquiries at the time the boy disappeared, so who was I to turn busybody and informer?

I'll try and explain what happened. But you must understand that all this took place over quite a time, and sometimes I was away from home or busy, and didn't go near the lake. Nobody seemed to take any interest in the couple living there but myself, so that it was only what I observed with my own eyes that makes this story, nothing that I heard from anybody else, no scraps of gossip, or tales told about them behind their backs.

Yes, they weren't always alone, as they are now. They had four kids. Three girls and a boy. They brought up the four of them in that ramshackle old place by the lake, and it was always a wonder to me how they did it. God, I've known days when the rain lashed the lake into little waves that burst and broke on the muddy shore near by their place, and turned the marsh into a swamp, and the wind driving straight in. You'd have thought anyone with a grain of sense would have taken his missus and his kids out of it and gone off somewhere where they could get some creature comforts at least. Not the old man. If he could stick it, I guess he decided she could too, and the kids as well. Maybe he wanted to bring them up the hard way.

Mark you, they were attractive youngsters. Especially the youngest girl. I never knew her name, but I called her Tiny, she had so much go to her. Chip off the old block, in spite of her size. I can see her now, as a little thing, the first to venture paddling in the lake, on a fine morning, way ahead of her sisters and the brother.

The brother I nicknamed Boy. He was the eldest, and between you and me a bit of a fool. He hadn't the looks of his sisters and was a clumsy sort of fellow. The girls would play around on their own, and go fishing, and he'd hang about in the background, not knowing what to do with himself. If he possibly could he'd stay around home, near his mother. Proper mother's boy. That's why I gave him the name. Not that she seemed to fuss over him any more than she did the others. She treated the four alike, as far as I could tell. Her thoughts were always for the old man rather than for them. But Boy was just a great baby, and I have an idea he was simple.

Like the parents, the youngsters kept themselves to themselves. Been dinned into them, I dare say, by the old man. They never came down to the beach on their own and played; and it must have been a temptation, I thought, in full summer, when people came walking over the cliffs down to the beach to bathe and picnic. I suppose, for those strange reasons best known to himself, the old man had warned them to have no truck with strangers.

They were used to me pottering, day in, day out, fetching driftwood and that. And often I would pause and watch the kids playing by the lake. I didn't talk to them, though. They might have gone back and told the old man. They used to look up when I passed by, then glance away again, sort of shy. All but Tiny. Tiny would toss her head and do a somersault, just to show off.

I sometimes watched them go off, the six of them – the old man, the missus, Boy, and the three girls, for a day's fishing out to sea. The old man, of course, in charge; Tiny eager to help, close to her dad; the missus looking about her to see if the weather was going to keep fine; the two other girls alongside; and Boy, poor simple Boy, always the last to leave home. I never knew what sport they had. They used to stay out late, and I'd have left the beach by the time they came back again. But I guess they did well. They must have lived almost entirely on what they caught. Well, fish is said to be full of vitamins, isn't it? Perhaps the old man was a food faddist in his way.

Time passed, and the youngsters began to grow up. Tiny lost something of her individuality then, it seemed to me. She grew more like her sisters. They were a nice-looking trio, all the same. Quiet, you know, well-behaved.

As for Boy, he was enormous. Almost as big as the old man, but with what a difference! He had none of his father's looks, or strength, or personality; he was nothing but a great clumsy lout. And the trouble was, I believe the old man was ashamed of him. He didn't pull his weight in the home, I'm certain of that.

And out fishing he was perfectly useless. The girls would work away like beetles, with Boy, always in the background, making a mess of things. If his mother was there he just stayed by her side.

I could see it rattled the old man to have such an oaf of a son. Irritated him, too, because Boy was so big. It probably didn't make sense to his intolerant mind. Strength and stupidity didn't go together. In any normal family, of course, Boy would have left home by now and gone out to work. I used to wonder if they argued about it back in the evenings, the missus and the old man, or if it was something never admitted between them but tacitly understood – Boy was no good.

Well, they did leave home at last. At least, the girls did.

I'll tell you how it happened.

It was a day in late autumn, and I happened to be over doing some shopping in the little town overlooking the harbour, three miles from this place, and suddenly I saw the old man, the missus, the three girls and Boy all making their way up to Pont – that's at the head of a creek going eastward from the harbour. There are a few cottages at Pont, and a farm and a church up behind. The family looked washed and spruced up, and so did the old man and the missus, and I wondered if they were going visiting. If they were, it was an unusual thing for them to do. But it's possible they had friends or acquaintances up there, of whom I knew nothing. Anyway, that was the last I saw of them, on the fine Saturday afternoon, making for Pont.

It blew hard over the weekend, a proper easterly gale. I kept indoors and didn't go out at all. I knew the seas would be breaking good and hard on the beach. I wondered if the old man and the family had been able to get back. They would have been wise to stay with their friends up Pont, if they had friends there.

It was Tuesday before the wind dropped and I went down to the beach again. Seaweed, driftwood, tar and oil all over the place. It's always the same after an easterly blow. I looked up the lake, towards the old man's shack, and I saw him there, with the missus, just by the edge of the lake. But there was no sign of the young-sters.

I thought it a bit funny, and waited around in case they should appear. They never did. I walked right round the lake, and from the opposite bank I had a good view of their place, and even took out my old spy-glass to have a closer look. They just weren't there. The old man was pottering about as he often did when he wasn't fishing, and the missus had settled herself down to bask in the sun. There was only one explanation. They had left the family with friends in Pont. They had sent the family for a holiday.

I can't help admitting I was relieved, because for one frightful moment I thought maybe they had started off back home on the Saturday night and got struck by the gale; and, well – that the old man and his missus had got back safely, but not the kids. It couldn't be that, though. I should have heard. Someone would have said something. The old man wouldn't be pottering there in his usual unconcerned fashion and the missus basking in the sun. No, that must have been it. They had left the family with friends. Or maybe the girls and Boy had gone up country, gone to find themselves jobs at last.

Somehow it left a gap. I felt sad. So long now I had been used to seeing them all around, Tiny and the others. I had a strange sort of feeling that they had gone for good. Silly, wasn't it? To mind, I mean. There was the old man, and his missus, and the four youngsters, and I'd more or less watched them grow up, and now for no reason they had gone.

I wished then I knew even a word or two of his language, so that I could have called out to him, neighbour-like, and said, 'I see you and the missus are on your own. Nothing wrong, I hope?'

But there, it wasn't any use. He'd have looked at me with his strange eyes and told me to go to hell.

I never saw the girls again. No, never. They just didn't come back. Once I thought I saw Tiny, somewhere up the estuary, with a group of friends, but I couldn't be sure. If it was, she'd grown, she looked different. I tell you what I think. I think the old man and the missus took them with a definite end in view, that last weekend, and either settled them with friends they knew or told them to shift for themselves.

I know it sounds hard, not what you'd do for your own son and daughters, but you have to remember the old man was a tough customer, a law unto himself. No doubt he thought it would be for the best, and so it probably was, and if only I could know for certain what happened to the girls, especially Tiny, I wouldn't worry.

But I do worry sometimes, because of what happened to Boy.

You see, Boy was fool enough to come back. He came back about three weeks after that final weekend. I had walked down through the woods – not my usual way, but down to the lake by the stream that feeds it from a higher level. I rounded the lake by the marshes to the north, some distance from the old man's place, and the first thing I saw was Boy.

He wasn't doing anything. He was just standing by the marsh. He looked dazed. He was too far off for me to hail him; besides, I didn't have the nerve. But I watched him, as he stood there in his clumsy loutish way, and I saw him staring at the far end of the lake. He was staring in the direction of the old man.

The old man, and the missus with him, took not the slightest notice of Boy. They were close to the beach, by the plank bridge, and were either just going out to fish or coming back. And here was Boy, with his dazed stupid face, but not only stupid – frightened.

I wanted to say, 'Is anything the matter?' but I didn't know how to say it. I stood there, like Boy, staring at the old man.

Then what we both must have feared would happen, happened.

The old man lifted his head, and saw Boy.

He must have said a word to his missus, because she didn't move, she stayed where she was, by the bridge, but the old man turned like a flash of lightning and came down the other side of the lake towards the marshes, towards Boy. He looked terrible. I shall never forget his appearance. That magnificent head I had always admired now angry, evil; and he was cursing Boy as he came. I tell you, I heard him.

Boy, bewildered, scared, looked hopelessly about him for cover. There was none. Only the thin reeds that grew beside the marsh.

239

But the poor fellow was so dumb he went in there, and crouched, and believed himself safe – it was a horrible sight.

I was just getting my own courage up to interfere when the old man stopped suddenly in his tracks, pulled up short as it were, and then, still cursing, muttering, turned back again and returned to the bridge. Boy watched him, from his cover of reeds, then, poor clot that he was, came out on to the marsh again, with some idea, I suppose, of striking for home.

I looked about me. There was no one to call. No one to give any help. And if I went and tried to get someone from the farm they would tell me not to interfere, that the old man was best left alone when he got in one of his rages, and anyway that Boy was old enough to take care of himself. He was as big as the old man. He could give as good as he got. I knew different. Boy was no fighter. He didn't know how.

I waited quite a time beside the lake but nothing happened. It began to grow dark. It was no use my waiting there. The old man and the missus left the bridge and went on home. Boy was still standing there on the marsh, by the lake's edge.

I called to him, softly. 'It's no use. He won't let you in. Go back to Pont, or wherever it is you've been. Go to some place, anywhere, but get out of here.'

He looked up, that same queer dazed expression on his face, and I could tell he hadn't understood a word I said.

I felt powerless to do any more. I went home myself. But I thought about Boy all evening, and in the morning I went down to the lake again, and I took a great stick with me to give me courage. Not that it would have been much good. Not against the old man.

Well . . . I suppose they had come to some sort of agreement, during the night. There was Boy, by his mother's side, and the old man was pottering on his own.

I must say, it was a great relief. Because, after all, what could I have said or done? If the old man didn't want Boy home, it was really his affair. And if Boy was too stupid to go, that was Boy's affair.

But I blamed the mother a good deal. After all, it was up to her to tell Boy he was in the way, and the old man was in one of his moods, and Boy had best get out while the going was good. But I never did think she had great intelligence. She did not seem to show much spirit at any time.

However, what arrangement they had come to worked for a time. Boy stuck close to his mother – I suppose he helped her at home, I don't know – and the old man left them alone and was more and more by himself.

He took to sitting down by the bridge, humped, staring out to sea, with a queer brooding look on him. He seemed strange, and lonely. I didn't like it. I don't know what his thoughts were, but I'm sure they were evil. It suddenly seemed a very long time since he and the missus and the whole family had gone fishing, a happy, contented party. Now everything had changed for him. He was thrust out in the cold, and the missus and Boy stayed together.

I felt sorry for him, but I felt frightened too. Because I felt it could not go on like this indefinitely; something would happen.

One day I went down to the beach for driftwood – it had been blowing in the night – and when I glanced towards the lake I saw that Boy wasn't with his mother. He was back where I had seen him that first day, on the edge of the marsh. He was as big as his father. If he'd known how to use his strength he'd have been a match for him any day, but he hadn't the brains. There he was, back on the marsh, a great big frightened foolish fellow, and there was the old man, outside his home, staring down towards his son with murder in his eyes.

I said to myself, 'He's going to kill him.' But I didn't know how or when or where, whether by night, when they were sleeping, or by day, when they were fishing. The mother was useless, she would not prevent it. It was no use appealing to the mother. If only Boy would use one little grain of sense, and go . . .

I watched and waited until nightfall. Nothing happened.

It rained in the night. It was grey, and cold, and dim. December was everywhere, trees all bare and bleak. I couldn't get down to the lake until late afternoon, and then the skies had cleared and the sun was shining in that watery way it does in winter, a burst of it, just before setting below the sea.

I saw the old man, and the missus too. They were close together, by the old shack, and they saw me coming for they looked towards me. Boy wasn't there. He wasn't on the marsh, either. Nor by the side of the lake.

I crossed the bridge and went along the right bank of the lake, and I had my spy-glass with me, but I couldn't see Boy. Yet all the time I was aware of the old man watching me.

Then I saw him. I scrambled down the bank, and crossed the marsh, and went to the thing I saw lying there, behind the reeds.

He was dead. There was a great gash on his body. Dried blood on his back. But he had lain there all night. His body was sodden with the rain.

Maybe you'll think I'm a fool, but I began to cry, like an idiot, and I shouted across to the old man, 'You murderer, you bloody God-damned murderer.' He did not answer. He did not move. He stood there, outside his shack with the missus, watching me.

You'll want to know what I did. I went back and got a spade, and I dug a grave for Boy, in the reeds behind the marsh, and I said one of my own prayers for him, being uncertain of his religion. When I had finished I looked across the lake to the old man.

And do you know what I saw?

I saw him lower his great head, and bend towards her and embrace her. And she lifted her head to him and embraced him too. It was both a requiem and a benediction. An atonement, and a giving of praise. In their strange way they knew they had done evil, but now it was over, because I had buried Boy and he was gone. They were free to be together again, and there was no longer a third to divide them.

They came out into the middle of the lake, and suddenly I saw the old man stretch his neck and beat his wings, and he took off from the water, full of power, and she followed him. I watched the two swans fly out to sea right into the face of the setting sun, and I tell you it was one of the most beautiful sights I ever saw in my life: the two swans flying there, alone, in winter.

242